Tessa's Flight

This is a work of fiction. All characters and events portrayed in this novel are either products of the author's imagination or are used fictitiously.

Tessa's Flight

Cover by Driven Digital Services
Map by Vicki B. Williamson
Editing and typesetting by Kingsman Editing Services

First Edition December 2019
ISBN: 978-0-9990605-3-7

vickibwilliamson.author@gmail.com

. . . the visionaries.

Tessa's Flight

The Pedagogue Chronicles
Book III

Vicki B. Williamson

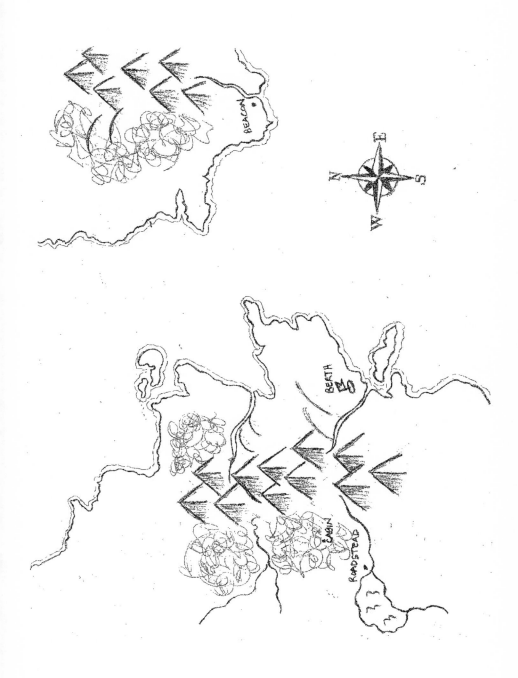

THE WORLDS WERE LAID OUT before the twins like multicolored playing marbles. Some displayed many hues. Those touched by Cassandra were dark, dead, and cold.

Cassandra spun in a circle, her arms at her sides. With a girlish laugh, she stopped to point at first one world and then another.

"Do you remember the day we played for that one?" She beamed at her brother, her face aglow. "I have always enjoyed playing with you, brother."

Caleb turned from her. From her laughter, from her arrogance, from her ridicule. It was time he put away the thoughts of what once was—the love of another millennium—and fought for the lives they gambled.

He'd allowed her to win in the past, thinking she would come back to him as the sister of their childhood. But now he realized that was not to be. She was no longer his Cassandra.

She was the consumer of worlds.

1

THE RAPTOR SCREAMED, DRAWING THE girl's eyes. She stood transfixed for a moment, watching the golden bird ride the warm currents, the subtle shifts of its tail feathers keeping its powerful body on an even plane.

It dipped a wing and plummeted toward the ground, loosing another scream of pure abandon. Tessa's green eyes remained on the bird as it swept up at the last moment to avoid a lethal crash with the hillside.

It soared toward her, her gaze never leaving it. As its trajectory took it over her head, she leaned back then moved to the edge of the cliff. Inhaling the fresh morning air, Tessa seated herself and scanned the blue and green valley before her. This was her favorite time of day. The sun, just breaking on the horizon, shot warm, yellow beacons into the dawn. Across the floor of the valley, early fog still rolled between the trunks of moss-covered trees, but soon the sun's heat would burn it off.

When the raptor gave another distant cry, the girl stopped daydreaming and concentrated. Pulling the image of the bird into her mind, she closed her eyes and took another deep breath.

First came the rush of wind in her ears and through her hair. Smells changed, becoming crisper, cleaner. When the bird screamed again, the girl heard it within her own mind, and opening her lids, she looked out at the tiny world below. Where before the fog moved through the trees, now it appeared to be a soup the puffs of trees tops floated upon.

2

"TESSA!" HER MOTHER CALLED, NOT surprised when she didn't receive an answer. Stepping to the door of their cabin, she raised her voice. "Tessa!"

In the distance, around the outbuildings, she heard a faint reply. Responding to the indistinct call, she yelled, "Breakfast is ready!" and then turned back to the home.

Watching the man who helped her bring food to the table, Maya shook her head. "It's a good thing we train every day, Sentinel, or you'd have grown soft these last sixteen years." The man, clothed in leathers, acknowledged her with a tip of his head. He had not aged as those around him.

Maya had grown into her beauty. Her frame remained thin but strong, and her hair still glowed like a red flame. Her cloth skirt made muted sounds as she moved, the clip of her boots soft on the earthen floor.

"That girl." She sighed. "By the time she gets in, breakfast will be cold."

"I hear her now," Sentinel uttered and placed the last dish

on the table.

When Tessa stepped through the doorway, the sun came with her. Hair, long and dark as pitch, flowed behind, but instead of absorbing the light, her tresses reflected it as if a nova surrounded her. She was always in motion, even early to walk and talk. Maya watched her closely for magics, but the girl she birthed and raised was just a normal mortal, or as normal as their family could be. Intelligent, precocious, and independent. And then she turned sixteen, and Striker had come into their lives.

"Wash up." Maya admonished the girl when she reached for a roll. Her face broke into a smile when Tessa and Sentinel started to discuss her morning over the washbasin. Their unusual lives were like everyone else's in other ways. Maya tried to give Tessa as normal an upbringing as she could.

After Mikel's death, with the loss of both her mother and Teck, Maya didn't want to go on. If not for the child growing under her heart, she would have curled up and died, consigning Sentinel to the same death. But she knew the babe was there, had felt her move, and the love that filled her kept her living.

As Tessa's birth neared, Maya knew she needed a plan. They'd need a home and a living. She couldn't contemplate returning to the area around Roadstead. She needed something new. With Sentinel and her dog, Rory, at her side, she stepped aboard the first ship leaving port. As luck would have it, they traveled south toward the city of Beacon. A beautiful land. Warm and fruitful.

Over the years, Sentinel had sold his skills as a mercenary.

But now, they existed much as Sylvan and Maya had — trading goods like vegetables, meats, and hand-spun fabrics with the closest settlements. They would never be wealthy like the people Maya's mother came from, but they were warm and fed. And most of all, safe. People had grown used to the funny trio — the exotic color and features of Sentinel, and Maya with a child but no husband. They came to appreciate the food and clothes they had to trade and welcomed them as part of the community.

"We'll need to pack for a trip to town," Maya began as they all sat to eat. "Our stock of furs and fabrics are overflowing, and we need supplies before the seasons change. I'm thinking to leave tomorrow before the sun is up. We should be back in a couple days." With no arguments forthcoming, Maya set the plan in motion.

* * * * *

THE CREAK OF THE WAGON and rattle of chains woke Tessa from a restless sleep. Up early and bundled in with their stores, they'd headed to town.

At least she was warm, she thought and burrowed into the furs, again welcoming sleep.

WHEN HER EYES OPENED, IT was to stare into a powder-blue, cloudless sky. A small spot high in the air turned up the corners of her mouth.

Faithful Striker.

Relaxing, Tessa caressed the length of the bow next to her.

It was a thing of beauty that used to be her mother's. When she showed an aptitude for the weapon, her mother had gifted the bow to her along with a quiver of steel-tipped arrows. They were her prized possession. Every time they went to town, people offered to trade for it. So many that Sentinel built her a case to conceal it across her body.

She would never sell the bow—never even contemplate it. Not only was it from her mother, but it was special beyond its beauty. Every time her mother looked at it, something passed behind her eyes. Tessa could never tell whether it was good or bad—it passed so quickly—but she knew it was special. She watched the passing countryside, daydreaming about what she'd talk her mother into getting her in town.

3

THE LATE SUN CUED THE coming night when the trio pulled into a large farm. Fat, happy sheep grazed in the far pasture, and all around the house, butterflies flitted among the wildflowers.

The Hampshires owned this property. They were the nearest neighbors and a good resting spot on the trek to town. They'd just reached the house when the door was thrown open and a young girl rushed out.

"Tessa!" she yelled and, jumping into the wagon, threw herself at the older girl. With a laugh, Tessa caught her in a hug.

"Sally, it's good to see you, too."

"Mama said you'd be here soon." The girl stood and pulled on Tessa's arm. "Hurry, come and see the new puppies. They're in the barn."

"Okay, okay . . . Don't pull my arm off." The girls' laughter pealed out over the valley as they tumbled from the wagon and darted across the yard.

Maya watched them go, a smile on her face. It was good for

Tessa to have friends. Sally, though younger, allowed Tessa the opportunity to be a child. Living with an adult and an eternal being, Tessa didn't often get the time to play the way she did with Sally.

"Maya," came the call from the porch. Maya turned from watching the girls to greeting Sally's parents.

THE FIRE BLAZED IN THE stone hearth, food filled the table, and laughter filled the air.

"Oh, Maya. It's always so nice when you all stop here. We wish you lived closer." Sally's mother, Anna, leaned into Maya and whispered, "Sometimes, I wish for another woman to discuss life with."

Maya laid her hand on the woman's forearm. She, too, missed the company of another woman. "I always enjoy our time together."

Anna laid her hand over Maya's. "Maybe, before you leave tomorrow, we can gather some berries from the hillside."

Maya figured Anna must want some privacy to talk, so she gave her an eager nod. "Of course. I'd love to take some berries home for canning."

4

EVENING HAD WELL SET BY the time their wagon pulled into town. It was mostly quiet, the citizenry compiled largely of farmers, but the tavern still emitted a tinny tune and raucous laughter as they passed. Maya directed the team toward the town stables. Their belongings, including those for trade, would be safe there.

Pulling the team to a halt, Maya jumped down, directing Tessa to help. "Get the team stabled. Sentinel and I will be back as soon as we secure lodging."

Tessa nodded as she worked the bindings free from the horses. They knew their jobs well and remained compliant as she worked around, between, and under them. Before her mother cleared the double door of the stables, Tessa was already leading one animal into a stall. She'd feed, water, and brush them down for the evening. Care of the working animals had always been an essential part of her life.

She was finished with the animals, her bow and quiver slung over her body and all their packs in a pile at her feet when her mother and Sentinel returned.

With a harried hand through her hair, her mother checked Tessa's work and then hurried back to the door. She bent to strap on her blades and grab her pack. Her mother's age lines showed now, and Tessa frowned when her mother spoke. "Mrs. Mangle's boarding house is full, so I got us a room at the tavern . . . Almost think we should sleep here . . ." she trailed off. "There's a large group of strangers in the back room of the tavern, so we'll go in and straight up. Don't stop. Don't mess around downstairs. Understand?"

"Yes, Mama," Tessa said softly. She'd never seen her mother like this. She was always calm and decisive. Now her eyes hardened as she cut her gaze to Sentinel.

"Anyway, I don't know. They just feel . . . wrong."

Sentinel nodded and pulled a short blade from his belt then straightened his pack on his shoulder.

"Yes." She nodded in agreement with his action. "Yes, let's be prepared for anything."

A shiver passed down Tessa's spine. Even though she trained with her bow, long knife, and even the twin blades her mother wore, she'd never been in danger. This awareness was new to her. She felt alive in a different way—her senses were on high alert.

When they entered the tavern, the shouts of drunken men in the back room drew all their eyes. Maya stepped to the side and gestured Tessa ahead of her and up the stairs. Pausing on the first step, her eyes swept the entire area before she preceded Sentinel to the second floor and into their room.

* * * * *

TWO MEN STOOD IN THE shadows for a moment more before moving out. One stepped forward to peer up the stairs.

The weapons, he thought. He never would have thought anything of the three except for the weapons.

Among men of his community, there was a general call to locate a particular girl—a woman by now—with particular weapons. He'd always thought it a fairytale. Not only the proficiency of the girl with the blades, but the description of her companion. Add that to the tales of her, and no one would believe it to be true.

Now, here they were. A woman with crossed blades accompanied by a black man. If they could speak with her, convince her to accompany them, they'd see more reward and acclaim than they'd ever thought possible. Glancing at his friend, the two men moved back across the room to sit by the fire and plan.

5

MAYA SCANNED THE TOWN. SHE couldn't dismiss the tingle at the base of her neck.

Their night had been quiet after the furtive flight to their room. Maya and Sentinel took turns on watch while Tessa slept the sleep of the young. Sometimes, she wondered if she were being too worried about security, but then she'd remember where they came from and decided she couldn't be too worried.

This morning, their business was completed to the satisfaction of all, and now, the animals were harnessed and ready to travel. Her caution brought her to take a last long look around, but everything appeared normal. Finally, she climbed up next to Sentinel and flicked the reins.

* * * * *

THE MEN SAT ATOP THE high outcropping and watched the wagon depart. They'd thought to approach the woman the night before, but between her rushing to their room, and her reputation, they decided to wait. They would need to speak with her—verify she was the one they wanted. If she were—and they were sure she was—they would need to convince her to travel with them.

Time was tight, and their need mighty.

* * * * *

MAYA LOOKED OUT FROM THE light of their fire. They should have left town earlier. Had they headed home with the coming of the dawn, they would now be safely in the Hampshires' home. She preferred Tessa to be behind walls rather than out in the open as they now found themselves. But if Maya's discomfort were warranted, the fight would follow them to their friends' doorstep.

Antsy, she jumped to her feet to prowl their camp's boundaries. She still wore her blades, though she kept them within their scabbards. Her long knife waited in her grip. At times like this, she longed for Rory's companionship. Nothing compared to a dog's senses, especially in the dark.

* * * * *

TESSA SAT BY THE FIRE, watching her mother pace around their camp, her eyes wide. There had been times when she'd thought her mother paranoid, but this was not one. Even she felt the tension in the air. Some hours ago, Sentinel had doubled back to come up behind whoever trailed them and to get whatever information he could.

WHEN THE RIDERS CAME WITHIN reach of the firelight, Maya and Tessa stood next to the bedrolls. Maya now had her twin blades at the ready. Tessa had an arrow notched on her bow, her long knife an easy pull from her belt. If they thought two women to be easy prey, they were in for a surprise.

It surprised Maya to see the men bundled in a group, not surrounding the women.

"Stop right there!" she called out.

The man in the lead put up his hand and, as a unit, they halted their horses. Slowly, the leader dismounted. The night was so quiet, all they heard were popping of the fire and the creak of the man's saddle. Maya took a step forward to place Tessa behind her.

"What do you want here? We have nothing for you."

The man held both hands up in a pacifying gesture.

"We're not here to cause you or the girl any harm." He took another step forward, his gaze sweeping the area. "Where is your man?"

Maya ignored his questions and his assurances for their safety. With a threatening raise of her swords, she took another step forward and demanded, "What do you want?"

The man kept his hands open and away from his weapons. "I just want to speak with you. We're in search of someone, and I think you're her."

At his words, visions of Mikel filled her brain. She always

knew this day would come. Now, though, she had Tessa.

"Get back on your horse and ride out. This is your only warning and only chance." She took another step forward, a twist of her wrist causing the blade to spin, its whistle loud in the still night. "I don't want to kill you, but I will. I'll tear you apart and spit you out."

"You're fearless, I'll give you that." The man kept his eyes on her but took another step forward. "And I've been told you can back it up. I'd prefer not to put it to the test." Again scanning the area, the man continued. "We've been sent for you. We're to bring you back."

"Who sent you?" A shiver went down her spine. Mikel was dead. She killed him, but still her fear pressed against her chest.

"A priest. A priest with one hand."

Maya's memories flashed. That day in Mikel's throne room, she'd been so upset. And then everything had happened so fast. She'd been focused on her mother, or what used to be her mother, but in the corner of her memory, she recalled Patrick. He was on his knees on the dais. Bruised and bloody, he cradled his arm next to his body. And that arm, she now remembered, was missing a hand.

"Patrick?" she whispered.

"Yes." He nodded. "Father Patrick hoped you would remember him after all this time."

"What could Patrick possibly want from me? It's been almost twenty years since I last saw him." With a quick shake of her head, she brought the sword up, effectively cutting off anything he might have hoped to say. "No. Wait. I don't want to hear anything he has to say. I left that behind me a long time ago."

"My name is Inger. I lead this band of men, and we've been instructed to find you and bring you back." The man took a hesitant step toward her.

"I have no intention of returning with you. No good can come of it." Maya shoved a sword into its housing on her back but kept the other at the ready. "The last time I was there, I lost almost everything I valued in my life."

* * * * *

TESSA WATCHED HER MOTHER, HER eyes wide. In this short time, she'd already learned more about her mother's past than in her whole life. She kept still and quiet at her mother's back, afraid if she were acknowledged, her mother would stop talking.

Who were these men? Who was the one-handed priest?

She strained to silence the questions burning inside her. The man took another step toward the women, his face pleading.

"Much has happened since you went away. Patrick needs you. The land needs you."

Maya took a small step back from the slowly advancing man, shaking her head. "What could I possibly have to offer him?"

"Your mother. He requires help to defeat your mother."

6

SENTINEL MOVED LIKE A WRAITH through the forest. He'd doubled back on the men who trailed them.

Now he hid in the trees, listening to a man speak with Maya.

The man sounded desperate to have her accompany them. Sentinel didn't think they should return to Berth.

When they finally left, he'd felt Maya's pain as if it were his own. The loss of her father, her mother, and even the boy, Teck, all affected her strongly. He didn't know what he would do if she had to face her past that way again.

Sentinel pulled himself out of his musings. When the man mentioned Maya's mother, Sentinel started, his brows drawing together. They had been certain Sylvan died in the destruction of the temple room. Maya and he had barely escaped with their lives.

Sentinel stepped carefully forward. The man's tone was changing now. He wasn't going to ask much longer. With another pace, Sentinel stood directly behind the last man in their group. He slid his arm around the man's throat, lifted him, and maneuvered him backward and into the cover of the brush.

When Sentinel laid the unconscious man down, he stood for a moment to consider him. Maybe he should slit his throat and be done with it. He had no problem killing this man and the others, but he wanted to ensure it was the best plan.

After sliding his knife back into its housing on his belt, Sentinel took a length of rope from his pack. He bound the man's hands behind his back then tied his legs to his hands. After he gagged him, Sentinel stepped from the brush.

SENTINEL CULLED DOWN THE MEN. By the time Maya pulled her second weapon back from its housing, only one man remained with the leader.

7

MAYA LOOKED AT THE MAN over her swords. She had been aware of Sentinel slowly taking out the others. She didn't know or care if he killed them. Either way, the fight could do nothing but go their way.

They would have won before. Now it was a doubtless conclusion.

"I think you should leave. Pretend you never found us." She sounded reasonable, but the leader shook his head and took another step forward. "Come on, mister. Don't be stupid. You don't want to end this day dead."

Once again lifting his hands in a pacifying gesture, the man scowled. "It's not my intention to fight you . . ." He turned to gesture to the men at his back. When he saw Sentinel's knife at his remaining man's throat, his scowl deepened, and he spun to face the new threat.

He sidestepped out from between them.

"Now wait a minute. Where are my men? We didn't come here to fight you."

Maya stepped forward until the tip of her blade rested on his throat. "I guess you came to the wrong place then."

BY THE TIME SENTINEL HAD the last two men bound, Maya and Tessa were in the wagon, heading home. Sentinel would catch up, but they wanted to get as much of a head start on the men as possible before they were awake and free.

This trip home, they would not stop at the Hampshires' farm. They'd move fast and far. The decision not to kill the men put them all in danger. Maya and Sentinel had killed when they had no other choice, but this was not one of those times. Tessa had never lived such a life. Maya didn't want to start it now.

* * * * *

WHEN THE RAIN STARTED A few hours into their flight, Tessa exchanged a smile with her mother. If the rain continued throughout the night, it would go a long way toward disguising their tracks from all the others. She scanned the night sky. The moon hid behind the heavy cover of clouds. She had a fleeting worry about Striker but assured herself he would be huddled somewhere to wait out the storm. He knew his way home.

Maya had always kept so much of her past a secret. Tessa had heard the man though. Maya's mother—Tessa's grandmother—was causing a problem. Some man, this Patrick, needed her to defeat her mother. Why?

Tessa peeked at her mother from around the hood of her cloak. She'd been so calm while confronting the men. Even before it became apparent that Sentinel was limiting their ranks, her mother was calm. So calm.

As she stood behind her mother, Tessa's hands had been shaking. The tip of her arrow quivered, and her knees had felt weak. She'd never had that sensation before. Her brows pulled together. Did this mean she was a coward? Maybe she'd never be brave like her mother.

She turned from her mother. In the distance, against the rim of the next hill, she saw the outline of a man. Her heart jumped, thinking it was one of the men who'd confronted them. The figure moved closer, and she relaxed when she recognized Sentinel.

When they pulled alongside him, her mother stopped the team and wagon and he climbed in the back. With a flick of the reins, Maya set the team in motion.

They'd travel through the night and most of the morning before reaching their home. Once there, things would return to normal, but with this glimpse into the world and her mother's past, Tessa didn't think she would ever be the girl she was before.

8

TECK STOPPED AT THE END of the gangplank and scanned the port. It had been almost two decades since he'd stood on the land of his birth. Now, looking at it, he felt an unfamiliar flutter in the pit of his stomach and pushed himself to take that final step. For a moment, the sounds of the dock intensified—seabirds and hawkers crying, the creaks of ships as they moved in their moors, and even the smells of fish and water. He felt light-headed and held the guide rope to steady himself.

He'd made a life elsewhere. Now, in the last few months, he'd thought of Maya again.

As a young man, he was prideful and jealous. It hadn't taken him long to realize he made a mistake. That he'd left Maya in haste. But he'd been unable to turn back and admit it. Just admitting it to himself had tested the boundaries of his courage. So inexperienced and angry he'd been.

Well, he thought, he'd spent the last twenty years using that anger to his advantage. He'd become wealthy doing the task one didn't talk about in polite company. Wealthy enough that he didn't have to work for anyone anymore.

Leaving the dock, Teck moved through town. The accents of the people, the clothing they wore, even the smells of food baking all reminded him of when he was a boy.

Now that he was here, he'd need to plan his next step. When his stomach growled, he decided a room and dinner would be the first thing.

The area around the port bustled with business catering to travelers and seamen alike. Traffic containing wagons, riders on horses, and travelers on foot moved up and down the streets. Men yelled, and dogs barked. Ladies plying their wares leaned out of upper windows of buildings, and a few even ventured out into the streets to lure in the odd passerby. Teck simply shook his head when one ran her hand down his chest. With a pretty pout, she stepped back but didn't argue as he moved past her.

After all this time, he wondered where he'd find Maya. Where to begin.

9

ALMOST A WEEK HAD PASSED when thoughts of Maya's mother plagued her mind. Images of her the last time she'd seen her—crazed, scary, swirling with the mass of her magic. But within the confusion and fear of those images rose the picture of the cottage in the woods. Her mother tending her flowers, singing her a lullaby, caring for her when she was ill. A lifetime of laughter and love.

Could she put all that out of her heart and not at least attempt to save the woman who'd raised her?

WHEN SHE ROSE TO DRESS, her mind continued to swirl. Stepping from the room, she gently pulled the door shut to give Tessa a few more moments of sleep.

Her lips curled to see Sentinel laying fresh logs on the fire. As they caught, he faced her.

"When do you wish to leave?" His whisper didn't surprise her. As her pedagogue, they had a bond that ran through their minds and hearts.

"As soon as possible." She glanced at the closed door. "Tessa needs to be kept safe. I want her to stay at the Hampshire farm."

"You know this will be a problem for her."

Maya was already nodding. "I know, I know. She'll think to go with us." As she spoke, Maya moved across the room, already gathering items they would need on their journey. "That's not going to be possible, though. We don't know what we'll be facing, and I can't be the one who puts her in danger." She turned to him. "She'll just need to understand."

At first, he didn't say anything, but then he muttered, "You have met your daughter, right?"

Maya pursed her lips and scowled. The girl would mind, or Maya would tie her up to keep her safe.

* * * * *

TESSA STEPPED OUT OF THE bedroom she shared with her mother and Maya barely noticed her amid the chaos. She and Sentinel stacked items near the door. They had blankets, food, clothing, and all manner of other items.

"Are we going somewhere?" Tessa asked.

"*We* are." Maya turned to continue her stacking, evading the heart of the question. Behind her, she heard Tessa grab some items and follow her to the door.

She knew it would be best to face Tessa's disappointment head-on, so with a sigh, she swung around.

"Tessa, my love— " The excitement in her daughter's eyes

stopped her, and the disappointment she was soon to impart weighed heavily on her shoulders. When she didn't immediately continue, Tessa stepped closer.

"Yes, Mama?"

"Um. Well, baby . . . you see . . ." How could she dash her daughter's hopes? The travel. The excitement. Tessa had never been far from home.

Maya concentrated on the danger and the simple fact that she could never ensure Tessa's safety. She couldn't take her with them.

Maya took Tessa's arm and led her to twin chairs by the fireplace. "Sit, please." Maya took the other chair.

"I've decided to travel back to the land of my birth." Maya had to drop her eyes when Tessa leaned forward. "Um . . . Sentinel and I will be leaving as soon as we are packed to go." Again, she had to stop and gather her courage. She leaned forward and feathered her daughter's forearm. "But you will be staying with the Hampshires."

Like a puppet with its strings cut, Tessa's entire frame fell. Dismay and confusion radiated from her face. "Wha— " She swallowed and tried again. "What do you mean?"

"It won't be a journey for a young girl— "

"But Mama," Tessa cut in, "I'm not an infant. I've trained my entire life." She slid from the chair to her knees in front of her mother. "I'll be an asset to you. Please let me go."

"No, Tessa." Maya stood, forcing Tessa to sit back. "My mind is made up. I will not risk you." She stepped from between the chair and her daughter to pace within the room. "The three of us will travel together as far as the Hampshire farm. You'll stay with them." Maya sighed, feeling her daughter's plea through the air.

"They'll appreciate your help around their place." She glanced up but returned her stare to the floor. "You all get along well. Sally will love to have you there.

"Anyway." She faced Tessa now, her hands clasped in front of her. "The decision is made, and it's how it'll be." She started to stack more items by the door. "Get what you'll need for an extended stay; we'll be leaving soon."

* * * * *

TESSA SAT ON THE EDGE of the bed, her mind in turmoil. She still couldn't believe she'd just sat there. Didn't argue harder.

She began to gather her belongings but continued to mentally bash herself. She wasn't a child any longer. She could make decisions for her own life. This was so unfair.

She had her pack filled with a change of clothing, a lightweight but warm blanket, an empty flask for water, a few tools, and a long knife. On top of the pack she laid her bow in its case and the quiver of arrows. When she studied what she'd packed, she realized she wouldn't be staying at the Hampshires'.

She stepped backward from her belongings until her legs bumped the edge of the bed and she collapsed on it. She stared at the ceiling while her mind whirled.

Was she really planning on following her mother?

Yes.

Her jaw tightened and she sat up to look at her belongings again.

What she'd told her mother had been correct. She had trained her entire life. She was capable and intelligent. But she also knew there was no reason to argue with her mother. She'd never get her way, never even get a word in. Her mother had always been a force to be reckoned with. And single-minded. Now that she had decided, nothing would change her mind.

Tessa stared blindly at the wall. She'd travel with them to the Hampshires'. She'd be agreeable. But after Sentinel and her mother left, she'd set out after them. When they were days away, she could join them. There wouldn't be time to backtrack, and her mother would have to allow her to come with them.

A small smile curved the girl's lips. The images of foreign lands and excitement filled her mind. Her heart picked up, and she jumped up to grab her things and get them into the wagon. Now that her decision was made, she couldn't wait to head out.

10

THE HAMPSHIRE FARM CAME INTO view through gaps in the trees.

When they rolled back in, moving along one side of the house, the door opened and Anna stepped outside, drying her hands on her apron. A smile split her face when she recognized them, and she stepped to the edge of the porch, her hand up to shade her eyes.

Sentinel halted the team and Maya jumped down. She climbed the stairs to give Anna a quick hug. Taking the woman's arm, Maya turned her, and they walked away from the wagon.

Tessa watched her mother, aware of Sentinel's gaze. She then looked at Striker who sat on a perch mounted to the wagon. His large eyes watched her, and then he shook. His feathers fell in disarray before they lay back down.

Tessa ran a hand down his head and back.

Striker would be an asset, too. She pressed her wrist against his lower chest, and he stepped on her forearm. Sharp talons tightened around her arm as she stood. If he'd wanted, he could cause mortal injury with them and his beak. He was beautiful but deadly.

Looking over his head, she saw Sally running toward the wagon. She gave his head a light kiss and lifted her arm. With this motion, Striker took to the air, which stirred the hair around her face and blew it across her eyes. When she moved it out of the way, Sally had reached her and was clambering into the wagon.

"Tessa." The girl was breathless.

"Hi, Sally," Tessa said warmly, but her gaze was on her mother.

11

MAYA AND SENTINEL AWOKE EARLY, ready to head out
in record time.

Tessa watched and helped where she could. But try
as she might, she couldn't keep the scowl from her face. She
knew she would be following them, but they didn't know that.
How could they not even give her a thought? Why was it so
easy for them to leave her behind?

When her mother and Sentinel were ready to leave, Maya
approached Tessa.

"You stay safe, okay? Be good for Anna and help out
around here."

"Yes, Mama."

Maya pushed a lock of Tessa's hair behind her ear. Her
voice caught, and a tear ran down her face. She grabbed her
daughter's shoulder and pulled her close. "We shouldn't be
gone too long."

Tessa pulled back. "I'm sure I'll see you soon."

"Yes." Maya nodded. "Yes, we'll see you soon."

Maya released her daughter, hefted her pack on her shoulder, and walked to Sentinel. When she passed him, he stood for a moment more, and Tessa fought to hide her growing anxiety. Then, with one nod to her, he followed Maya.

Tessa watched until they were out of sight. Even knowing she would be following, her heart felt as if it would break.

Her vision blurred, and a tear ran down her cheek, so she ran away from the homestead into the forest. Sally called out behind her, but she stretched her legs and left the girl behind.

Deep in the wood, she sat under an old tree. She wiped her cheeks with stiff fingers. Willing herself to be calm, she listened to her breathing and the breeze whispering in the leaves. Heavy lids fell, and Tessa reached first inward and then out.

A pool of calmness surrounded her. Right after came the rush. Wind, sounds, her senses alive in a way she could never be when she was alone.

When she opened her eyes, she was skimming over the treetops, the sun glinting on a far-off lake.

She could see for miles. The edge of the great forest was within her grasp. With a tip of a wing, she circled around and scanned below for her mother and Sentinel. Small clutches of birds startled at her passage, and below, a herd of deer fled through a stream and up a hill. Not many moments later, she saw what she sought on a broad path, heading to the far shore.

Her mouth opened and a scream issued forth, echoing back at her. Her mother turned, putting her hand up to shield her eyes in the early sunlight. Tessa maneuvered around them and overhead again to see her mother raise a hand in farewell. With a final circle, Tessa released her hold on Striker to allow him his freedom.

Tessa still sat beneath the tree, her back straight, legs folded, hands on her knees. Her breath was even and steady. A sudden breeze ruffled her dark bangs. Her wide, white eyes didn't so much as flicker.

Another moment passed before her lids closed and she tilted her head forward wearily. She hugged her legs to her chest and leaned against the tree trunk. When she opened her eyes again, she looked out of shimmering pools of green.

Striker would stay with her mother, but at a distance. This evening, when she left to follow them, she'd call him to her and have him take the lead. It wouldn't be too long before she'd catch up. She needed to make sure not to join them too quickly, or they would simply send her back.

Satisfied with her plan, she stretched her legs out before her. She was already packed and didn't plan on unpacking anything at the Hampshires'. After everyone was asleep, she'd leave a small note for Anna so as not to worry her and follow her mother.

* * * * *

MAYA TURNED FROM THE HAWK as he soared overhead. She patted Sentinel on the arm as she passed him. "She'll be okay."

When he didn't say anything, Maya looked over, her eyebrows raised. "You don't agree?"

"Tessa is very capable. I'm sure she'll be fine."

"But?"

He shook his head. They'd went on for about a mile when she again spoke.

"We should be at Beacon in a couple of days. From there, we'll catch a ship. Try to get as close to Berth as possible."

Sentinel nodded.

12

THE SOFT SNORES COMING FROM the other room convinced Tessa it was safe to make her escape. She shared a bed with Sally, and the young girl had fallen asleep as soon as they'd gone to bed. She slumbered with the abandon of the young, her body taking up most of the mattress, her breathing deep and even.

Tessa pushed the covers to the side and slid from the bed, sure not to wake the other girl. After standing, she pulled the quilt up around Sally's back. When Tessa made her way toward the doorway, she peered back. The moonlight fell on half of the mattress, partially illuminating her friend. Her hands rested under her chin as if praying, her mouth partially open.

Tessa realized there was the real possibility she might never see her young friend again, and for just a moment she doubted her decision to follow her mother. She recognized her indecision for nerves and turned back toward the door.

When it creaked upon opening, she froze, sure Sally would wake. She was ready with a quick lie about visiting the privy, but the room behind her remained quiet.

She hefted her pack from the floor, freezing again with a hiss as the weapons clanged together.

All quiet, she slipped from the room, closing the door behind her.

The main part of the house was in complete darkness with the moon behind it. Tessa knew the layout well, but now her mind spun to remember if anything was out of place. Anything on the floor that might cause a trip or noise.

Sliding her feet, she moved across the room to the table where she deposited a brief note to Anna then moved to the front door. She eased it open and slipped out, pulling it closed behind her before exhaling a calming breath.

With her head high, she marched across the porch and down the stairs. When her feet hit the dirt, she stopped to look around.

The night was calm and quiet. Everything was thrown into a play of shadow and light under a glowing moon. It looked magical.

Frogs called through the reeds, and a cool breeze stirred the grasses at her feet. Scents of dew carried in the cool air that drew a chill up Tessa's spine.

She let the night unfold around her as she collected herself. Then, with her mother at the forefront of her mind, she shifted her pack and headed down the lane.

13

THE FIRST NIGHT, MAYA AND Sentinel found shelter in a thicket off the side of the road. The summer night was warm, and unconcerned with animal predators, they didn't make a campfire. Predators of the human variety were more on their minds, and a fire was more likely to draw them than keep them away.

Even under the cover of darkness, they knew they were still vulnerable to danger, so they took turns on watch.

While Maya slept, Sentinel sat a small distance from her, deep within a patch of night shadow. The sounds and smells called to his spirit, prompting him to go forth and stalk some prey. He imagined moving through the forest, steps soft, limbs loose, eyes keen.

These introspective thoughts pulled Sentinel back into memories. They'd been lucky to survive the temple in Berth. Now they'd be returning to it.

It was almost two decades ago, and still he could recall the fear he'd felt at almost losing Maya. It had been the first time in his existence he'd felt such a strong, uncontrollable emotion. It had filled him, making him dizzy. They would need to be prepared.

Feeling the sensation of being watched, Sentinel gave a start, pulling himself back to the present. He looked around his area and, when he didn't see anything, he studied Maya. Her sleep was deep and unbroken. Nothing bothered her and no threat presented itself. Still he couldn't shake the feeling.

When he looked up, it was without surprise to see the hawk on a branch above him.

"Striker," he muttered.

The bird stared at him for a moment, its head moving from side to side, eyes intense. Then it took to the air almost soundlessly. Sentinel watched until the bird disappeared in the dark sky, his mind on the bird's owner.

Maya turned over, yawning before she moved to sit beside him. "Night quiet?"

Deciding to keep the visit of the hawk to himself, he said, "Yes. This far out, the road to Beacon is empty."

She nodded. Sentinel's lids drooped, and with Maya beside him, he felt calm. He rarely let down his guard, but she'd grown into a strong woman and warrior. So had her daughter.

WHEN THE SUN PEEKED OVER the horizon, they were already walking toward the coast. Their companionship came naturally. Since he'd first appeared to her in the caves with her father's men, they'd grown closer, merging, the bond of the pedagogue strong.

14

PATRICK READ THE MISSIVE AGAIN. Could it be true? His men claimed they'd found Maya. But then, they stated they'd lost her. She was traveling with a man, dark of skin—it had to be Sentinel—and a young girl. He didn't know for sure who that might be. Perhaps a friend, or servant. They said they would continue to search until they found her again.

Now, his mind filled with possibilities.

He'd hoped Maya would aid them against the beast her mother had become. With this news, his hope blossomed into certainty.

He knew she was alive.

Patrick pushed back from his desk and crossed the room. In the past years, he'd become an important man within the resistance. What was left of it, anyway.

That day in Berth, men had scattered. No one knew who was still alive and how they would come back together. He had remained hidden, healing from his many wounds.

When he'd approached men he knew—lords and other

leaders—they hadn't been interested in challenging Sylvan. And with Sylvan, her man Orson. Together, they were a formidable team of death and cruelty.

With Lord Bathsar dead, it seemed the true leader was gone. All the bravery had been leached out with his murder. Men wanted to keep their heads down.

Then Patrick discussed Lord Bathsar's dream. A dream of a land without oppression. First it was Mikel, his brother, but now, it seemed Sylvan had become the real threat, her magic subverted to the point that nothing seemed able to stop her.

He began slowly—sitting in a tavern with men whose allegiance he was sure of. But then he moved into the community. He opened a small house of worship, and within its walls, they discussed resisting the norm. Making a better life for all people of this land. He had failed once to be the man of courage like Lord Bathsar, and he had a second chance at redemption.

Now, after so many years, they were close to springing the trap. Patrick felt Maya's presence would sway the last few. And that might be the difference between winning and losing.

15

TESSA MOVED IN THE UNDERGROWTH near a fast stream. The sun sank on the distant horizon. She needed to find a secure spot to spend the night. She just needed the right tree.

When she found it, her palms pressed flat against the rough bark, she looked up. For her, the safest place was up.

She took a moment to better secure her pack and weapons before she climbed. She'd always been good at climbing trees. Heights didn't scare her, so she eagerly scaled to the higher branches until they were thinner, their girth almost too small to safely hold her weight. Her view towered over many trees, and she could see for miles. It wasn't quite the same as being one with Striker, but it still gave her a sense of freedom. And, at this height, she was virtually invisible from the ground.

She threw a leg over the branch and settled in the crook against the trunk. A length of rope secured her to the tree. The sun would wake her early, and she needed rest.

Still, she stared into the twilight. Tomorrow, she figured,

she'd catch up to her mother and Sentinel. The timing was good—they were too far from the Hampshires' to make her return or to return with her. Too much time would be lost. They would have to allow her to accompany them.

The thought of the surprise on her mother's face made her smile.

It would be a great adventure. Soon, she'd be with them heading to another land. One she'd only dreamed about.

Tessa snuggled into her spot, the night sounds lulling her to sleep.

16

WHEN THE SOUNDS OF HORSES filled the air, Maya and Sentinel were already pulling weapons and turning back-to-back.

Within seconds, Maya recognized the leader and her sword tip dropped.

When he dismounted, she stepped forward. For all his talk of searching for her, he didn't look happy to see her.

"Inger." She gave a small smile as she faced him. "Surprised to see you so soon."

At first, he didn't say anything, visibly struggling with his irritation. She was sure her smile and sarcasm weren't helping his ego. When he muttered something under his breath, something she was sure wasn't complimentary, she let it go.

"I thought you would show at some point." She scanned his men. Few met her eyes; most watched Sentinel. She kept her humor to herself, knowing how intimidating he could be, even if he hadn't already bested them. "Just kind of surprised it didn't take you longer."

"You will be coming with us."

When she glanced back at him, she couldn't contain a full smile any longer. He was fluffed like a hen, but he kept throwing worried glances from her weapon to Sentinel.

"Yes," she said to him and sheathed her sword.

His eyes opened wide, his brows lost under his bangs. "Yes?"

"Yes. We were heading back to Berth. Heading to see Patrick. It's only smart to travel in a group. Safer that way." She gave him a wide-eyed, innocent look.

He stared at her for a moment longer. Chatter began within his ranks. Then, like a bladder of air without a stopper, he deflated. His shoulders lost their rigidity, his gaze fell to the ground at her feet, and his breath came out in a whoosh. He nodded.

She couldn't help but be impressed by his adaptability when he lifted his head, still nodding. "Yes, safer to travel together."

He faced his men. When he had all their attention, he raised his voice. "We will be traveling with these two. They are the people Patrick sent us to find. It has been many long years, but now we can go home."

Maya glanced at Sentinel. No wonder he'd appeared so upset when they left him trussed up. How long had they been at this?

"We will return to our homes victorious. We will be the motion that sets our worlds back to right." At this, the men gave shouts, smiled, and pounded each other on their backs.

He turned from his men, left them to give each other congratulations, and walked to Maya. "We'll camp here for the night, then tomorrow we'll head toward the coast."

Not usually content to give someone else the lead, Maya decided to allow him this small victory. She nodded once. Maya and Sentinel headed in the opposite direction to gather dry wood for their fire. They might be traveling with these men, but at least for now, they would keep themselves apart.

MAYA STEPPED FROM THE FOREST, her arms full of wood, a freshly killed rabbit hanging from her hand. Sentinel sat by a fire, and behind him the group of men made camp.

She dropped the wood in a pile with some Sentinel had gathered then began to clean the rabbit. Seeing what she brought, Sentinel set up a roasting spit.

At the sound of footsteps, Maya looked to see Inger walking toward them. She continued to prepare the rabbit. When he stopped but didn't speak, she glanced at him before returning her attention to their dinner.

"What can we do for you, Inger?"

"The men were talking. They were wondering if the queen were indeed your mother."

Maya handed the carcass to Sentinel who skewered the rabbit and set it to roasting. Leaning back, she regarded the other man.

"How long have you been on our trail?"

When he didn't answer, she indicated he should sit with them.

The man sat, watching the rabbit roast. He didn't meet her eyes or answer her question.

"So," she tried again, "you can ask your questions, but you won't answer one of mine."

He studied her as if taking in her words. Finally, he dropped his eyes. "I have been away from my home for almost five years."

"Five years? Is your group the only one Patrick sent out in search of us?"

At first, she didn't think he was going to answer her, but then he said, "No. There were many groups sent out to the far reaches of the known world—possibly even to parts unknown. I don't know how many are still in contact with Patrick."

The last of the sun set, and a lone owl hooted. Maya watched the smoke from the fire drift up until it disappeared into the darkness. The fire hissed as juices from the rabbit dripped onto burning brands, and the smell made her take a deep breath. She relaxed back against her pack and crossed her feet near the fire. The darkness and small fire created an intimacy that had her asking, "How did it come that you went on this mission?"

With a glance at his men, he said, "I was a small lad when the temple fell. But my parents spoke of it often enough. It became the thing of legend around town.

"I remember the ruins smoldered for weeks. And even after that, the green grew wild and untamed. At that time, I ran with a group of children and we'd play among the vines and brambles. It was great fun for us. We couldn't understand the fear in our parents' eyes and why we were told not to play there.

"One day, weeks later, we went to play, but some of the growth had blackened and died. We poked it with sticks, throwing the charred remains at each other. The next day, two of the children were kept home, sick in their beds. Within the week they'd died."

Firelight reflected in his eyes, making them appear to shine. The cadence of his voice, the intimacy of the camp, and the darkness made her shiver.

"It was some time—and after a couple more of the children had died—before we realized the blackened growth was killing them. Anyone who touched it became sick and withered like the green. People moved out of their homes, away from the location of the temple. The city of Berth, which was once a vital, thriving center, is now a ghost town. It was years before travelers began to report contamination outside the city walls. Spots, first very small, in all the forests of the land. Spots of sickness. Everything that lives is dying."

Sentinel sat forward to pull the rabbit from the fire. He did nothing else, though, sitting back to again regard Inger. Maya looked from her companion to the man, captivated by his tale.

"It was around this time that a man began to preach in the streets. He wore a monk's cloak and had only one hand. People seemed to know him—or at least know *of* him. Some referred to him by name. Patrick. The priest had been thought to have died the day the temple fell. Now to have him back and inspiring hope, people flocked to him. His words led the elders to again begin thinking of the future. A future without the rot.

"Patrick told us of a woman. A woman subverted by evil. It was her and the magic fueling her that we needed to best. But to do this, we needed to find another. A champion." Inger sat forward, his gaze intent on Maya. "You. Patrick instructed us to find you. He believes, and we believe, that you will be able to end your mother's subversion. We were charged to find you and bring you back."

Maya reached for the rabbit, tearing some meat from it. Filling her mouth, she gave herself time to think. She swallowed hard then looked from Sentinel to Inger. They both stared back.

"This is all fine and good, Inger, but did Patrick ever give any indication of how I am supposed to overcome my mother?"

When he didn't answer her, she looked away, her lips pursed.

"The last time I saw my mother, she sent a gray mist that killed everything it touched." Maya stood to walk from the fire. She stopped at the tree line, her back to the two men as she remembered her mother's rage.

She spun and walked back to them. "This is a fool's errand. My mother became a being I don't know. She doesn't know me—did you know she tried to kill me that day? You talk about the day the temple fell, but I was there." She gestured to herself. Her voice rose. "If not for this man here"—she pointed at Sentinel— "I would have been dead long ago. I have no weapon for this. No defense against her magic."

She plopped back down in her spot and again ripped meat from the rabbit. "We shouldn't even be here. There is no help I can give."

17

WHEN TESSA WOKE, THE SUN was just cresting the edge of the world. Its light caught her eye as she sat up.

Rubbing her eyes, she watched and listened for any sign of danger. After a time, when all seemed quiet and normal, she shimmied down from her tree.

She wasn't hungry yet. She'd watch for berries, roots, and the like, and stop later to break her fast. Shouldering her pack and her bow case, she headed in the direction of her mother and Sentinel.

Yesterday morning, when she'd linked with Striker to check on them, their track had taken a direct course to the coast. She had no reason to think they'd veered from it.

IT WAS ALMOST NOON WHEN she heard a scream.

Tessa knew she was coming near an area where she should meet with her mother and Sentinel. Her head was down, looking for traces of their passage, when the scream made her head wrench up, eyes wide.

Her only thought was her mother, and she was in trouble. Taking off at a run, the girl crashed through the underbrush. When another scream came to her, this time a man, she slowed to silence her progress.

She snuck closer, moving the branches out of her way, aware of where she stepped to make sure she didn't make a sound.

She heard the laughter of men. Crouching, she peeked between the foliage of a fern. Her life with her mother and Sentinel, though designed to train her to defend herself, had never put her in a situation to come up against the cruelty of man. Now she saw it in all its blatant vulgarity.

Two dead horses lay tangled in front of an overturned wagon, still bound in their harnesses. Tessa couldn't discern where one animal began and the other ended. The horses and wagon must have been crashed to bring it to a halt.

A young boy lay sprawled on the wagon and the dirt. Blood and brain matter seeped from a crack in his skull, and his leg was bent at an odd angle. An old woman was attempting to hold him. Her face was distorted with the ravages of her crying. Their goods were strewn about, and two highwaymen rummaged through their belongings.

Partway across the road, a man lay face down, another of the robbers stooped with a knee between his shoulder blades. The man grasped the farmer by his hair and pulled backward. He slit the man's throat with a knife. Blood spurted, wetting the ground in front of them.

The scent, a coppery, earthy smell, came to Tessa and she fought a gag in her throat, tears rising to her eyes. With her fingers to her lips, she turned from the sight. Then, more afraid to look away, worried she wouldn't notice if they headed toward her, she again faced the barbarism.

When the killer dropped the man's head, it plopped into a pool of blood, making a sucking sound. He stood, wiping his blade on the dead man's pants and looking toward the woman. She was gently sobbing now, crooning to and rocking the dead boy.

"Ain't nothin' here." One of the men kicked some belongings out of his way. He turned in a circle as if trying to locate some hidden cache of goods.

"Farmers," the killer muttered in disgust.

He seemed to be the leader. He walked around the wagon and disappeared from Tessa's view. Moments later, he was back leading a string of saddled horses. The robbers must have left their mounts below the hillside to conceal them while they ambushed the wagon. Tied by a long rope to one of the horses was a dog. It was medium in size with a stocky, powerful body, and a short snout and ears. When they passed the old woman, the dog strained at his leash, snapping at her. She was oblivious to this, continuing to sing softly to the boy.

Tessa, who had before bemoaned smelling the scents of the dead, was now glad the wind was blowing from them to her. Perhaps the dog wouldn't scent her.

She crouched lower, curling into herself, trying to become invisible. Her mind worked furiously. She feared the woman would be killed. She had been too late for the man and boy, but she couldn't sit here and let an innocent woman die.

When she heard a shout from farther down the hill, she closed her eyes and concentrated on Striker.

WIND. THE WARMTH OF THE sun. A lightness.

All these feelings came to her in an instant, each familiar as her own. She scanned the world from a vantage high above. Below, the wagon and people appeared as toys.

She turned a wing and circled the crash. Two more men on horseback moved toward it. They wore the same clothing and hats and carried similar weapons as the robbers.

She flew past them to perch on a tree just off the road. She studied where she knew her body kneeled. Even to her it was unseen behind the curtain of foliage.

The newcomers came into the clearing, and the first men welcomed them with familiarity.

"Homer," the leader called. The mounted man raised a hand and headed in his direction. When he reached him, close to where Tessa in Striker's body sat, he alit from his horse and approached the leader.

"Anything further on?"

The man shook his head. "Nah. All the roads is clear. Not much pickins betwixt here and there."

The leader was already nodding before the man ended his reply. "Gonna have to go on further. This here area's gettin' too picked over for my likin'."

Tessa listened intently to the men's words. She needed to

find a way to ensure the woman's safety. She couldn't just sit and do nothing.

When the hawk ruffled its feathers, the man's mount looked up. The bird and horse caught each other's gaze.

WEIGHT. POWER. FEAR.

Tessa's world shifted, and then she was looking at the hawk in the tree from a vantage point she'd never experienced. Her control slipped as the horse threw its head and whinnied in panic. When the horse reared to its hind legs, the rein fell from the man's grip. He turned, grasping frantically for the straps. The other horses shifted, a moment's panic passing through their ranks, but they were tied securely to a branch. Men came running, and the hound strained at his rope, barking at the commotion.

Now free, the horse went to bolt, but Tessa exerted pressure to control the animal. She'd never shared this bond before with any animal but Striker—never realized she could. The horse's instinct told it to flee, panic filling it at her intrusion. Again it reared and spun. Tessa projected her will more intensely than she'd ever tried just as the horse planted its hooves to run.

Men surrounded the frenzied horse, throwing up their hands and shouting. The dog, barking and twisting, broke his lead and entered the fray, snapping at the steed's feet. The horse reared again, coming down. Its front hooves almost landed on the dog. When the horse dropped its head to kick, it locked eyes with the dog.

STRENGTH. INTELLIGENCE. THE INTENSITY OF sight, sound, and smell.

The dog turned and ran, dropping its hindquarters as if it were being nipped at. When it stopped, whined, and ran the side of its head along the ground, Tessa felt as if she were in a big vat being mixed. She couldn't control herself. Emotions swirled with the new creature whose mind she shared.

Chaos ruled the clearing. No one noticed the dog, all eyes on the horse, who was now quieting. It blew large breaths out, head hanging down.

In the head of the dog, Tessa spoke gently.

It's okay. Good boy.

The dog calmed and quit trying to tear its head off along the ground. It turned and sat, panting hard. Drool ran from its mouth. Every few seconds, it would make a loud slurping sound, lick its nose, and then return to panting.

Tessa kept up the monologue of calming words, but her mind worked furiously. She'd never imagined she would be able to jump animals. The knowledge was exciting and scary at the same time.

With the horse captured, the men began to gather their things. It looked as though they would soon be leaving. One of the men stopped in front of the old lady, watched her keening to the boy, and then turned to the general group.

"What we wanna do with her?"

The leader stopped what he was doing to regard her, and then, as if dismissing her from his thoughts, gave a small shrug and muttered, "Kill her."

The man advanced, pulling a knife from his belt.

The dog jumped and latched on the man's forearm. Bearing down, Tessa tasted blood. She would have thought this action repulsive, but enough of the dog's instincts remained that all she felt was excitement and hunger. Lunging with its large body, the dog pulled backward, shaking its head.

The man screamed a high-pitched wail that didn't even sound as if it came from a man. He shook his arm and hit at the dog to dislodge it, but its jaw clenched harder. Tessa felt the sensation of the dog's teeth sliding along the bone in the man's arm.

When the man went down on his back, arm still in the canine's mouth, the dog's owner ran up and grabbed the collar. He hit the dog, pummeling his head.

Concern for the dog warred with concern for the woman and Tessa released the man. He cradled his mangled arm, moaning in pain.

Again, the clearing was in chaos.

The canine's owner pulled it away and tied it securely to the wagon. Tessa observed the men through the dog. What could she do now?

The men were yelling, the leader gesturing at the dog. One man stooped down and began to bind the injured man's arm. When he helped him up, with his good arm around his shoulders, the leader stopped yelling to help him rise.

In no time, the men were mounted, the leader saying, "Just keep that cur away from me," and they headed out.

When the leash pulled tightly on Tessa's throat, she closed

her eyes and concentrated on her own body. She had a pulse of fear when she realized she hadn't thought about getting back into herself, but then the familiar sensation of shifting filled her, and when she opened her eyes, she was in her body, still crouched behind the blind of vines.

When she stood and looked, the last of the riders were just disappearing around a bend in the road. She waited a moment more before skirting the vegetation and stepping out to the woman. As with the men and dog, the woman seemed oblivious to her presence.

Tessa bent down beside her, and after placing a gentle hand on her shoulder, she gave her a slight shake. She had to shake her again, and harder before she got a response. When the woman quieted and turned to look her way, she didn't focus on her. Her attention was far away.

"Ma'am," Tessa began, moving to try to catch the woman's eye. When the woman didn't respond, Tessa tried again.

"Ma'am let me help you. We can bury your loved ones. I can help you get to the next town, if that's what you want."

The woman looked up. She laid the boy gently to the side and stood. She only took one step toward Tessa.

When the woman plunged a knife into her own stomach, Tessa's head swiveled to the empty scabbard on her own belt. Disbelief filled her mind and for a moment, she couldn't move.

The woman fell to her knees, her hands still on the hilt of Tessa's knife.

"No." Tessa dropped beside her. She never imagined the threat to her would be from the woman herself.

Blood ran from the wound to soak the woman's dress. Out of power, the woman lay back on the dirt, her hands falling from the knife to her sides. Tessa leaned over the woman, grabbed her by her shoulders, and tried to sit her up. Without the woman's assistance, she couldn't move her and had to lay her back down.

"No. No, you can't. We were going to get you to town."

The woman stared at Tessa, her eyes beginning to dim. Shock froze Tessa's thoughts.

When the woman's head dropped to the side, she muttered, "Robert," and then nothing.

WHEN TESSA HEARD THE BIRD caw, the blood on the woman had thickened. She didn't know how long she'd been sitting in the road. After another caw, she looked over her shoulder and saw a couple of large black birds on the man's back. One pecked his cheek, removing a piece of flesh.

Her stomach churned, and her body threatened to throw up the small amount of food she'd eaten that morning. Jumping to her feet, she rushed the birds and they flew off, voicing their complaints at her intrusion. She thought about sending Striker after them but realized the birds were just being birds.

She would need to bury the family.

Searching through the belongings strewn about the clearing, Tessa located a hoeing tool she thought she might be able to dig with. The birds were back, though.

Sweat rolled down her back by the time she got the family pulled together and covered with an old ratty blanket. The family would be safe from the ravages of the birds until she could get them buried.

OFF THE ROAD, OUT OF sight of the crashed wagon, Tessa stood over the three graves. She'd done the best she could. The graves were shallow, so she'd gathered large stones to cover the dirt to keep scavengers away.

She was exhausted, dirty, and hungry. She was no closer to her mother. In fact, she was even farther behind them.

She stood, her mind in a stupor, and stared at the graves. All she'd been able to think since coming upon the crash was how to save the woman. Nothing had worked out as she'd planned.

She didn't have any words to say over the graves, didn't have the energy to think of any. She dropped the hoe and walked back to the road and the wagon. There, lying in the dirt, was her knife, dried with the woman's blood. Tessa bent to pick it up, almost falling in her exhaustion.

Her entire frame hurt as she stared at the weapon. Blood had covered the blade before—the blood of animals she'd hunted. But this stain, this woman's blood, made her heart ache. She'd need to gather her pack, find a place to clean up, eat something, and get some rest.

Tomorrow she'd need to travel fast. She needed to get to her mother.

She needed a hug.

18

MAYA REALIZED VERY QUICKLY THAT traveling with a group of men was no fun.

She was tired, bored with their discussions, and she missed her daughter. The best part of it was because they were traveling by horseback, she could tell herself that this experience would be done quickly, and she would be home again.

She longed to sit with Tessa and visit about her day. To work together around the warm fire in their cabin. To hunt together, gather berries, or tend to their garden. Practice with their weapons. There were times over the years when she thought her life was boring, but now she longed for the normal routine of day-to-day life with her child.

What if it were months before she saw Tessa again? Years?

What if she never returned home to her daughter?

Thinking that maybe this decision to travel back to Berth was made in haste, she kicked her horse into a faster trot to move alongside Inger.

"Tell me," she began, catching his attention. "Tell me more of what is happening in and around Berth. Why do you think my mother is still alive, and what does it have to do with her?"

Inger looked at her for a long moment, his body swaying with the steps of his steed. Then he blinked, dropped his gaze, and with a slightly trembling hand, he wiped his mouth.

"When Patrick first called people together, his intent to conscript groups to search for you, he didn't tell us of all he knew or planned. Perhaps even that he didn't have a plan. We all knew or had heard bits and pieces about that day. The death of Mikel Bathsar. The freeing of the land from his tyranny. We also knew the land continued to die. People were dying.

"He made us feel as if we could do something. That *we* were the answer. That the future was ours for the taking." Inger studied the far hill, his eyes narrowing. "He never told us that we might be gone for years, or maybe never come home at all."

Maya felt a sense of guilt as if she should apologize for the hardships created by her family.

"When Mikel Bathsar was in power, he had a man who served him."

She leaned forward in her saddle. Excitement colored her voice when she interrupted his tale. "Yes. I remember him. The little man."

He nodded. "Orson. The man's name was Orson, and in many ways, he was worse than your uncle."

She sat back, her eyes taking on a far-off gaze. "Orson . . . Yes, he was a bad man. Scary."

"He is still alive."

Maya's eyes flashed. "Alive? How? I thought he died that day in the temple."

"No. He now serves your mother."

They rode together for a while, neither saying anything. The sun bore on them, but Maya felt a chill in her bones. She had thought she was finished with this business. She thought she'd be allowed to live her life, safe and happy with her daughter and Sentinel.

"As I said, for the longest time—years—people thought your uncle's oppression was vanquished. The ruins of the temple spoke to the people's strength. About the time of Patrick's return, the small man also made an appearance.

"At first, it was just whispering from some folks. They'd say they saw him walking through town in the dead of night, or maybe standing afar and watching, but when they looked again, he was gone. People told them they were crazy. Imagining things because of the black rot. That was at first."

A shiver ran down Maya's spine. She remembered him all too well—his face, the sound of his wheezing, wispy voice. When he'd called her *pet*. Being chained at the mercy of his less-than-tender care.

"He began to come around more and more. And then, the children began disappearing. No one knew for certain he was behind it, but we all knew he had to be. The coincidence was too great. People talked, whispered in corners, afraid somehow he would hear. They remembered how it had been. His perversions. His cruelties. And they wondered how they could have forgotten. How could they have gotten complacent? An evil such as his. They should have dismantled the ruins of the temple, stone by stone, to ensure he was indeed dead."

Again, Inger's story stalled, and in the quiet, he and Maya rode, neither willing to break the silence. Each lost in their memories.

A while later, Maya asked, "And my mother? When did you know she still lived?"

"One day, there she was. Walking down the road, obvious to all. Some, the younger ones, didn't know who, or what, she was. All they saw was a finely dressed lady — old and hunched but finely dressed. With her she carried a basket of goodies. As soon as one child received a treat, all of them flocked to her. The parents tried to call them back, but the lure of her treats . . . sweets being such a rare thing . . . they would not come.

"When she left, many of the children went with her. Some were held back by their parents. Everyone thought the children were lost forever. But the next day, they returned. It became apparent very quickly that they were not as they left. But none of them could remember what had happened. They would speak achingly of Nav-lys. That was when we first began to refer to her as that. We didn't know whether this was her name or just what the children called her."

Maya's memories flew back to her mother tending her flowers. Her large bonnet shaded a portion of her face, but still the freckles popped on her skin. Under the freckles, her skin would take a honey glow from the loving touch of the sun.

And another memory. One of Sylvan on a small stool, milking the old cow. Hauling the pail of warm milk into their cabin. Baking for her child.

No. She wasn't Sylvan any longer. Not the mother she remembered.

"So, what made you realize she needed to be stopped? It doesn't sound like she was doing anything."

"When she came again to the town, the children again went with her, but this time, a man followed them. Nav-lys and the children went into a cave in a hillside outside of town. The cave has always been there, but no one goes in it. No one even goes near it. There is an old tale of bad things happening there. Even the air has an oppressive taste."

"Did the man follow them? Did he go into the cave?"

Inger nodded at her questions, though his face had paled. "He went into the cave. He heard voices. Chanting. Laughing. We don't know what he saw within the walls. He came back to the town, running. He was stumbling over his own feet. The terror on his face and in his eyes . . . He could never tell us exactly what he saw." Inger shook his head and wiped his hands over his face and into his hair.

"Later, the children came back, and they were worse. Like empty scarecrows, no longer children. Everyone was afraid. People got together and said we had to do something. Nav-lys, witch that she was, needed to be killed. We couldn't continue to sacrifice our children. That night, the man who'd spoken out the loudest was killed in his bed. His daughter, a small child of no more than seven years, wielded the knife that sliced his throat. When he was found the next morning, blood covered the two of them. The girl still had the knife in her hands.

"When I left with these men"—he looked around them at the group— "the people of the town were tying their children up at night. That was years ago. I don't know what's happening now. All I know is, when we send a missive to Patrick, we get an answer. He pleads for us to continue our journey. To help him in his fight against Nav-lys and her man."

"And why do you think I can be of help to you?"

"Patrick told us that you vanquished your mother when you faced her before." He looked at her closely, his expression hopeful. She thought he was almost holding his breath waiting for her answer.

"Why would he say that?" She shook her head at him. "I ran." She shifted in her seat to better face him. "I ran from my mother. I was lucky to get out of the temple that day."

His eyes narrowed and he eyed her. "He says you have magic."

She broke his gaze to stare off over the riders in front of them. Without giving him the answer he seemed to want, she mumbled, "What am I doing here?"

* * * * *

AT THE FIRST CLANG OF sword against sword, the men sleeping around the fire leaped to their feet. Sleep still clouding their minds, swords were pulled.

Inger spun and stepped toward the sounds of battle only to see Maya and Sentinel sparring in the field.

In the morning light, the four swords shone with every

move. Men stepped up to Inger, a question apparent in their expressions.

Maya and Sentinel moved back and forth across the grassy expanse, neither willing to give to the other. Their abilities were equal and like nothing Inger had ever seen.

The motion of the combatants and their expertise with their weapons was like a dance. He didn't know when Maya began to gain an upper hand, but suddenly, Sentinel was being driven back across the field toward the men.

Like the buzz of an insect, an incessant sound dug into Inger's mind. He tore his gaze from the fight, unsure what he heard. He saw the other men looking around, curiosity in their expressions. As the tone increased in volume, Inger returned his attention to the duo.

Maya's swords were now moving so fast, he was unable to track them. All Sentinel could do was bring his weapons up in defense. As he watched, spellbound, Inger realized the sound was coming from her weapons. With every arc, they sang.

With wide eyes, he looked from the flash of steel to Maya's face. Her red hair flamed around her head where the sun caught it. A smile of pure pleasure lit her features.

Without warning, she stopped her forward momentum. Sentinel dropped his arms, deep breaths moving his chest.

When Maya looked toward the watching men, Inger would swear her eyes shone blue.

19

THE PAIN IN PATRICK'S KNEES and hips broke through the haze of his thoughts.

Patrick told himself that he would stay here, on his knees in supplication, until he received an answer to his prayers.

It had been years since he'd received direction from Caleb. How was he supposed to know what to do? He had sent men out. Groups of men—some of them sent to their deaths. Only two of the groups still made contact with him. What if it were all for nothing? What if Maya couldn't stop her mother? Maybe, bringing her here would just ensure her death, too.

The door to his chamber banged open, a young servant hustling in.

"Father," he said, screeching to a halt when he saw the priest on his knees, arms pulled to his chest.

Patrick kept his head lowered, giving himself another moment.

When the boy didn't leave, Patrick sighed. He raised his

head to look at the boy, only to see he too had bowed his head. The corners of Patrick's mouth rose.

"Yes, Samuel?"

The boy looked up, barely meeting the priest's eyes, and then he scanned the room. "Um . . . Father Patrick. There's been a message. Chester bid me come and get you."

With a nod, Patrick placed his good hand on the floor. He wondered how he'd rise when his lower half felt numb.

Before he could get a foot under him, he felt the boy at his side. With a surprisingly strong hold, he grasped the priest's arm, the one without a hand, and looped it over his shoulders. He held the older man around his waist and helped him to stand.

"Thank you, Samuel." He stood for a moment, his arm around the boy's shoulder, and allowed the blood to flow back to his extremities. The pain of it, he deserved. It was only right that he should feel pain when so many others would never feel anything again. No pain, no joy, no love, no anger.

He limped slightly as he and the boy made their way from his chamber, but he resisted leaning on Samuel for assistance.

Halfway down the hallway, they met Chester coming from the opposite direction. He hustled, panting slightly. He held a small scroll. They stopped when they came together, Chester giving a small bow to the priest.

"Father Patrick. This message just arrived. I thought it might be important."

Patrick took the scroll. Everyone had been on edge waiting to hear if Inger and his group had relocated the woman they thought was Maya. He turned to wander back down the hall, slowly opening the scroll. He could feel the two men at his back.

"It is from Inger," he said, confirming their thoughts. He finished it, feeling a bit light-headed. He turned and handed the paper to Chester who wasted no time in reading it.

"He found her," Chester said, his voice breathless and wispy. He reread the message, then looked from Samuel back to Patrick. "He found her. Now what?"

Now what, indeed, Patrick thought. "They will bring her back with them."

"How long do you think?" Chester pressed. "How long before we'll be able to confront Nav-lys and her man?"

Patrick held up a hand. He was getting ahead of himself. "Why don't we just wait until Inger returns with the woman. *If* she is Maya, then we'll take it from there."

Chester nodded his agreement, but Patrick could tell his words meant little. He could practically see his wheels turning with ideas as they again started down the hall.

When they passed a window, which was really an arrow slit in this old castle they now found themselves housed in, Patrick stopped to stare out. The sun shone on the surrounding forest, and it should have had an inviting feeling, but he shivered. Nothing had happened as he'd planned.

From the time Caleb had first come to him as a small boy, he'd had in mind how he would succeed, how he would fulfill the wishes of the man who'd raised him from the squalor of his youth. All he'd ever wanted to do was to please Caleb, to show he was worthy of the charge he had instilled in him.

Now, he thought he was heading in the correct direction, but it was so hard to be certain. Confusion warred with devotion. Each tried to overtake the other.

If only Caleb would speak to him again. It had been so long.

But it seemed, no matter how often or fervently he prayed, he received no response. Caleb was silent.

20

THE HAWK RODE THE AIRWAVES. As it circled, its head shifted toward the terrain below.

With a dip of a wing, the raptor flew toward the mountains, taking an indirect line toward the shore.

When it spotted the riders miles ahead of the area it searched, it angled its body to better utilize the warm upward currents. Soon, it was near enough to identify the red head of a woman who rode in the midst of the men. Behind her sat an exotic black man.

Striker dipped and turned, watching to ensure the woman and man weren't under any duress. When it seemed they rode willingly with the group, the bird turned back the way it'd come, heading for its mistress.

* * * * *

TESSA BLINKED AND LOWERED HER head, breaking contact with Striker. Her mind spun.

No wonder she hadn't been able to locate her mother and Sentinel. When had they come back into contact with the group of men on horseback? And why were they now riding with them?

She didn't see any way to catch them. On their steeds, they would outdistance her in no time — they already had. She thought for a moment about returning to the Hampshires'. She could be back within the week. Her mother would never know she'd followed them. She could, if she wanted, be back within safe walls, burrowed in a warm bed, secure in her days.

The thought fled quickly.

To follow her mother and Sentinel, she would need to keep an eye on them with Striker and continue to follow them, moving as fast as she could. She hadn't anticipated making the trip to the coast on her own, but she was secure in her ability to feed and water herself, to fight if necessary, and to flee when she must.

She took her pack and weapons from beside her. Shouldering all, she looked toward the mountains and the coast. In the far distance, she thought she saw Striker winging toward her.

She took a deep breath, and with it she centered her mind. Her mother. She would track and locate her mother. Then she could make the trip across the dark sea with her and Sentinel. She would prove having her would benefit all.

21

THE WOMAN WHO ONCE WAS Sylvan Singh wandered through the cold, dark cavern. She had many hours of downtime, many days where all she did was dream of killing.

Sometimes, in the dark, she would listen to the Other in her mind. The true Sylvan. She would listen while she screamed or cried. Sometimes, the Other was perfectly quiet. Those times made her stop and listen, wondering what she might be up to.

Never did she allow the Other to be out. To be in the light. When the Other had almost won back her freedom, Nav-lys realized all was not as it appeared. She was not as invulnerable as she wished. And the Other was not as defenseless as she thought.

Today was not a quiet day, though. As she moved through the cavern, the echo of the Other's screams rang in her ears. The reverberations were so loud, she didn't at first hear the man. When she realized he neared, she turned partially to face him.

"My love," he whispered, ever careful of her, ever wary of

making her angry.

When she turned fully, she looked down on him. He had been a good servant. She didn't trust him, but of all her property, he was the one she dealt with most.

She didn't answer him, but he knew she wouldn't speak with him.

"The new children are here." To locate new blood, the young, he'd had to search abroad. Villagers hid their children. Now it was harder than ever to come by what she needed.

She turned to sweep back toward the main cavern. Before they arrived, she could hear the faint echo of them crying. This delivery, their life forces riding hot and high, was another promise of what could be. When Cassandra came, she would take the land. She would take all the life in the land and if pleased, as promised, Nav-lys would leave this place. She would be taken with Cassandra.

22

MAYA LAY ON HER BELLY next to the men, Inger on one side, Sentinel on the other. They looked over the outcropping at the massive man-camp below. They needed to get by the bandits, to continue their trip to the coast and home. There didn't seem to be any other way than this cut in the mountains. And to use this mountain pass, they would need to get by the bandits.

With a look and a motion at each other, the three slid down the back of the hill, keeping themselves out of sight.

"What do you think?" Inger asked her and Sentinel. Somehow, in the last few days, they had become the leaders of this group. Inger and his men seemed more than happy to follow her lead.

She raised an eyebrow at Sentinel. "I don't see any way to get through the pass other than to go right through the camp."

Sentinel nodded his agreement.

"Do you think we could sneak through the camp once darkness has fallen?" She sounded hopeful, even to her own ears.

"No," Sentinel replied bluntly.

"I guess we could go in prepared to fight but see if they will allow us to pass through."

The men just looked at her. "Doing that will give up the element of surprise. We may need it. There are many more of them than of us."

Maya nodded and walked off, muttering, "I know. I know."

WHEN THE SUN BEGAN TO sink, Maya still didn't have a workable plan to get them through the mountain. She really didn't want to have to fight alongside these men, not against a greater force and for something that really wasn't that important. If they could just find another way.

Just as she was getting ready to head back the way they'd come, Inger came to her with one of the men from his group.

"This is Migog," he said. "He joined our band not long ago. He was traveling alone and said he didn't have anyone." He turned toward the man, motioned him forward, and said, "Tell her what you told me."

The man, who looked unhappy at being put in the center of attention, mumbled, "I grew up around here. Was tell, back then, of a way through the mountains."

"Through the mountains, like the pass?"

"Nah." He shook his head. "Like right through the mountain."

"Like a tunnel through the mountains?"

He nodded, the look on his face one of slight annoyance.

"Times told, it was a long hoof, but doable. More than one said they went that way."

"Is it big enough to bring the horses?"

He scanned over her shoulder, thinking. "Well, now, I don't know if anyone took rides into the mountain. Gonna be a few days or so."

"You can lead us to where the trail begins?"

"Yah, sure." He nodded vigorously. "We're gonna need light. Gonna need plenty of light."

Maya looked at Inger, and he wasted no time getting the men busy making torches.

"We'll take the horses as far as the beginning of the tunnel and look there if we're going to have to release them. If our luck holds, perhaps we'll be able to take them with us."

All the men and Maya got their belongings together and mounted. Migog led the way around the back side of the hill. The farther they traveled, the less they could hear the encampment. After a while, sounds of voices, pans, and swords clashing were a distant threat.

The birds sang high in the trees as the horses plodded along in a line, and the hot sun shone down. Maya watched the birds jump among the branches, their movements hypnotic. When a horse moved alongside her, she gave a small start and looked back over her shoulder at the rider.

Sentinel moved even closer. When he leaned toward her, she leaned to meet him. "What do you think of this man of Inger's?"

She considered his words and then looked up and down the

line of men, Migog in the lead. She sat flatly back on her saddle, pulled her cape from her shoulders, and laid it in front of her.

"I think," she said and she leaned into him again, "that you and I should watch ourselves with all of these men."

Nodding, his lips pursed, Sentinel allowed his horse to fall back.

23

THE SUN WAS SINKING ON the horizon when they reached the cave entrance. It was hard to see in the dark, and even harder to see within.

With a stream nearby, Maya went with some of the men to replenish their water jugs. Sentinel went with the rest to investigate the cave to see if they could bring the horses.

When she returned, some of her companions were arguing. She walked to Sentinel.

"I think we should spend the night and enter the cave in the morning."

"Nah," another one voiced, "we'll waste hours that way. We might as well get started now."

Another said, "We aren't going to be able to bring the horses. The ceiling is too low."

"Maybe we shouldn't go this way. There's got to be another way through the mountains."

Maya watched the argument for a moment before she turned to Inger. He was the leader of this band. He should be the one to decide—at least for his men. When Inger noticed her, he cleared his throat and stepped forward.

"It's been pretty easy traveling today with the horses and all. I think we should unload them and let them go. We can pack up all we can carry, get some torches lit, and head into the cave. It's going to be dark in there whether it's night or day." When he finished, he looked at Maya. She nodded and turned to her horse. The men babbled behind her, some agreeing and some complaining while they gathered their belongings.

After removing the tack and supplies from her horse, Maya pet the animal's nose. She laid her cheek against the beast, breathing in the warm, earthy scent of his fur.

When he blew out a breath and tossed his head, she leaned back. "Whoa, that's a good boy."

She gave the horse one final pat on the neck and slipped the harness from around its head. It stood for a moment, but with her urging, it turned and walked into the night. Around her, other horses were released. Watching them disappear into the forest, she felt heavy.

Branches threw shadows in the light of the newly risen moon. She wondered if Tessa was looking at the moon with her. Was she wondering where her mother was? She thought of her daughter, warm in the Hampshires' home. Safe. She needed to keep it that way.

"We are ready."

Maya looked past Sentinel at the torches being lit by the mouth of the cave. She gathered her pack and weapons and slung them comfortably on her back. She checked her long knife to make sure it sat properly on her waist and then nodded at Sentinel. Together, they moved toward the men and the blaze.

24

WITH ONE STEP INTO THE cave, Maya had misgivings. She'd never been a fan of being underground. The cold and wet made her feel trapped. If it came to it, fighting would be very difficult, if not impossible, within the confined area.

She didn't trust the men they traveled with, and she didn't know what was coming. Not the best place to be.

She gave Sentinel one last telling look and then followed the men.

The oppression deepened immediately. She only saw the backs of the next two men before the darkness enveloped her vision. A steady habit of looking down and around kept her less anxious. The walls were so close, she could touch them. The men's breaths came from all around her, and her breaths came harder as she imagined that they were using up all of the air.

The tunnel floor was surprisingly smooth. Occasionally, a rock tripped one of them, or a motion caused someone to start, but mostly, it was quiet and easy. Maya liked it even less for all its seemingly benign qualities.

The longer they walked, the warmer and staler the air became. Maya didn't know if this had been such a good idea. How many days would it take to pass through this mountain?

THEY'D WALKED FOR SOME TIME, the men relaxing and visiting after they felt more comfortable. They kept their voices low, however, perhaps bothered by the echoing quality of their surroundings.

Maya still found it hard to breathe, the air having become drier. She was more used to the confinement, however, and moved along easily beside Sentinel. Occasionally, he dropped back when the opening narrowed, but then he would move beside her again. They spoke little, both attentive to any changes.

Inger called a halt. They didn't know how far they'd gone or how long they had to go, but each was tired.

Maya moved to the band's leader, and when he finished a conversation with one of his men, she said, "I think we should have a sentry tonight. Sentinel and I, along with a couple of your men, can take first watch."

Inger nodded and regarded a pair who he dictated would stand sentry.

Maya and Sentinel took the opposite direction of the other watch, which put them back down the tunnel the way they'd come. A couple of the firebrands were laid beside the men to allow some light while they slept.

Maya rolled her torch in the loose soil. She moved out of the edge of light and then a bit farther down the tunnel. When she was no longer in the light, she dropped her pack and sat on it. A moment later, Sentinel sat next to her.

"I've never been in any place like this before," she whispered.

"Nor I."

"I wonder how long it will take to get through the mountain."

"Days."

She nodded and looked back down the dark hall they'd come from. "I'm going to lose my mind before we get out of here."

He didn't answer. When she glanced at him, he was also staring at the encroaching darkness.

25

TESSA LOOKED DOWN AT THE camp of men. They were everywhere.

Even having been to town, this was the largest group of people in one place she'd ever seen. Just the noise and smell were enough to warn others of their presence.

Once again, she'd lost track of her mother. She didn't know how they kept eluding her, but they were heading toward the coast. She figured she'd keep heading that way herself and keep an eye out for them. She was confident she would find them.

This camp made her rethink her plan, though. What if the coastal town were bigger than even this camp? She couldn't imagine it. Maybe, she wouldn't be able to locate her mother or Sentinel easily. What would she do then?

She again studied the men below her. There was no need worrying about what would be. If she couldn't get past this camp, she wouldn't be looking for her mother in any city.

The sun was sinking on the far hill, its light throwing streaks through the tents and concealing people with smoke from the fires. She wondered if they'd even know she didn't belong, there were so many. If she waited until after dark, though, many would be asleep and seeing her would be harder.

She decided that would be the way to go. She'd stay until well after dark and then make her way through the camp.

TESSA STIRRED, HEARING THE CALL of a distant owl. When she opened her eyes, she realized she'd fallen asleep.

She looked up to scan the camp below her. It looked much as it had, though fewer bodies moved around. She scooted backward until she could stand and remain concealed. With a glance, she noticed the half-moon high in the sky and realized it was later than she thought.

She put the bow case on and then pulled her cloak around her, pulling the hood up. She took her long knife from her belt, keeping it hidden within the folds of her cloak. With her pack on her shoulder, she could have been one in a thousand other people.

As she moved toward the edges of the camp, her heartbeat increased. Before long, she felt it in her ears. She wiped her palms on the underside of her cloak.

When she saw the first man in the distance, she lowered her hooded head and walked straight into the camp. He never even glanced at her. A small smile curved her lips.

One down, a few thousand to go.

SHE'D MADE HER WAY THROUGH about half of the camp when she realized she was being followed. Keeping an eye on him, she sidestepped and headed deeper into the camp and then back to the edges of it. He not only stayed with her but moved even closer.

Her thoughts spun. She walked as if aimlessly moving to the other side of the camp but continued to shift toward the outside. Fewer figures crossed her path, and when she moved into a grove of trees, she slowed.

"Hey, you there," the man trailing her called, but she ignored him and kept walking. A bit farther and she slipped behind a tree. With a shift of her shoulders, Tessa dropped her cloak, pack, and weapons. She kept only her long knife in her hand, reversed it to hold the hilt up, and waited for him.

She figured she could knock him out with the butt of her knife. By the time he came to, she would be long gone.

The man stopped just out of reach. He looked into the darkness and then paced slowly forward. With her back pressed against a tree, she held her breath. He was so quiet. She almost peeked out from around the tree when the snap of a twig had her halting. In the next instant, the man stepped past her.

She sprung onto his back, one arm wrapped around his throat. He bent at the waist and, with a spin, flipped her from his back. The impact expelled air from her lungs. She gasped, unable to catch her breath.

The man's foot caught her in the ribs. With a moan, she rolled to her side, the hood of her cloak falling back, and black hair tumbled out.

"Well, lookie what we have here."

Tessa rolled to her hands and knees to look through the falls of her hair. When he reached down to grab a handful and wrench her head back, she rose to her knees, a gasp forced from her. He stepped closer, placing his other hand under her chin to jerk her face up.

She couldn't breathe. Her strikes feeble, she hit out at him, but he just laughed.

She couldn't catch her breath. Couldn't get his hands off her. She flailed around, ineffectively swatting at him. Her hand scraped the ground and she felt a stone. She grasped it with her nails and swung wildly, only to miss. It brought her body around, and the man shook her by the hair and slapped her across the face.

For a stunned moment, Tessa didn't know where she was. The ringing in her ears was so loud she couldn't hear anything else, and then the sound of her breathing filled her head. She cried out, feeling pain in her jaw and lip.

"You're a scrapper, ain't yah?" His voice rasped in her ear as he sniffed her hair. She hung by her neck, arms limp, barely staying on her knees. He shook her again, causing pain to arc across her neck and down her back.

A sharp sting had her pulling her hand up before she realized it was the edge of her knife. Splaying her fingers, she strained for it again.

The man leaned down to her, this time licking her face, his tongue poking in her ear. A shiver of revulsion shook her frame just as she felt the edge of her blade. She touched it again with the tip of her finger but was unable to grasp it.

She stretched, pushing against the man.

"Oh, now you're wantin' it, huh?" he mumbled, rubbing her hair in his hand.

When she stretched forward again, she pulled the blade to her, slicing her palm. The blood made the handle slick, and for a moment, she thought she was going to lose the weapon. She grasped it firmly. Through sheer will, she got a foot under her.

Tessa pushed with all her might to drive the blade into the man's belly.

He gasped. She cemented her stance as she stared into his eyes, smelling his breath, the flow of his warm blood on her hands.

When he reached for her again, she shoved on the knife hilt. The blade, still buried in his gut, cut upward. This time he moaned and slowly fell backward to the ground. In the partial moonlight, Tessa could see him spread-eagle, a wet mass of entrails just sliding from his body.

When the smell hit her, she spun away to wretch. She took two steps and fell to her knees.

Shock turned into tears and her frame shook with sobs, her bloody hands clasped together. The blood on her skin felt like it burned, and she couldn't collect herself as she continued to sob, dry heaving and gasping for air.

WHEN SHE CALMED, SHE SAT in the dirt and turned to again look at the man. In the speckled moonlight, his guts and eyes shone unnaturally. Already, small flies were gathering.

She had to get up, to get moving, but she just sat and stared at what she'd done.

It took another moment before she pushed to her hands and knees and then wobbled to her feet. As she stood over the man once more, her mind cleared, and sanity returned.

She needed to get rid of the body, and she needed to get out of here.

Trying not to look at him, Tessa grabbed the man's wrists and pulled him deeper into the woods. It was hard—he was a big guy—but she was desperate. She reached a slope and a ravine that broke through the forest floor.

She got on her hands and knees and pushed him until the slope of the coulee caught his weight and he rolled down the hill. She watched him fall, snapping branches and knocking loose rocks on the way down.

When everything was quiet, she stumbled to her feet and made her way back to her belongings. Reaching for her pack, she stopped. Her hands. In the waning light, her skin looked black. She rubbed them on her pants, but the blood wouldn't come off. It was now quite dry.

She grasped her shirt between two fingers and pulled it out, surprised to see it was caked with dry blood and dirt. There was nothing she could do about it now. She'd need to make certain no one saw her.

Again, she reached for her pack and bow case. Slinging both around her, she pulled her cloak on and the hood up before clasping the front with one hand. Just as she was going to step out of the forest and into the camp, she scanned the ground for her long knife.

It remained in her free hand as she headed back into the

camp.

HOURS LATER, WITH THE SUN shining on her face, Tessa left the bandits' camp behind her. The image of the man she'd killed haunted her vision, but she tried to think only of finding her mother.

26

"WAKE UP."

Maya sat straight up, her eyes on Sentinel. They'd ended their watch sometime in the night.

"What? What's happened?"

Sentinel laid his hand on her arm and looked over his shoulder where Inger and some of the men gathered. "The man, the one who would lead us through the mountain."

"Migog?"

He nodded. "Yes. He is gone."

"Gone? Gone where?"

"I don't know. I heard the men talking."

Maya looked around Sentinel's squatting form to where the men gathered. They whispered forcefully to each other. She walked toward them, Sentinel right behind her.

Inger saw her coming and shushed the others before he stepped forward.

"Where has he gone?"

Inger put up his hands in a pacifying manner. "We don't

know. Maybe he's scouting ahead and will be right back."

"How long has he been gone?" Her voice, though low and calm, had a sharp tone to it.

"W-Well, we don't know. No one saw him leave."

"No one saw him leave?" she repeated. "Is he the only one gone?"

Inger's brows rose, and he scanned the area. "Um. I think so. I didn't think— "

"You didn't think. That's just great." Maya turned in a circle. "Get your men together. Let's see who we've still got."

As the men clustered together, even before Inger said anything, Maya could see not only was Migog gone, but one other man.

"Who was standing watch last night?"

Inger stared down at the ground, then with a sigh, he looked at her. "Migog and his friend. They volunteered to take one end. The end we just came in from." His shoulders fell. "His friend was getting nervous. Kept asking Migog about people not getting out. I guess it got the better of them."

Maya nodded. Without saying anything more, she returned to her bedroll and pack and rolled it up.

"What now?"

She angled toward Inger. "What do you mean, what now?"

When he didn't say anything else, she stood to face him. "Get your stuff together. We're going on."

He nodded and ordered his men to prepare.

Sentinel came to her. "Is this the right decision?"

"I don't know," she answered. "I just hope this tunnel continues on."

27

HANDS ON HER HIPS, MAYA stared at the tunnel where it branched into three.

She moved closer to each, leaning slightly to peer down each of them in turn. They all appeared the same. No scent or feeling set one apart from the others.

"Gods," she muttered. What were they to do now?

"Um, well . . ."

She looked over her shoulder to see Inger behind her, wringing his hands.

"What?"

"Well. It is said you have magic."

Maya rolled her eyes. She'd gotten by for the better part of her life without falling back on magic. Now, all of a sudden, she was being thrust into a predicament where she was going to be forced to rely on it.

Without answering him, Maya turned from the young man. She paced to Sentinel. She felt him looking at her. She felt them all looking at her. When she caught Sentinel's eye, all he did was raise a brow.

"Gods," she muttered again.

When she turned from him to again approach the junction where the tunnel diverged, she felt Sentinel at her back.

For a moment, she looked down the dark tunnels. Then she dropped to one knee and shoved a claw of fingers into the soil.

Instantly, sensations came to her. Motion. Life.

For a moment, she just felt. It had been too long. The life-giving energy in the plants and trees flowed through her as if they were one. Fresh air and renewed energy. She'd been wrong to retreat from this part of herself. She hadn't even realized how much she missed it.

Sensations ran from her hand up her arm to fill her body. She wobbled, her anchor to the ground the only thing keeping her upright.

Lights burst behind her closed eyelids, and her breath quickened.

A warmth—a coming home—overflowed, and with it tears ran from her eyes.

It was a moment before she gathered herself enough to add a wish to her presence. As if in a vortex, something lured her consciousness down one of the tunnels. She whisked by something she tried to capture, but she was moving too quickly. Then, with a jolt, she was at the end of the tunnel, sunlight shining on her face.

She'd just registered the stop, the warmth, when she was sucked back into her body.

She kept her eyes closed and head down as she fought away

the dizziness. Then, taking a deep breath, she raised her head and released her hand from the earth.

When she went to stand, she faltered, but Sentinel was there to catch her. He stood with her while she got her feet under her. All the men stood close by. They watched her, eyeing her as if she were something foreign.

"The right tunnel leads to the outside."

A murmur began immediately, and she had to speak up to be heard. "There is a threat."

All conversation died, making the tunnel feel hollow again.

"We're going to have to make our way past it—possibly fight. But there is no other way to the other side of the mountain."

"We could just go back," came a voice from the rear.

"Yes. I've given that some thought. But then what? How are we to get through the camp?"

"Do you know how long this tunnel is? When will we face this danger?"

Maya looked toward the man who spoke. She'd never talked with him before and didn't even know his name.

"It appeared to be a few days until we have to face whatever it is, and after that, again before we escape this mountain. We have food. We have water. We have fuel to keep the torches going. We'll be able to continue on."

Inger stepped up. Facing his men, he said, "We all came to this country to find this woman. She must be returned to our homeland. You all know what Patrick said. She is the only salvation for our people. The only way to stop the evil of Nav-lys." He paced forward, looking them each in the eye. "We've faced dangers and trials before these past years. This is just one more that we must face to do what we must."

He faced Maya and Sentinel. "We'll continue on with you. We'll do what is necessary to see you back to Patrick."

Maya nodded, moving her gaze across the men to finally rest upon Sentinel. "Let's get started, then."

28

TESSA STOPPED ON THE LOW rise and looked back at the camp she'd left.

The memories of what had happened there would stay with her, she knew. Since she killed the man, she'd been trying to drive the thoughts, the feelings, from her mind. It wasn't working though. Nothing she did gave her any release.

She was changed. She would accept that fact. She would find her mother, and things would be better.

TESSA TURNED HER BACK ON the bandit camp and faced the coast. She had many miles to cover before she'd see the sea. Before she could locate her mother.

She scanned the sky, looking for Striker, but she didn't see him right away. She closed her eyes, concentrating, but not digging too deeply. She felt a sensation of water running over her skin, and when she opened her eyes, she spotted him.

Winging toward her, the sun reflected on the primary feathers of his wings until he appeared to be on fire. When he neared, he called. A scream of such rapture, even after her recent trials, she smiled. He was her love. Her saving grace. More than a mere pedagogue, he was truly a part of her.

She watched him for a moment more, and then setting her sights down the hill, she headed out.

29

PATRICK PACED THE MAIN HALL of the old keep. Each time he passed the table, his eyes were drawn to the ancient parchment. Finally, he stopped and reread what he had already committed to his memory.

> *In a time of strife, in a world of fear,*
> *age will come for three of the blood.*
> *When the core is joined,*
> *Three and Three become One,*
> *and darkness will be consumed by light.*

What did it mean? How could he aid in defeating Nav-lys when he didn't even know what was required?

These words, written an eon ago, were given to him as a child. At the time in his life when Caleb was a presence. He'd always known the words, but he never understood them. Even when he asked, Caleb had been inscrutable, any information so cryptic.

Today, he would check on the people. The world. The rot was accelerating. Its blackness traveled farther and faster. Groups of villagers cut and burned the rot, but it was a temporary fix. The source, Nav-lys and Cassandra, was what he needed to cut and burn. And for that he needed Maya.

30

TIME PASSED WITHOUT CHANGE.

Maya trudged along, occasionally wiping her forehead to catch a drip of sweat. The air seemed to be a barrier she had to push through. Even conversation had halted.

When Inger called a halt to their day, packs were dropped, and men flopped beside their belongings. Maya stared down the tunnel.

"Do you feel as if our daytime, the time we spend walking, is growing shorter?" she said.

Sentinel shifted. "Perhaps."

"I feel as if all I'm doing is sleeping. Even when I'm walking."

"Yes, there is an aura of being suspended in this time and place."

She turned on him, tapping him on the chest. "Yes. Exactly. I'm not sure how to break this . . . lethargy. We need to get out of here."

"Do you know how much longer it will be?"

She shook her head and sat next to her pack. "No. I've tried to look again. To feel the plants. But I think we're too far underground. I'm not able to pick up anything. It's as if we're buried alive."

She peered around them as he took a seat beside her. A shiver racked her frame and she scooted closer to him.

"I would have rather fought our way through the camp than be here."

He nodded and glanced about the tunnel. "At least that would be an enemy we could face."

WHEN MAYA WOKE, SHE REMEMBERED fragments of a dream. It was odd, disjointed.

She was walking through a dark forest. A full moon crested the horizon.

She hadn't felt fear, just confusion. Alone, she'd wandered for many miles. Then, without knowing how it came to be, her swords were in her hands. They felt right as if they were the only thing right in this dream world.

She struck out at something before she woke.

Maya sat slowly, willing her breathing to quiet. All around her, men slept. She strained her eyesight into the tunnel and finally caught movement from one of the men on watch.

Her dream continued to fade into an impression. She didn't know how long she'd slept but knew she couldn't return to slumber. She stood, sure not to wake the men around her, and went to relieve one of the sentries. She would rather spend the time thinking.

31

TECK STOOD FOR LONG MOMENTS staring at the ruins of the cabin, his mind awash in memories.

Maya standing within the corral, awe on her face at the bow he'd made her. Walking hand in hand later that evening. Her face in the soft moonlight. Their first kiss among the rocks. Her body moving through the water toward him.

Damn her.

Kicking himself, he stepped toward the wreck of the once lovely cabin.

What had he hoped to find coming back here? He didn't even know if she was still alive. The thought of never seeing her again filled his heart with pain.

Teck took a deep breath and turned from the memories. He'd just have to keep looking. He'd cover this entire country if he had to until he either found her or found someone who knew something about her. Her father, maybe. Lord Eldred Bathsar. People might not know anything about a lone girl, but someone had to know about Lord Bathsar. If he still lived, he'd know where Teck could find her.

As he made his way through the edge of the forest, Teck gathered dry fall for a fire and made his plans. He'd head to Berth. In the city, he'd ask around about Maya and her father.

He needed to see her again. For his own peace of mind, he needed to see if reality matched the memories.

IT DIDN'T TAKE AS LONG as he remembered to get to the village of Roadstead, and it seemed smaller. Back when it was his entire world, it seemed to hold all he would ever need.

He sidestepped to the edge of the road when a wagon rattled by, its driver yelling for him to move out of the way.

Partway down the main street, off to the side, he heard music and identified a saloon. The volume leaking from the place heightened when he pulled the doors open. Along with the sound came the smell of stale ale and cigar smoke.

Some things did change, he thought. When he was just a lad, there was no establishment like this in town. The puritan town leaders would never have allowed such a place to stand.

Walking through the doors, he let them swing closed behind him and, for a moment, observed the room. Many times, he'd been in this type of business. Everything was for sale, for the right price. He'd completed deals in just this type of place.

He dropped his head and made his way around the outside of the room. He had to step back when a young, drunk man almost ran him down in his pursuit of a working lady, who gave Teck the once-over. Her eyes shone in interest before her arm was captured by the young man. Turning her back on Teck, she strung her arms around the man's neck and went with him to the bar.

As he continued through the room, several men eyed him, but no one approached him. As soon as he sat at a table, a barmaid came over and splashed a tankard of ale in front of him.

"Anything else, honey?"

He looked up at her and then down at the stein wallowing in a puddle of amber liquid. "No. That'll be all for now."

"Just give a yell when you need another," she said and was gone, moving back through the crowd.

Teck sipped his ale, disparaging its warmth, and watched the room. He was at home in establishes like this as if he were in his mother's kitchen—maybe more so. He could practically say what was going to happen next in each situation.

So, it was with no surprise that he watched three large, drunk men make their unsteady way to him.

"Ah, look at the pretty man," one of them slurred, elbowing his friend. The three of them laughed at his humor. When it didn't get a rise from Teck, they leaned in and tried again.

"What you doing in this town, mister? We don't take kindly to strangers in these here parts."

The man leaned back into his companion, almost knocking him over. As he righted himself, he pushed back at his friend, upsetting his stance and causing him to splash his drink down his hand and on the floor.

"Yo, oaf." He set his stein down on Teck's table, shook off his hand, and pushed his friend on the shoulder, which caused him to knock into the third man.

Teck sipped his drink. When the third came back at the second, the three of them turned from the table, Teck forgotten in their irritation with each other. They yelled and shoved until they were back near the bar that ran the length of the room. When it appeared it may become serious, a young woman wandered by. She stopped, hands on her ample hips, and looked the three of them up and down.

Some words that Teck couldn't make out were exchanged, and the four of them headed up the stairs. Teck was sure the men would be passed out before they were able to perform, so the woman might be the smartest in the room.

As Teck watched the foursome go unsteadily up the stairs, the hairs on the back of his neck rose and a shiver ran down his spine. He took another sip, looking over the rim of his mug to the room in general, trying to decide what he was sensing.

Still unable to locate anything out of the ordinary, he sat against the wall, his body half in the light and half in shadow.

When the waitress made another pass, he ordered a second beer and some supper. The food and drink came back quicker than he would have thought. The scent drew his attention from the main room, smelling better than he imagined. He pulled the bowl close and dug in, pleasantly surprised. The food was good.

It had been some time since he'd had a stew this satisfying. The coarse, dry bread was a perfect accompaniment. He lost himself for a moment, his attention fully on his meal.

When a man slid into the seat beside him, he froze but only for a second. With a swallow, he picked up his mug, sat back, and regarded the man. "Help you with something?"

Teck's heart leaped when he recognized his uncle. With his elbows on his knees, he looked at Teck from his dusty boots to his messed-up hair.

"You look like a man who can get stuff done."

Teck's eyes rose from his uncle to glance around the room. Did he not recognize him? It had been twenty years, almost, but Teck was surprised when he continued to look at him as if he were a stranger.

Deciding to go with it and see what his kin wanted, Teck nodded. In his life, he had been the man to get things done. He needed to search for Maya, but his uncle's question had him wondering what was happening with his family.

"You have a problem you need solved?" he asked when his uncle didn't say anything.

His uncle leaned back and studied the room. "Might be I have a need for a service. If the right man came along. A man who charged the right amount and could keep his mouth shut when the deed was done."

Teck relaxed. Now he was curious. And he was used to negotiations. This was familiar territory.

He nodded and took another sip of his beer. "I might be that man. Since I'm a stranger to these parts." Teck thought for sure the man could hear the outright lie in his words. "I have no plans on staying here any longer than I need to."

"Well, that sounds good."

The man discussed his needs with Teck. When they came to an agreement about the cost, and how it was to be done, the man stood.

"I'll meet you back here, then. In two days' time." He tossed a small bag onto the table that hit with a jingle. "Here's half. I'll have the other half for you next time I see you—when the deed is done."

Teck nodded and pulled the bag of coins to him. The man gave him another long look and then, with a quick turn, walked out of the inn.

Teck flagged down the maid and ordered another ale. He had thinking and planning to do. What could his father possibly have done to so anger his uncle?

32

THE MILL THAT HIS PARENTS owned still stood along the river just out of town. The wheel moved with the force of the water, and multiple men worked in the yard. Some came and went from the building.

If anything, it seemed more prosperous than he remembered. In just the few minutes he'd been here, two loads of grain had been dropped off, and one wagon was picking up sacks of processed flour.

Did his parents still own the mill? Did it have something to do with his uncle wanting his father dead?

Teck turned from the mill and the memories it invoked to head toward his childhood home. It lay between the mill and town, just down a dusty road.

When he turned off the main thoroughfare and headed down the tree-lined path, he couldn't stop the memories. He and his brothers running through the woods, whooping, pretending to hunt bear, and the not-so-pleasant memories of the switch and his father arguing with his older brother before he left home.

His emotions came to the surface, somewhere they hadn't been for years.

He neared the house when something on the hill caught his attention. A small square of white picket fencing covered an area atop the hill. Teck turned off the path to climb the grassy hillside.

When he neared, the gravestone became evident, and it was only as he drew close to it that he saw his mother's name. His heart became leaden as he reread the words. The last he'd seen his mother, he'd told her good night right before he left their house for the last time. That night, he hadn't given any thought to her feelings. He was going with Maya, and his only thought had been for himself.

What had she felt all those years ago to find her son gone?

Now, he would have no opportunity to see her again. No opportunity to tell her how much she meant to him, how much he appreciated their times together. Her gentle care.

When a tear slid down his cheek, he jolted and touched the salty drop. How long had it been since he'd cried?

He heard the footsteps coming up the hill behind him. When his father stopped next to him, Teck acknowledged him.

He looked old. That simple fact surprised Teck more than anything else.

"Hello, Father," he said.

"Teck."

Minutes passed with both men standing, looking at the grave. Teck wasn't sure how much time passed before his father broke the silence.

"Come on down to the house. I'll make us some coffee." He turned from the monument on the hill and, slowly, his steps showing his age, he made his way down the slope. Teck waited a moment more before he followed him.

33

TESSA STOOD PERFECTLY STILL. SHE was poised on a log that stretched out into part of a lake. She stayed a step back to ensure her shadow didn't fall over the water and warn the school of fish. She had an arrow notched and partially drawn.

Earlier, she had tied a spool of twine to one of her arrows and made her way out onto the log.

Feeding herself was never going to be a problem if wildlife flourished. In addition to the meat she hunted, her mother had taught her about which plants were good to eat. She'd also taught her the ones best utilized for medicines and ones that were dangerous.

She decided on a nice plump fish, and with a slow pull, she primed the arrow for release. A small twang sounded right before a splash. Reeling in the arrow, she held up her dinner. The fish threw small droplets of lake water on and around her as it writhed. She wiped one hand over her face and looked up as Striker landed on a nearby branch.

"Just in time for some dinner, I see."

"Who are you talking to?"

She spun from the lake, almost slipping off the log. Behind her was a man dressed in forest-colored clothing.

"What do you want?" she asked and placed a hand on her knife.

"Hey," he said, putting his hands up. "Calm down." When she retained her stance, he took a step back. "I don't mean you any harm. Was just passin' by."

"Well, keep passin'," she answered and pushed her chin forward to motion him on his way.

When he took another step backward, he dropped his hands and turned to disappear into the forest. She waited another few moments. When she didn't hear anything else, she peered at Striker in the branches. He was preening his feathers and appeared relaxed, so she relaxed. The man must have indeed left the area.

She rolled up the twine and, holding the fish by the arrow, made her way gingerly back across the log. She'd planned on staying tonight by the stream. Had thought to have a fire and cook a hot meal. Maybe it wouldn't be such a good idea. She didn't know where the man had come from, or where he'd gone.

She watched Striker for a moment then decided to go with her original plan. A small fire would be welcome, as would a cooked meal. She had a long way yet until she reached the coast, and some comforts would ease her travels.

LYING BY HER FIRE, STOMACH full, she thought about how far she'd come. She was farther from her home than she'd ever been or ever thought she would be. Already she'd done things she hoped to never repeat and spent too much time alone. Striker kept her sane, but he wasn't like a companion she could talk to.

She drifted to sleep beside hypnotic flames and thoughts of where she'd find her mother.

34

COLD TENDRILS OF FOG CREPT down the tunnel to wrap around men's legs. Almost as one, the group stopped. They held torches aloft, staring at the mist among them.

Maya took a step forward as the group took a step back. With a deep inhale, she tried to learn something about the vapor. She didn't smell the moist, earthy scent of fog. There wasn't a breeze. How was it moving?

As she and the men moved in different directions, Maya stood alone within the blanket of mist. It halted its advance, and soon there was a sizable area between her and the rest of the group.

Looking down, she turned in a circle, the mist rising and falling with the motion of her body. When she looked at Sentinel, he took a step forward, away from the group. Just as she opened her mouth to speak, the mist closed around her, and in an instant, she and the fog were gone.

* * * * *

SENTINEL FROZE, HIS MOUTH AGAPE.

When thought and motion again filled his body, he grabbed a torch from one of the men and took off at a run in the direction of the fog. He heard footsteps behind him but didn't look back.

The tunnel only went in one direction, so even though he couldn't see mist in front of him, he knew which way it went.

He swung the torch left and right, his eyes following the light. From ahead he heard a scream. His head came up, eyes alert. Accelerating to a sprint, he flew down the tunnel toward the sound. As he rounded a sharp corner, a wall of mist blocked his way.

He slowed but didn't stop and stepped within the fog's boundaries.

White enveloped him. After just a few steps, he lost all sense of direction, unable to discern which way he'd come or which way he was going. He spun, peering into the soupy mist. It moved, not just with his movement, but seemingly on its own.

"Maya," he said, only to hear his voice bounce back to him.

What are you?

As the words echoed, Sentinel sank to one knee. Dropping the torch, he grasped his head. The loud voice bounced within his skull.

What are you?

A cry was forced from his lips, and on his neck, he felt a trickle of blood.

"Stop," he gasped and held up a hand.

For a moment, he simply inhaled, trying to get on top of the pain. When the voice didn't again speak, he dropped his hands and peered into the fog.

"Please," he said. "You are too loud for my body."

Another voice, this time softer and more feminine, spoke.

Interesting. What do you think it is?

Two or three others chimed in, a bubble of voices that Sentinel couldn't make out.

When he stood, the voices died down. The fog wrapped around him.

"I am Sentinel," he said. "I wish to have the woman back."

The babble began again. He heard some words.

Woman.

Stranger.

Magic.

Insect.

Eternity.

"Please, do you know where she is?"

The original voice returned. This time it was a lot quieter, though no less powerful.

She is with us.

Sentinel realized he was hearing the voices inside his own head. Even with them speaking softly, his skull felt as if it would split. He reached up again to touch at the base of his ears. His fingertips brought back blood.

Dropping his hands, he lifted his chin. "I must have the woman back."

Come.

The mist parted. He couldn't see the tunnel walls and knew he no longer traveled the path they'd been on. His torch was no longer the only light. The fog itself seemed to be illuminated.

Just out of sight, within the wall of mist, he saw movement. Many entities shifted and flowed through the expanse. Like fish glimpsed below the surface of a lake, they were there and then gone.

Fog closed behind him as he advanced. Sentinel faced forward and quickened his pace.

35

WAKING IN HIS PARENTS' HOME the next morning, Teck had a moment where he thought he was in a dream. But the sun streaming in through the window and the sounds of his father calling to the chickens were really happening.

The night before, they'd stayed up late. When the topic had turned to his mother's death, the coffee had turned to a distilled alcohol his father made.

Teck had been at a loss when tears reached his father's eyes. He and his sire had never been close. His father worked long hours, and his parenting skill was discipline.

But he hadn't had to do anything but listen.

His father had grown into an old man in the years Teck had been away. They'd thought him dead. That hurt the worst. He would never be able to let his mother know that her son was alive. Not only alive, but Teck had prospered.

Sitting up, he dropped his head into his hands. Now, he had a bit of a headache. And he still needed to talk to his father about his uncle. With his mother dead, and he and his brothers gone, his father alone owned the mill. He wondered if that was what was wrong.

He made his way to a bowl and pitcher of water against the wall. After he splashed water on his face and upper body, he felt more alive. He'd see if his father needed any help around the homestead. Teck was sure there would be plenty of repairs for him to take care of.

* * * * *

"TECK," HIS FATHER SAID FROM behind him.

"Sir." When he turned, Teck had to catch his surprise again. This old man was his father. Gray, thin, and stooped, he was a small version of the man he was when Teck had last seen him.

His father placed a hand on his arm and nodded toward the house. "Come and have some lunch. The rest of the chores can wait."

Teck wiped a hand over his forehead. He set down the axe and nodded. The old man turned and headed toward the house, Teck on his heels.

When they walked across the porch into the house, Teck smelled bread and a spicy meat. Platters sat on the table, and beading mugs of ale were a welcome sight.

He was halfway through his sandwich when he opened the subject of his uncle.

"How is the rest of your family?"

His father looked at him, chewing. When he swallowed, he

said, "Good."

"Just good? Is your brother still living close?"

"Yes. Just over the ridge." He indicated the direction with a tilt of his chin. "He built a house figuring on a wife, but that never happened." Teck's father took a long drink from his mug and then added, "So, he lives there alone. Always been alone."

Teck nodded. He let the silence spin out for a bit. Then, just as his father was finishing his meal, Teck said, "You and he get along?"

The old man choked on the last remnants of his bread, coughing so hard Teck thought he might have to help him. When he caught his breath, he grabbed his mug and took a long drink.

He cleared his throat, set down his drink, and mumbled, "Well sure. Why would you ask that?"

Teck shrugged and looked at the remainder of his meal. He didn't know how much to tell his dad.

He hadn't told his father that he wouldn't be staying. But even knowing that, he couldn't leave while his sire was in danger. His uncle would just approach someone else.

He could stay for a day or two, get the old man set with repairs, but then he needed to be on his way. His whole purpose for coming back was for Maya. He wouldn't hang around here too long. He needed to deal with his uncle.

"Dad . . ." he began, but when the old man looked up at him, he saw the knowledge in his eyes. Something bad had come between the brothers, and his father knew about it.

36

LATER THAT EVENING, COMING DOWN the lane to his uncle's house, Teck rode boldly up to the gate outside the kitchen. He'd borrowed his father's horse under the pretext of getting some air.

Pulling the horse to a halt, he was just swinging down when the door opened. His uncle stepped from the house, a questioning look on his face. When he saw who his visitor was, his face ran pale.

"Uncle," Teck addressed him as he stepped from around the horse.

"Uncle?" The man took a pace closer to Teck, a frown on his face. "Do I know you?"

"I'm Teck, Uncle. Barry and Maybell's youngest."

"Barry and—" He stepped closer to get a better look. Finally seeing something he remembered, he stood tall, his face even more ashen.

Teck walked up to the gate and swung it open. "I think we have something to discuss." His uncle turned and ran back into the house, slamming and locking the door behind him. Teck breathed out a deep sigh. This was not going to go well.

* * * * *

TECK POUNDED THE LOOSE SOIL down with the back side of the spade. He was dirty and tired and disgusted with this day's work. But the threat to his father was taken care of.

Even after all the things he'd seen and done, he'd been surprised by the venom his uncle had regarding his father. He thought, perhaps, the man had gone insane.

Hardships, deaths—all manner of atrocities. Teck didn't believe it. His father had been a hard man while Teck was a boy, but nothing like what his uncle had said. He had been delusional. And now it was done.

His uncle would be missing, but no one would find him. Teck made certain of that. His father would be safe.

He'd done all he could. Now, Teck would leave in the morning.

37

FROM THE HILL, TESSA STUDIED the town. It was small. There was no movement, but it should allow her to replenish her supplies.

Striker perched on her forearm, his feathers glossy in the sunlight. She gave the town another glance and then, with an upward thrust, sent the hawk into the sky. For another moment she watched him catch an updraft. Then she set her sights on the buildings below.

AS SHE WALKED DOWN THE track that represented a main street, Tessa felt eyes on her. She remained alert for threats but kept moving. A bit farther, she saw the building she figured must be the general store.

She pivoted through the door into a dimly lit room. A few shelves took up space within, most of them empty. Maybe this wouldn't be a place to provide her with provisions. Viewing the room through a scattering of dust motes, she took a step forward.

"Hello," she called.

No one answered. Only silence reigned, and when no one came forth, she continued to wander through the shelves. Occasionally, she'd pick something up, look it over, look around, and set it back down. She wasn't sure what to do if no one showed up.

"Hello," Tessa called again. But again, she was met with silence.

She ran her finger across one of the shelves, displacing a thick layer of dust. It didn't appear as if anyone had been here for quite some time. The town seemed abandoned.

When motion caught her attention, she walked to the window. The man by the lake walked in the street.

Was he following her? What could he want?

She watched for a moment more, craning her neck to keep him in her sight. As he walked farther away, she moved to the door and went out.

She followed him down the street but kept to the far side of the walkway, her back to the storefronts. When he stopped and peered around—almost seeming to sniff the air—she froze against the building. She followed him when he kept walking.

As he rounded a corner, Tessa hurried to trail him. But when she rounded the corner, he had disappeared.

Shock filled her and she stepped away from the building to scan the street.

Nothing.

She might have been the last person on earth, the town was so quiet. She didn't even hear birds. Just the low hum of the wind above her and the sound of her own breathing.

When a sound did come—a creak of the plank behind her—it was like an explosion in the silence.

She spun, already pulling her knife from her waistband, only to have a fist cuff her on the side of her face. She saw the dusty road coming up and then nothing.

TESSA MOANED, PUTTING A HAND to her face.

It hurt to open her eyes, the light cutting into her head. She touched her jaw gingerly. When pain shot to her temple, she moaned again.

"Sorry I hit you so hard."

Tessa froze. She peeked from under her hand, squinting against the light. The man sat across from her. The one from the lake and the street.

Now she remembered. She dropped her hand and glared at him.

"What do you want?"

"Why you followin' me?"

"You were following me."

He shook his head.

She pulled herself to a sitting position, another moan forced from her lips.

He'd laid her on a platform, slightly elevated off the floor. With her legs hanging down she leaned forward to cradle her head in her hands.

"Again—sorry."

"What's going on?" She looked at him through her splayed

fingers. "Where have you brought me?"

"Somewhere safe. You can't just wander around out there."

"I do fine on my own, thank you." When she went to stand, her world tilted, and she sat down heavily. "Gods. You didn't have to hit me so hard."

"I didn't," he insisted. "Maybe you have a weak jaw."

With another glare, she turned away from him, only then realizing her belongs were missing.

"Where are my things?"

With a gesture over his shoulder, he said, "In the other room. They're safe."

She scowled, sure she couldn't believe him, and leaned into her thighs so she could try to stand. This time, she made it to her feet.

She walked into the room. She didn't get far since the room was small and had to turn and head back to where she'd begun.

"I need to get out of here."

His hands rose in a staying gesture. "Now's not a great time to be outside."

"Why?" Her voice came out clipped. This whole situation made her angry.

"Well, now, there's a couple tribes of folks that would like nothin' more than to come across a morsel like you."

"And do you belong to these 'tribes'?"

"Me?" His eyes widened and he shook his head. "Nah, I hang alone."

When he stood, she stepped back to keep some distance between them.

"Here." He moved to the side of the room and opened a cupboard. "I got some fresh water and some biscuits. The bread might be a bit stale, but they're still good." He turned with a water jug in one hand and a wrapped package in the other.

She was stopped by the look on his face. His eyes were wide and guileless, a small half smile curving his lips.

She stepped forward and took the things he offered. Giving him another glare, she walked back to the sleeping platform.

Keeping an eye on him as he sat with his own biscuit, she took a tentative nibble. When the food hit her tongue, her stomach growled. Her cheeks warmed, more so when he chuckled.

"See, told you it's good. My name's Jax."

She stared at him for a moment and then, with a nod, leaned back and took a bite.

THE MAN SNORED SOFTLY. SHE could sneak out now. Find her things in the other room and leave.

The problem was, what if he had told the truth? What if she walked out of here right into a deeper danger?

She could connect with Striker. Jax was asleep. She could take a look around and be done before he woke. If the coast was clear, she could head out. He wouldn't be the wiser.

She watched Jax for another moment until she was sure he was sound asleep.

She sat up, careful not to make any noise. Tucking her legs under her, she relaxed against the wall. With a deep breath, she turned her mind inward.

38

THE NIGHT WAS COOL. WHEN the breeze picked up, the feathers on his neck ruffled.

He knew the girl was with him. Felt her in a way he could never describe. He felt completeness. She didn't have to tell him her wants or needs; he just knew.

Even in the black of night his eyesight and hearing were extraordinary. The world around him was thrown into stark relief, small lines of light streaking across the surface of the land.

Taking his cue from the girl, her need above his own, he opened his wings and dropped from the branch he perched on.

Light and agile, currents caught him. With barely a flap or two, he soared high. He ignored his instincts—the desire to hunt and feed—and looked for what she sought.

It didn't take too long when, miles away, he saw movement. The size, the disruption of the night, a plume of dust flowing behind, could only be from man.

He stayed high, buoyed by the air currents, to pass over them. A spark of the girl's alarm filtered through him to see them heading in her direction.

He circled the valley and pulled the girl with him—like a gentle tug of her hand. They soared, the night full of scents and intrigue. He felt her calm. The bliss of their union filled her. When she released and floated away, he felt the separation cut.

* * * * *

JAX OPENED HIS EYES AND stretched his arms above his head. His first thought—why his bed was so hard—was replaced by the memory that he shared his room.

He stopped mid-stretch and jerked toward his visitor.

"What the— " He caught his whisper, not wanting to disrupt her.

Keeping his gaze on her, he sat against the wall.

In the pale light of his lamp, her head was thrown back and her eyes reflected white. Steady, deep breaths came. Her hands were turned up on her thighs and, occasionally, a finger would twitch.

He didn't know how much time passed when her chest rose in a deep, waking breath. She blinked, looked forward, and opened her green eyes.

Neither of them said anything. Then, dropping her eyes, she turned her head.

"What was that?" His whispered words sounded loud in the small room, and she cringed.

She didn't even acknowledge his words. After a moment, she reached down to retrieve her mug of water. As she drained her glass, he thought, whatever it was had made her thirsty.

"You gonna tell me?" he asked again.

She turned her head to look at him. "Are you going to tell me your secrets?"

He gave her a small shrug. "What do you want to know?"

"Nothing." She looked away again. "I don't want to know anything about you."

"Tell me your name."

"Why?"

"Why not? We have time to spare. At least a little." He angled his head toward the door and mumbled, "We might be able to go out soon."

"No," she said. At her sharp tone, Jax's brow furrowed.

"No? How do you know that?"

"I just don't feel like it's safe. Not yet."

After a long stare, he nodded slowly. "So, what do I call you?"

She took a deep breath. "Tessa."

"Tessa. Nice to meet you."

* * * * *

THE NIGHT PASSED SLOWLY.

He would ask her questions, and she would ignore him.

Tessa thought once or twice they might have dozed, but she couldn't be sure.

When the morning broke, a beam of light filtered through a crack in the ceiling. Jax blinked up into it and then blinked at her.

"Think we can go out?" he asked.

"How would I know?"

"Figured you had your ways."

She looked from him, to the light, to the door. "I would have no idea."

The light came from a different angle when Jax opened the door. He inched it ajar and listened with his ear to the opening.

Tessa shifted with every move he made. When he didn't do more than stand and listen, she tapped her fingers and breathed a deep sigh.

"Well?"

He shook his head.

A moment more of that and she'd had enough. She dropped her feet to the floor and scampered up next to him. With her lips near his ear she repeated, "Well?"

He popped his head around, and she stepped back to avoid his nearness.

"I can't hear anything." He listened again. "I think it's okay to go out. Before, they've always been gone by daybreak."

Tessa figured that was good enough for her. She placed a hand on his arm and pushed him to the side then opened the door. She stopped and listened, and silence greeted her.

"All right, where are my things?" She stepped from the inner room and walked into the larger one.

"Yes. Where are her things?" a voice said from within the dark of the exterior room.

Tessa froze, and Jax grabbed her arm and pulled her out of

the open doorway. He threw his body against the door, but it was already being thrust open by multiple people. The force of their combined muscle drove his small weight back into the room where he hit the far wall. He looked up with horror as men filled the room.

Different colors, textures, and patterns adorned the tribe. Their hair, long and scraggly, was braided in multiple strands. Feathers and beads decorated it.

Tessa couldn't believe their size and strangeness. She couldn't tell the color of their skin since each was painted a different color.

She gained her feet and rushed to Jax. Kneeling beside him in the corner, she helped him sit.

When she turned wide eyes to the group at the entrance, it was to see them part and another individual come into the room. This one was like them in his dress and colorings but stood a bit shorter. He strode through the mass of men, touching arms and patting them like pets. He scanned the room before turning his gaze to Tessa and Jax.

"Well, now," he said as he squatted in front of them, "what do we have here?"

Tessa leaned back, pressing into Jax. She was afraid to break her gaze. Afraid he might strike like a snake.

Then, as if dismissing them from his thoughts, he stood to walk around the room. He picked things up, shook them, studied them, and then dropped them again. One or two items, he placed within his clothing.

Behind her, Jax took her hand in his quaking one. She

chanced a glance from the tribe leader. His eyes were glassy, and he was visibly shaking.

What was going to happen here?

When the leader stopped in front of his band again, he turned back to face her and Jax. The room, even with so many in it, was silent as he studied them.

"Take them," he ordered and walked out as the group rushed in.

Hands pulled her to her feet. A bag was crammed over her head, and she found it hard to breathe in the confines. The bag smelled of onion and vomit, and she thought for a long moment that she was going to add her own to its history. Breathing through her mouth was marginally better, but now she tasted the scents on the back of her tongue. Her hands were wrenched and bound together behind her back.

Pushed and shoved, she was bounced between bodies. She could only assume Jax was experiencing the same treatment.

A moment later, she felt the cool fresh air of outside. It teased her, allowing just a taste to permeate the cover. Then she was moved forward and placed on a broad back. The horse under her shifted, and instinct had her tightening her knees to grip its girth.

Someone mounted behind her. Strong arms came around her, her body pressed into his. She attempted to pull forward only to be roughly pulled back. There was a crack of reins, and her ride jumped into motion.

39

WHEN SENTINEL ENTERED A LARGER room, he only knew it as the fog dissipated. A pedestal and altar stood alone in the room. On the altar lay a body.

He broke into a run, but the fog swirled around his feet. Mere yards from the body, he ground to a halt, his eyes riveted to the altar.

"Maya."

It was her. For a moment fear filled him and he couldn't move. He pushed the emotion down and stepped forward.

When he saw her chest rise, his breath expelled in a rush. He touched her arm. She was warm. "Maya." He shook her gently. She didn't move, though behind her lids, her eyes shifted.

"Maya," he said louder, and he shook harder. When she still didn't lift her lids, he spun into the room. "Free her!"

The sudden influx of voices had him on his knees.

Impertinent.

Punish him.

Interesting.

Kill him.

Fate.

"Stop!" he yelled, and the room became quiet.

For a moment, he stayed on one knee, his head in his hand. Then with effort, he pushed to his feet.

"Please." His voice came out a whisper. "Please, you must release her."

The original voice, the one who had spoken to him the first time, said, *Why?*

Because they must. Not for the land, not to defeat her mother, not even for Tessa . . . They must release her for him. If she died, he died, but he didn't wish to live—he wished not to live without her. They were each part of a whole. Only one with one another.

"Because," he whispered, "I love her."

Silence answered his declaration. Then, gently, he heard, *Interesting.*

A small noise had him spinning around.

Maya's hand was on her forehead, her other reaching for the edge of the altar. When she shifted, a moan escaped her.

Not even realizing he'd moved, Sentinel was at her side.

With a hand on her back, he assisted her to sit. She eased her legs over the edge of the platform, her head held in both hands.

"What happened?" He could barely understand her words—so slurred was her speech.

"You are fine. Everything is fine."

He turned back to the room, keeping her to his back. He allowed his gaze to cover the room, not having a solid object to focus on.

"Thank you," he said. "Thank you for returning her to me."

But nothing answered. The fog had vanished.

He put an arm around Maya to assist her. When her feet hit the ground, her knees buckled, and he grabbed her around the waist. Through sheer force, he walked her the way he'd come. An echo of voices came to him down a far hallway. As they neared each other, he recognized Inger's voice in the lead.

* * * * *

MAYA HELD ONE HAND TO her head, the pounding so fierce, she worried her head would split.

If it had been anyone else who pulled her along, she would have planted her feet and swung a fist. But she knew Sentinel had her—knew it in a way she could never explain. She allowed herself to be taken, putting her energy into keeping her skull together and her stomach down.

The rhythm of Sentinel's pace turned the pounding into a roar. When she heard many male voices through the static in her head, she eased up and listened.

"You found her."

"Yes," the timbre of Sentinel's voice rumbled. She turned into his body, a small whimper escaping from between her hard-pressed lips. "We must find a place for her to rest."

Inger's voice came very near her. "I believe we've found a

way out of this mountain."

"Show me." With his face close to Maya's, he whispered, "Just a little longer, my girl."

Maya nodded into his chest, one fist clenched in his shirt and the other in a death grip on the back of his belt. She could do this.

She imagined Tessa's face, her daughter's visage keeping her mind off the pain radiating in her brain. When she caught a whiff of fresh air, her head rose, but she couldn't open her eyes. She felt Sentinel's face near hers as he pressed a small kiss to her forehead.

A little farther and the warmth of sunshine bathed her in a welcome embrace, and her mind relaxed.

The ground under her feet changed. The hard rock became spongy, and each step brought the fragrance of grasses and petals.

"Here," Sentinel said in her ear. "Sit here."

She did as she was told. Tree bark met her hand and she lowered herself to the ground. Soft, dense grass surrounded her.

"Lie down, my girl." Sentinel was right in front of her, his hand urging her to lie to the side. Doing so, she put her head on his coat. A deep breath filled her lungs, bringing with it the scent of him and the comfort of the outdoors. Finally, the pain diminished to a mere pinprick.

"Sleep. I will keep you safe."

She believed him. He would always keep her safe. She drifted off to the sounds of distant bird songs and the hum of low voices.

40

MAYA CRACKED HER EYES OPEN, momentarily confused. In front of her, a fire blazed and men sat around it. She squinted, sure she should know them. Their voices rose and fell with the evening breeze. The scent of roasted meat wafted to her and her stomach cried, making her wonder when she'd last eaten.

When a shadow cast from the fire fell across her, she saw Sentinel. He squatted and, with a gentle hand, pushed her hair behind her ear.

"You seem better."

"I think I feel better. In truth, I can't remember much."

He sat next to her, and she pushed herself to a sitting position. She rubbed a hand over her face and combed her hair down her back with her fingers. He handed her a cup. She sniffed it, the crisp, cool smell of water making her salivate. After drinking it, she asked, "What happened?"

"You don't remember?"

"No. Almost nothing."

"The mist came, and it took you with it."

She nodded. "Yes, I remember the mist." She stared at the fire, rubbing her temple. "And the pain."

"The beings. The ones in the fog. Do you have any recollection of them?"

She looked off into the night. After a moment she shook her head.

MAYA THOUGHT SHE CONSUMED HER weight in food. It felt as if she hadn't eaten in a month, and her body was making up for lost time. Inger brought her another trencher of stew, and with a smile, she took the meal.

"You're going to pop if you continue to eat this way," he said, chuckling before he sat beside her. "It's good to have you back with us. For a while, we weren't sure we would see you or Sentinel again."

Maya put her spoon down and turned to Inger. She hadn't heard this part of the story.

"What do you mean, Sentinel? I thought you were all together."

Inger shook his head and leaned over to pluck a root from her stew. Tossing it into his mouth, he spoke around it. "No. When you disappeared, he ran to find you. We lost him within the tunnel. When he came out carrying you, it was the first we saw either of you. It's good to have us all together again."

41

TECK STOPPED ON THE ROAD in front of his parents' home and looked back. He studied the lay of the land, the roof of the house and barn, and the far-off hillside. He knew he would never return. His father would die here, alone.

When he walked away, Teck put it behind him. Doing a task and moving on was something he was good at. Now he'd put his sights on Maya. It was a big land, and she could be anywhere. He stopped, little puffs of road dust blowing past his feet. What if she were dead? He'd never thought to truly consider this before.

He shook his head. He wouldn't think that way. She was strong. She had Sentinel with her the last he saw. Together they were formidable. More than formidable—unstoppable.

Convinced, he began to walk again.

Berth, he supposed. There might be some information about one or the two of them in or around Berth. A red-haired woman and a black man each sporting crossed blades would have to draw attention. All he had to do was ask around. Ask around and follow the information. Her father had always been an important, well-known man. He would ask for Eldred Bathsar.

His head up and face forward, he was sure someone would know where to find her.

42

THE TILTING OF HER WORLD woke Tessa. When she hit a hard surface, the explosion of air from her lungs and the bolt of pain in her shoulder had her wide awake.

She moaned and tried to roll, but with her arms still strung behind her, she was stuck. Someone grabbed her by an elbow and yanked her up. Pain streaked from her fingers to her shoulders. She rose to her toes in an attempt to alleviate the tension on her arm.

"Ouch," she called out. "Wait, wait," but her captor didn't listen. She stumbled over something but was kept on her feet. She heard many people walking and talking quietly. Horses were being moved away.

"Jax," she called but didn't receive an answer. "Jax!"

"Quiet." The one leading her cuffed her on the head.

Her head spun, and for a moment she was truly dragged by her arm. Then her captor stopped and wrapped an arm around her midsection to lift her like a sack. Dizzy, nauseated, and confused, she hung on his arm.

When the sounds changed, she thought they might be in a building. She was set on her feet and the bag pulled from her head.

Tessa squinted up at the man in front of her. He was a giant. She was tall for a woman, but he'd picked her up like she were a child. She barely reached his chest.

He pointed to a corner of the room. "Sit."

Tessa scanned the room, not seeing anything she could use to get free. When she didn't immediately sit down, the man put his hand on her shoulder and shoved.

She turned back to him and flipped her hair out of her face. "I would like my hands to be untied."

"Sit."

"Not until my hands are untied. My arms are numb."

The giant pushed her again, but she resisted.

"No. And where is my friend Jax?"

"Little man gone. You sit." He pointed to the corner.

"Gone?" She stepped forward, a tremble in her voice. "What do you mean gone?"

The giant took her arm, walked her to the corner, and forced her to the floor. Tessa dropped her head to her knees, tears welling in her eyes. She hadn't known Jax long, but how could he be gone? What would become of her now?

She wiped her face on her knees and looked around. It appeared to be a storeroom, but one with very few items in it. Two windows were placed high on the walls. She wouldn't be able to get out of them, but they let in sunlight.

The giant left, so she moved to her knees and got her feet

under her. She paced the room, looking for something she could use.

She'd made two circuits of the room before a box caught her attention. The sun's rays had moved far enough into the room to reflect on brass hinges.

With her arm, she knocked the box off the stand. She turned it with her boot and then stomped on it. It was old and worn and came apart easily.

She sat on it. Feeling behind her, she scooted a bit and located one of the brass hinges. She held it firmly in her fingers and made her way back to her feet. After kicking the remnants of the box out of the way, Tessa moved back to her corner, stood against the wall, and began to saw at the ropes binding her hands.

TESSA WORRIED SOMEONE WOULD COME before she could free herself. The rope was looser, strands of it hanging from her bindings, but she wasn't really any closer to being free.

Throughout the day, she heard noises outside the building. People talking, horses—even a wagon went by. Each time, she'd pause her ministrations on the rope, waiting to see if anyone would enter. No one had come back for her. She didn't know if they ever would. And if they did, she wondered if she'd wish they hadn't.

BY THE TIME THE ROPE came free from around her wrists, it was slick with her blood. Multiple small cuts from the edge of the brass covered her fingers.

With no time to spend on the small things, Tessa wiped her hands on her pants legs and scanned the room again. This time, she looked for a way to open the door or perhaps get up to the windows.

She'd begun to pull a table and boxes to the wall under one of the windows when she had a thought. She gave the door a long look and then, setting a box down, she walked to it. Her steps remained slow and measured as if she might chase it away. After she grabbed the knob, she paused. Blood coated the metal, making it appear as if she held a small heart.

"Please," she whispered and twisted the knob. When it turned, her head dropped, and she breathed a deep sigh.

She stepped back and pulled the door open a fraction. With her eye to the gap, she peeked.

In the dusky light, no one was around the building. She waited a moment, but outside everything stayed silent.

Opening the door, she stepped through and pulled it shut behind her. She hustled around the corner and down the back of the building. Now that she'd moved closer to the center of their town, she heard voices. A loud babble of them, a hum that reached into the evening.

She looked back the way she'd come. It seemed to be her escape. She even took a step in that direction. Then the image of Jax's face—standing in his room, water and biscuits in his hands—made her stop and move toward the center of town.

Buildings and tents were deserted. She didn't pass another person. The closer to the hum of voices she got, the more uneasy she felt. Soon, she was jumping at shadows and anticipating someone around every corner.

She cleared the buildings and crested a hill, looking down on a makeshift arena. People stood all around the circle. They were cheering, their arms raised in celebration. Something was happening in the arena, something she couldn't make out over their bodies.

A tingle lanced her spine. She knew what was happening. She should take this chance when they were occupied and run.

Indecision halted her footsteps either way. She couldn't run, couldn't live with herself if she abandoned him, but fear kept her where she was. At least until the fervor died down and a few people sat.

Then she saw him. Jax.

43

EXCEPT FOR THE MAN-CAMP in the mountains, the arena housed the most people Tessa had ever seen. They were all the same tribe, which was obvious by their dress, plaited hair, and painted skin. One man, the smaller one from yesterday, stood in the center, his voice rising above the roar of the crowd.

As the shouting died, he again addressed them, walking in a circle, his back to a pole sunk into the middle of the field.

"We will feast. We will give our enemy to the gods. We will lie with one another. The gods will be pleased. The coming seasons will be prosperous."

The crowd again screamed their approval.

"Women will be taken. Children will be born. Our lives will be filled with plenty."

Tessa's heart beat so hard in her chest, it vibrated in her throat. For a moment, she saw stars, then she gasped, sucking in gulps of air. Bending at the waist, she thought she might be sick.

"This sacrifice will lead us all to prosperity." She looked up again in time to see him slide a knife along Jax's ribs. Jax screamed as his flesh fell open, and the crowd roared their approval.

Tessa charged forward, her mind a whirlwind of white, all self-preservation forgotten.

She shoved through the crowd, not aware when they fell back from her. Stumbling, she pulled herself back up and rushed to the weeping boy.

"Jax!" she cried.

When she reached the center of the arena, she collapsed at his feet. His brows drew together over his tear- and blood-streaked face.

"Tessa, you shouldn't be here."

She pressed a hand to one of the many wounds that covered his torso.

"Oh, Jax." Her voice broke with tears she couldn't control.

"She has come."

Tessa spun toward the voice. Only then did she realize the arena had fallen perfectly silent. The man raised his arms, circling them.

"She has come!" he said, projecting his voice over the crowd.

Tessa looked left and right, only now seeing her folly. The man in the circle wore a cape and headdress. Feathers covered the surface. In one hand he held a long staff, the end covered with more feathers and something that shone in the fading light. His other hand held the knife he'd been using to cut Jax.

He raised his arms, tilted his head back, and again yelled, "She has come!"

As his words faded, the crowd answered in a unified voice. "Mother."

The volume and power of the word caused Tessa to jump, her gaze skittering around the crowd. When the man grabbed her arm, she started back but was unable to break his grip. Afraid and angry, she threw a punch that caught him in the mouth.

The man dropped her arm and she retreated closer to Jax. When he raised a hand to touch his mouth, his fingers came away coated in blood. He looked from his fingers to her and smiled—his teeth were red. He spun from her to face the crowd and raised his bloody fingers. "She has come!"

To which the crowd answered, "Mother."

He smiled again, turning back to her. Then he spun back to the gallery. "She will give strong babies."

"Mother."

Tessa moved backward, her thoughts in turmoil. She felt Jax at her back and looked over her shoulder.

"Run, Tessa."

Her mind spinning, she faced forward, and the man was right in front of her. She didn't have time to react before he hit her. Her lip split and she tasted blood. Only the fact that she fell against Jax stopped her from hitting the ground.

The man grabbed her by her shirt, hauling her upright and causing her shirt to rip down the side before he flung her to the dirt.

She twisted, but he was already on her. His entire weight holding her down, he grabbed her flailing hands and held her by the wrists.

She looked up, struggling, and his smiling face covered her view. She bucked, flailing her legs, digging her heels into the dirt, but she was overmatched.

Anger, terror, futility all filled her like a black cloud moving across her brain. She couldn't contain it. She stiffened, threw back her head, and screamed. Long and loud, she thought her throat would bleed. The final note came out in a whimper, a tear sliding down her temple to disappear in her hair.

Another scream filled the void. Her assailant's head snapped up, his eyes wide and searching, nostrils flared.

When the shadow of a raptor passed overhead, the man scuttled off Tessa to squat in the dirt, his gaze sweeping left and right.

Tessa rolled to the side and gained her feet. She wobbled, ragged and dirty, hair hanging to obscure part of her face. Blood and saliva ran down her chin and dripped onto her torn shirt.

Silence filled the air and the man straightened to stand, his gaze moving around the sky.

Tessa felt Striker in her head and lifted her arm. He swept in and alit on her forearm, talons leaving small punctures in her skin. His wings extended, and he issued another call. Silence filled the arena. Then, as one, all the audience members and the chief dropped to their knees.

Tessa stood, her breath coming in great gasps. She wanted to kill the man but told herself to get Jax and get gone.

Through the strands of her hair, she saw the knife in the dirt. Striker flew from her arm to perch on the pole that held Jax. Her friend looked over the crowd, his heavy brows lending an intensity to his stare.

Tessa kept a wide berth around the man who still kneeled in the dirt. She stooped to retrieve the knife, almost falling as a wave of dizziness caught her. Her vision grayed for a moment, and she had to feel around on the ground for the knife.

She stopped behind the man, breathing heavily, fingers clenching and unclenching the hilt.

She could kill him now. He was bowed before her, back turned. Ripe for the picking. His neck slicing under the blade. The gush of warm blood. The sight of him collapsed in the red dirt.

Jax coughed and moaned, and her attention was pulled from one man to another.

Deliberately, she stepped away from the chief to walk to Jax. She stood in front of him for a moment. Motion above her caught her eye and she looked up to see Striker staring at her.

Was he a god to them? Who knew where the pedagogues came from?

Then he shook, ruffling his feathers, and he was again the bird she knew.

Focusing her attention on Jax, she sliced through his bindings, catching him when he fell from the pole.

"Come on, Jax. We're leaving." She pulled one of his arms over her shoulder and kept the knife in one hand while grasping him around the waist. Together, they moved to the edge of the arena.

They were almost at the exit path when the crowd stood as one. Tessa whipped around, dragging Jax with her. Behind them, the chief stood, his staff in his hand.

She brandished the knife. "Stay away from us."

He raised a hand, palm forward in a pacifying gesture, and said something she didn't understand. When he lowered the staff and began to untie something from the head of it, her gaze scoped the crowd. All eyes were on them. The chief took a step toward her, and her gaze swung back.

He kneeled again, offering something. In his hand rested a stone about the size of his palm. Clear with speckles of metallic color inside, light reflected and glistened off it.

When she hesitated, he stood, said something else, gestured at Striker and her, and pushed the stone at her. She hesitated a moment more and then moved the knife to her waistband before deftly plucking the stone from his hand.

He nodded and bowed his head, once again falling to his knee.

Her gaze swept him and the area and then she partially dragged Jax away.

Every few steps, Tessa glanced behind them, but no one followed. They turned a corner, heading toward the building she had been imprisoned in, when she saw a large figure in the street. She slowed but kept moving forward, not certain what else to do.

Closer and she saw it was the giant. Attempting to keep the giant in sight, she shifted her gaze. Off to one side of the road, two horses were tied. They had packs tied to their backs.

The giant watched them until they were mere feet from him. Even there, Tessa had to look up to meet his eyes.

"What do you want?" she demanded.

He dropped to one knee, now level with her gaze, and held out a hand to the horses.

"For the Mother."

Tessa gave it a moment. Worried but not dumb, she hustled Jax to the horses.

"Jax." She shook him. He wasn't unconscious, but he wasn't really with her. "Come on, Jax. Let's get on the horse."

When he reached up to grasp the horse's mane, she considered herself lucky. She bent and threaded her fingers together, grasping him under the knee. With more muscle than she felt she had, she hefted him on the horse.

The giant remained kneeling. She slipped under the horse's neck, untied the reins, then gave them to Jax.

"Hold these for a minute, buddy." Another bolt of relief went through her when he grasped the reins and his gaze met hers. "We're almost out of here." She tied the other horse to the one Jax sat on and slipped back under. Grabbing the mane, she stepped back and threw a leg behind the boy, pulling herself up behind him. She wrapped her arms around Jax and took the reins from him. With a pull on one side and a small kick, she turned the horse and moved into the street, the other horse following docilely by its reins.

As they rode by the giant, she looked down on his bowed head. When she heard the faint sound of wings overhead, she glanced up then aimed her gaze down the road.

44

PATRICK HELD UP BOTH HANDS, but the assembly of men continued to shout and argue, ignoring his efforts to gain control.

"My lords," he said with a raised voice. "Sirs, please."

Most of the men in the room quieted and looked toward the front of the room, but some continued with their heated discussions.

"Please, gentlemen. If I might have a moment of your time." At this, the remainder of the men looked toward the priest.

"Thank you." Patrick stepped closer to the assembled men. He needed to stay in control of them or they would accomplish nothing. "I appreciate you all coming together today. We must decide what is to be done about Nav-lys and her poisoning of the land."

A babble of voices answered his statement. In the clamor, he heard an accusation.

"I thought you told us you had this handled. That you had the answer."

He again held up his hands. "I told you I felt I knew the answer to our dilemma."

"It's been years," someone yelled.

Patrick nodded and moved closer. "Yes, I am aware of how long we have had to live with this poison in the land. It isn't something any of us want to continue."

"You don't have children."

"Or property."

Patrick was fast losing control of the room. He wished he knew something solid to tell them. How was he supposed to have all the answers? And even what he did know, he couldn't share.

"Not long ago, I received word from one of the groups we sent in search of Maya." This information hushed them. All eyes on him, their looks of hopefulness broke his heart. What if Maya didn't come? What if her coming didn't heal the land?

"They told me they were bringing her back with them." A little lie couldn't hurt, not at this juncture. "I'm afraid I don't know their current whereabouts. We just have to be patient."

The room erupted again, but not quite as loud. Patrick made his way to the other room. Perhaps he could find some peace and quiet and even get a bite to eat.

When he entered the adjoining room, there was too much activity there for him to think. Servants milled about, cleaning and gossiping.

HE HADN'T STROLLED LONG WHEN an idea came to him. A problem. What if Inger arrived with Maya? They'd been thinking of the coming for so long, no one had given any thought to what would happen when she came.

Perhaps, now in the light of day, he should take a trip to the temple. They thought Nav-lys and Orson had left the temple. The children had been taken to the cave outside of town, so he should be safe. He could check it out, see if there was anything that might aid them.

Once the idea set in his mind, there was no turning back. The temple wasn't too far. The keep was close to town. He could be there within the hour. At least, he would feel as if he were doing something.

The day was sunny, and now his disposition felt bright. Oh, to be doing something constructive.

WHEN HE REACHED THE TEMPLE, the sun was straight above him. He'd been in the temple many times and thought there would be plenty of time to investigate. The main hall had the large dome, which had been smashed when Maya and Sylvan fought years ago. Daylight would pour in. He easily convinced himself of the safety of daylight and the fact that he would be well out of the temple by nightfall.

The area around the temple was deserted. Any citizens of Berth who still lived within the walls moved far away from the temple area.

He climbed the stairs to the front entry, memories already assaulting him.

"Don't be a child. An empty building can do you no harm." But as he moved down the empty hallways, the echoes made his nerves jump. The building was empty. It was as if something kept all that might enter, out.

When a bead of sweat ran down his temple, he stopped to wipe his brow. The heat had increased in the enclosed spaces. Add that to his nerves, and it created a veritable oven. His cloak clung to his back and shoulders, catching on his legs with each step he took.

It wasn't too much farther to the throne room, and the closer he got, the more flayed his nerves became. The memories of the torture he had endured at the hand of Mikel Bathsar jumped to the front of his mind. He couldn't look anywhere without seeing the pitiful mess he had been when he fled this building.

Patrick pulled the sleeve of his cloak up to reveal the stump of his wrist. Some days, it still pained him. Sometimes, he still felt the removal of his fingernails.

He rubbed his remaining hand over the well-healed stump, his thoughts on his last visit to the temple. He still felt shame when he thought of how he'd run. Maybe, success in defeating Nav-lys would alleviate his feelings of inadequacy. Maybe, he would be able to sleep through the nights not haunted by dreams.

Patrick kept his hand firmly around his stump and continued down the hallway. When he came to the broken frame of what used to be the golden door, he stopped for a moment, afraid to enter the chamber. His gaze rested on a large hole in the far wall. A hole where the golden door had once rested. The door hadn't lasted long in a community where people starved. At first, they'd been afraid to enter the temple, but the lure of the gold had brought them. And when they had successfully navigated the theft of the door, others had come. Now, the temple was just the bones of the building.

With a deep breath, Patrick entered the throne room. It too had been emptied by looters.

His footfalls echoed within the empty space. What had he hoped to find here? Clarity? Did he really think there would be anything left in this husk of a building? Anything but his memories.

When he stepped onto the dais, he was again assaulted with the recollection of being here, on his knees. Bleeding. Battered. He thought his life was at an end. He thought, in that moment, that he had failed at the one thing that had been asked of him.

Now, the sun filtered in and birds flew throughout the room. More plant than building, it still grew with the offspring of Maya's magic from that day.

Patrick stepped down and sat on the stair. He concentrated, coming to terms with his emotions, his fear.

He was so focused inward, he only noticed when his ears popped. Startled, he leaned back. The birds were gone. Even the sun seemed to be leaving, the heat and light drained from it.

"Little priest."

He jumped to his feet, shifting to locate the speaker.

"Do not be afraid, little priest." This time, he had no trouble pinning where the voice came from. Out of the hall behind the dais, a woman strode. She was hunched, crippled with what seemed to be a great weight. Her long brown hair hung past her waist, gray streaked through it.

As she approached him, he fell back. He knew her for the evil she was.

Nav-lys.

Why would she be here? She no longer resided in the temple. No one did.

She looked him over, her black eyes reflecting his image. He wanted to turn and run, but his quaking legs wouldn't respond.

As she neared, the motion that impeded his lower limbs moved up his torso. By the time she stopped inches from him, he was visibly shaking, his teeth chattering.

"Little priest," she hissed. She ran a chipped black fingernail down his cheek.

He felt as though his bowels would release. Pure fear filled his body.

Somehow, he managed to speak. "Are you Sylvan?"

Her eyes veiled and nose crinkled, and she took a step back. "Sylvan?"

He took courage from her reaction. He didn't know what that meant but went with it.

"Yes. Are you Sylvan?"

"No," she hissed again. "I am Nav-lys. Sylvan is gone."

"Gone?" Now, bolder, he stepped toward her. "What do you mean gone?"

"The Sylvan. She was soft." Nav-lys turned from him. She moved across the dais area, seeming to float over the debris strewn in her wake.

Patrick waited for her to say more, but she didn't. He thought she might be leaving and, although he couldn't believe it, he followed her.

"Wait. What do you mean she was soft? Aren't you Sylvan?"

"No." Her voice was angry, and she turned on him. He stumbled back a few steps, almost falling over a mass of vines. "Sylvan sleeps. She is no more."

Patrick didn't push anymore. He'd seen firsthand what happened when she was angered, and he didn't want to end up a puddle for her to step over. This time, when she walked away from him, he let her go.

A second passed, and the sun again shone brightly. Birds sang.

He sat, this time on the floor. He couldn't believe he'd not only seen Nav-lys but spoke to her. And lived. He must be one of the few to come out on the other side of that conversation.

As his breathing returned to normal, he gave some thought to what she'd said. *Sylvan sleeps.* What could that mean? If Sylvan's consciousness were still within, could they wake her?

Once again, he wished for Caleb and his direction. He'd been given information he couldn't act on. He was just a man; how was he supposed to defeat this evil?

45

J AX RETAINED CONSCIOUSNESS LONGER THAN she thought he
would, but when he slumped in her arms, it still caught her
by surprise.

Now, her arms were beginning to shake from holding his
weight, and his blood continued to flow and drip down her leg.
It had slowed, but if she didn't do something soon, they were
going to have an even bigger problem.

She hadn't wanted to stop or quit before they put more
miles between them and the village, but when she heard
running water, she figured she'd been given her answer. She
kept the horses moving down the bank of the stream until she
saw what she was looking for.

"Jax." She reined the horse to a halt and shook him gently.
She needed to make sure he didn't fall from their ride. When he
stirred, she thanked the gods. If she'd had to manhandle him
from the horse and to a campsite, she'd surely injure him more
than he already was.

"Jax, I'm going to slip from the horse. I need you to hold

on." When she felt him tighten his legs and saw him grab the mane, she sighed in relief. He was still with her. She slid a leg back and dropped off the animal, keeping a steadying hand on his hip.

"Okay. Easy now." He slid his leg, and when gravity caught him, he almost fell. Tessa used the horse to push and keep him upright. With a deep moan, he clenched the horse, who sidestepped, causing him almost to fall again.

"Whoa," she said and gave the rein a small jerk. "Okay. Let's get you settled." She pulled one of his arms around her shoulder and grasped him by the waist. There was a small clearing near the stream, and she directed him there. As she seated him, he groaned.

"Will you be okay for a moment? I need to get some stuff and see to the horses."

He nodded but kept his head down, one hand over a wound on his side. Red seeped between his fingers. She would need to act quickly. The jarring horse ride didn't help the clotting.

She pulled the packs from the horses and created makeshift hobbles to keep them from wandering off. She was surprised by the amount of drying blood on the horse's flank. Jax was losing more blood than she'd thought.

The grass was plentiful near her chosen campsite, and the horses were already grazing, so she hoped they'd be good.

She dropped the packs next to Jax and pulled the knife from her waistband. She left to find the plant she'd seen and to look for another. When she saw the small stand of mockiweed, she gave a silent thanks to her mother. Tessa had never wanted to learn about plants, preferring to be out with Striker or weapons training, but Maya had insisted. Now, she was glad.

The mockiweed, first dipped in water and then crushed to release its sap, was a great coagulant. She cut plenty, and as she was heading back, she saw what else she wanted.

After plucking the blossoms from another plant, being careful of the thorns, she put them with the leaves in the turned-up edge of her shirt.

Jax was asleep or passed out. She wasn't sure which and guessed it didn't matter. Dropping her gatherings, she pulled the mockiweed leaves and headed to the stream. She saturated them and then moved back to Jax to scrub them between her fists. They released their sap, foaming like soap.

She kneeled next to him, and when he didn't wake, she began to lay the leaves on his wounds. Warm from her hands, the leaves didn't rouse him.

The blossoms, when boiled, created a broth that would help him heal—strengthen his blood, lessen his pain. She didn't know if she should light a fire, but the tribe did let them go, so why would they be looking for them?

She sat watching Jax for another moment and decided the benefit for his health was greater than the risk. Checking him again, feeling for a fever, she went to gather wood.

She realized she didn't have the means to light a fire. Holding her breath, she searched first one pack and then the other. When she found the fire-making kit and a small pot, she thanked the gods. She couldn't quite bring herself to thank the giant.

Fire started, blossoms boiling, Tessa sat. Then she realized how much her own body hurt. She manipulated her jaw, which felt bruised, and hoped it wasn't broken. Scrapes on her back carried a steady burn, as did those on her elbows when she scanned her arms. Even the puncture marks from Striker's talons pulsed and throbbed.

She pulled the blossom broth from the fire to cool and decided to save some for herself.

Now that the immediate danger passed, Tessa mourned the loss of her bow. She felt she'd disappointed her mother by not taking better care of it. Its loss made her miss her mother even more. She shook her head. She'd always thought, with all the training she, Sentinel, and her mother did, that she would be able to hold her own against a foe. These last few days had proved to her just how disillusioned she'd been.

Her mother and Sentinel would never have found themselves in this predicament. They would have cut a swath right through that tribe. She would never be able to live up to the warrior her mother was. She should have stayed at the Hampshires'.

A tear ran down her face and she slapped her thigh in frustration.

If she found them, she'd be more liability than asset.

"What are you crying about?"

Jax's voice pulled her out of her cloud of self-deprivation.

"Jax." She scooted to him. With the back of her hand, she checked his forehead and cheek, and smiled when she pulled the edge of a leaf aside. "You're looking good."

"Well, I feel like I've been run over by a herd of cattle."

A laugh exploded from her. Hearing him talk to her—joke with her—made the cloud of a moment before dissipate.

"Here," she said and grabbed the broth. "This will help with your pain."

She supported his head and kept one hand on the pot even though he held it in both of his. After he took a couple large drinks, he pushed it away, breathing deeply to catch his breath. When she tried to get him to take more, he shook his head.

She sat back and checked his color and breathing while sipping on the remaining liquid.

"What's this on my side?" he said as he started to pull it off.

"No," she admonished. "Leave them be. They'll help you to heal and stop your bleeding."

He looked down his nose at her with a small wrinkle in his brow but let the leaves alone. "They itch."

She nodded. "That's good. Leave them be."

He sighed and, leaning back, stared at the stream.

"You shouldn't have come—shouldn't have come after me." His voice was so low, she barely heard it over the babbling of the water. A small scowl marred her expression.

"How dare you think I would leave you."

"You don't know me. You could have run."

"We got out. It all ended up all right."

He shook his head, not looking at her. "We were lucky. Lucky, Tessa. Gods, it could have been so much worse."

At his words, Tessa had a flash of the chief. His weight on her, his breath in her face. She shivered in reaction. "Yes," she agreed.

THE FIRE WAS JUST COALS, the horses' breaths sounded warm and calm, and Tessa watched the night sky. The quiet welcomed her, calming nerves still stretched tautly.

"Where do we go from here?"

She'd thought him asleep but found she wasn't surprised that he wasn't. "I was on my way to the coast before all of this. I'm trying to catch up to my mother."

He nodded. "Okay. The coast, huh? I've never seen the big water. Always wanted to."

"Are you telling me you want to go with me?"

"Guess so. Don't have anything to stick around this area for."

"Well, okay." She rolled on her side to face him, his face dim in the low firelight.

"Yep," he added. "Guess you're stuck with me now."

"I just wish I could have gotten my things before we left the village. I know that's silly." She shook her head. "But the bow was my mother's. It was special to her."

"It's not at the village."

She sat up, leaning toward him. "What do you mean? The tribe had our things."

"No, they didn't. I told you I had them somewhere safe."

"You have my things?"

Nodding, his expression dull as if she were not quite smart, he repeated, slowly, "Yes. I had your stuff, and a lot of my stuff, hidden in the outer room."

"You're sure they didn't find it?"

"I'm sure. When they grabbed us, we left right away. The whole group. They didn't search anywhere but the inner room."

"Oh, Jax!" She jumped up and grasped his face, kissing him on the lips.

"W-Well." He smiled big and gave a small chuckle. He cleared his throat and shifted. "Do you know where we are? I was a little out of it yesterday."

"I think we're heading back the way we came." She sat back and leaned on her elbows. "I know it's not smart. Thought I should take us away from the area that the tribe went, but I didn't know where we were."

"That's good. We'll keep on this path. I know where we are. We should reach the town later tonight." He seemed to be thinking. "We'll get our stuff and head straight to the coast. Where are you meeting your mother?"

"I know where she's going when she gets across the water, but I'm not sure where they'll leave from."

"They?"

"Yes." She nodded. "She's with a—I'm not sure how to explain." She shrugged. "A friend, I guess."

THE SUN WAS JUST PEEKING over the hills, spooling through the trees and shining off the water. They hadn't slept much the rest of the night. Once, Tessa reapplied leaves to Jax's wounds, and she made them another pot of broth.

Now, he stretched gingerly as he stood, moving his body side to side.

She watched him, ready to admonish him to be careful, but he didn't overdo. When he stopped, she looked for what caught his attention.

"What? What is it?"

"Can you explain that to me?" He pointed up with his chin.

Striker was perched on a branch in a nearby tree. She looked down, thinking furiously.

"He's with me."

"I kinda figured that back at the village."

"Yeah. Well. He and I travel together. We're friends." She peeked at him from behind the fall of her hair.

"Okay. I guess I owe him. Seems like he saved us back there."

Tessa breathed a sigh of relief. It looked like Jax wasn't only going to accept Striker without prying, but he was going to see him as a positive.

When he struggled to get to his feet, she hurried over and helped him with a hand on his arm.

"Thank you." His voice sounded weak again—pained.

"Do you think you should travel today? Maybe we should wait."

"No," he said. "We need to be moving. I'll be all right."

She nodded, not really agreeing with him but not willing to argue. They did need to get moving. And she was anxious to make sure her bow was still within her reach.

When she moved from under his arm, she put a hand on his shoulder to ensure he was going to stay on his feet. He looked at her and nodded, so she released him. He wobbled for a moment but then found his place.

She left him standing but kept an eye on him. When she approached the horses, they raised their heads from a bank of lush grass.

"Whoa, girls," she whispered to them. She slipped a rope around the neck of one and then the other and led them back to the camp. They were docile, munching on mouthfuls along the way.

When she had the packs loaded and bridles ready for riding, she went to get Jax. He stood by the stream, gingerly pressing his side. The leaves stayed in place under some rags she'd ripped and wrapped him with.

"How does it feel?"

He first stared at her and then looked back at his side. "Surprisingly good." He poked again just low of his last wound. "I thought for sure I was dead. Didn't think there was any way I was going to get out of that one."

"Me too." She rubbed his arm. "We should be leaving."

He turned to walk with her to the horses. "I've been in some tight places before, but that was the worst."

She nodded and let him talk as they walked. He laid a hand on the bandages, his steps slightly unsteady.

When they approached the horses, the nearest one lifted its head and blew a breath from her nose, ears pricked forward. Tessa thought maybe the smell of blood, still heavy on Jax, had startled the horse. She spoke gently to the mare, patting her neck and holding one of the reins, then assisted Jax to mount.

When he was settled, she handed him the reins. She slid

under the neck of his horse, and before getting on hers, she reached up to check his wounds. Nothing seeped from his bandages. She gave him a small smile and then mounted her own horse before they took their next path.

46

I T SEEMED MAYA'S EYES HAD barely closed when she was once again in the mist.

She wandered blindly. Bodies rubbed against her, and voices whispered to her. Neither able to see or hear them clearly, something called to her, pulling her forward. In her mind was an expectant sensation, an answer to an unasked question. If she could just keep moving forward, she was sure to find it.

The sensation of motion flowed around her and in her as if she were floating in a boat on a moving sea. White, wispy fog moved like a current.

"Hello," she called. The sound of her own voice echoed back to her. Where was everyone? Sentinel must be near. Tessa must be near. She would never leave either of them. This world in which she found herself was silent, like a void. She couldn't even hear her own breathing.

The mist moved faster and swirled. Dizzy, she stopped walking forward. Even standing still, she shifted with the mist.

Faster and faster it spun until she had to close her eyes.

With no sight, no voices whispering, she was truly lost in this silent world.

She was just about to open her eyes again when a burning began in her breast.

No, she thought. Not in, but rather, on. Her lids still closed tight, she raised a hand and felt an object in her pocket. It was hot, burning through her vest.

When she grasped the item and pulled it out, all the motion, all the swirling in her head, came to a halt.

She looked down at the object, and it shone so brightly she had to squint. As the light faded, she made out a greenish-brown stone. Flecks of gold reflected the light.

In her head, she heard the words, *Find the Three—become the One.*

MAYA SAT UP STRAIGHT, SUCKING in a breath like she'd just surfaced in water. The dream, the mist. She remembered now. The entities within the mist.

With a shaky hand, she dug into her front vest pocket. She felt the weight before she touched the item and her breath quickened. She grasped the object and looked at the same stone in her hand. Oval, the size of her palm. In shades of brown and green with metallic striations shot through.

In the light of a new day, she watched it. When it didn't do anything, she grasped it between two fingers to turn it. Seeing something on the reverse side, she held it up, squinting in the fading light of the fire. On it were three equal lines with their ends touching. Across one of the points was another line.

Beautiful, she could admit. Like nothing she'd ever seen before. But what was it? Why was it?

She heard the men stir, and she hid the stone in her palm. She didn't want to share it until she knew what it was.

She looked left and right. A sinuous sensation flowed through her unlike anything she'd ever experienced. Bending her head, she placed her lips to her fists, the stone entombed within them. Words came from her in a whisper. Words she didn't know. Words she didn't remember.

When she finished speaking, she looked up and blinked rapidly, scanning the area, not sure what happened.

With an inner shrug, she took her hunting knife and sharpened it, not noticing the bulge in her shirt above her heart.

47

"**W**HAT DO YOU SEE?" TESSA leaned in the door, scanning for Jax.

"I told you to wait outside," he said as he pushed by her.

"I know what you said." She spun to face him, her hands on her hips. "I don't want to stay outside, and since when do I take orders from you?"

"I just want you to be safe."

"Yeah, yeah . . . Did you find our stuff?" She pushed at him, looking through what he held. When she didn't see her bow, she looked behind him as if it would magically appear. When that didn't happen, she turned back toward the building.

"I see you have an armful of your things. Where are mine? Where is my bow?"

He dropped the items he held and grabbed her arm. She stopped, turned, and he released her but stepped between her and the building.

"Jeez, give me a second, why don't you. I'm getting it, I'm

getting it."

"Get it quicker, Jax, or I'll do it myself."

He held up his hands in a pacifying manner, turned, and ambled back inside the building.

Tessa didn't know what he didn't want her to see. She thought they were past keeping secrets, but apparently not.

"Well hurry up, or I'm coming in." To occupy herself, she paced up and down the front of the building. Not too many moments later, Jax exited the doorway, his arms once again full of items. Strung over his shoulder and held partly under his arm, Tessa saw her bow case. She leaped to him, grabbing at it with vigor.

"Wait, wait. Let me set everything down." But he had to dump all the items in the dirt so she could get to the case.

She clung to it, giving it a hug, and she spun in a circle, a wide smile on her face. "Oh, Jax, you are the best. The very best," she said. She opened the case and drew out the bow. She spent some time looking it over, ensuring it wasn't damaged. After notching the string, she again reached into the pile and withdrew her quiver. From it she took an arrow and loosed it.

The arrow struck a tree some distance away, pinning a red leaf to the bark.

"Wow," he breathed, drawing a smile from her. "You're really good."

"So, what? You didn't think I would be?"

"No. That's not what I'm saying." His cheeks blushed. "I just didn't know you were that good."

"That's nothing," she said, her chest puffed. "I can hit a bird in flight pretty much every time."

"That's great. You must practice all the time." He moved closer, his fingers running over the etchings in the bow.

She held it out for him to hold. "My mother says I took to the bow like a bird to flight." A small smile came at the reference to her mother. "She hunted with a bow as a girl. It was natural for her to train me."

"This is a beauty." He held the bow to the sun, studying its contours. "Did your mother make it?"

"No." She reached for the weapon. "I'm not sure where she got it, but I know it's special to her."

A bit reluctantly, he handed the bow back. She unstrung the string and put it all back into its case. When she turned and began gathering her other belongings, he bent to help her.

"Do you know how far it is to the coast?" she asked.

"Only a day or two. We could still leave tonight. It's early enough, don't you think?" He looked up into the sky, turning in a circle. "It would be good to keep moving."

She looked back at him, noticing that he wasn't favoring his side anymore. Between the mockiweed poultices and the broth, he seemed to be healing right up. He seemed to feel her watching him and looked at her.

"What?"

"Nothing," she said, though she gave him a small smile. "I agree we should keep moving. I would like to get to the coast as soon as possible. With all this delay, I've probably already missed my mother."

"But you said you know where she's going, right?"

"Yes." She stopped to look around before stooping again to pick up her items. "I heard her say she would be going to the city of Berth. I don't know where that is though."

"If we don't find them on the coast, we'll just have to ask which ship is going there."

"Yes." She nodded. "I guess that should work."

"Sure, it'll be simple. You'll see."

"Well, let's just hurry, and hopefully we'll catch them before they leave for Berth." Tessa had a feeling she was going to be too late to meet up with her mother and Sentinel. She was going to have to cross the big water without them. But even before that, she was going to have to figure out a way to pay for their passage. She didn't have any money—she thought she'd be with her mother by now. She hoped something would come up.

SHE AND JAX WERE SOON packed up, all their belongings strapped to the horses except weapons, which they had strapped to their own bodies.

Tessa had her bow and quiver crossed over her body and a knife in her belt in place of the long knife she lost.

She watched with fascination as Jax hid various small blades among the folds of his clothing. When he finished, she couldn't tell they were even there.

"Are you any good with those?" She indicated the blades he'd been hiding. Before she could even blink, he pulled one and hurled it just past her ear. She heard the thunk of it hitting a tree behind her and, turning, she looked at the quivering hilt.

She turned back to the boy then sauntered up to the knife, jerking it from the bark.

"Okay. I can see you're good." When she walked back toward him, she held the blade out. "Maybe you can teach me?"

He took the blade from her, hiding it deftly within his clothes before looking into her eyes. "Sure. Trade you for lessons with the bow?"

Tessa's face broke into a large grin. "Of course. That's really a great idea."

Jax nodded his agreement, walked to his horse, and pulled himself up. A small groan escaped his lips as he sat. Tessa hurried to him, her hand on his leg.

"Are you all right? I asked you not to overdo."

"I know. I'm good."

She looked at his side, reaching up to poke at his bandages. "If you start to bleed again, I'm going to be angry."

"Yes, yes," he said, a sigh in his voice. "Let's get going."

Tessa decided there was nothing else she could do. She couldn't force him to be careful. He'd just have to deal with the pain if he overdid. She gave her horse a pat then grabbed the mane before she pulled herself up. When she turned her horse, Jax was already starting down the road away from the deserted town.

She kicked her horse to catch up with him, at the last moment glancing back. She would be glad to leave this behind.

48

THE BLADE HIT THE STUMP with a solid thunk.

Jax had marked a circle with a dot in the middle. Tessa kept trying to hit the middle of the circle, but her blade ended up just low of center.

When the blade hit again, her eyebrows pulled toward her nose.

She knew her aim was good. Her proficiency with the bow was proof of that.

She threw another one and still it was off the mark.

A whistle went by her head and a blade hit dead center.

"Jax!" She turned on him. "You could have hit me with that."

"Don't be silly. I'd never hit you with it." He sauntered over to her. "*I* know how to throw a knife."

"Ha, ha. Aren't you funny? Maybe if you were a better teacher, I could get rid of this drop I have." She tugged the knives from the stump and turned to him. "Did you ever think of that?"

He stepped right up to her, his body almost touching hers, and took the knives from her. With a quick spin, he dropped to one knee, the knives flashing as they hurtled toward the target. Three knives whacked within inches of each other around the middle dot.

"You make me insane." Tessa walked across to retrieve the blades, Jax chuckling at her frustration.

"Bring them back. Let me see what you're doing." He gestured to her, and grudgingly, she walked back in front of him. "Turn around," he said and turned her with his hands on her shoulders. "Okay. Throw one for me."

She glanced back, and he moved farther back and to the side. She focused on the target. With the blade in between her fingers and thumb, she swung back. When her arm shot forward, she released the knife. And it hit below the circle.

"Ah!" she moaned and stomped her foot.

"Tessa, don't get frustrated. I see what you're doing."

She turned to him with a scowl but remained hopeful. "What? What can I do?"

"You're releasing too late."

"Too late? I'm eyeing the target."

He nodded. "Yes, but you need to release before your arm comes through the arch. Trust me, I'm the expert, right?"

"Okay, okay. I'll try."

She lined up again, knife lightly gripped. Only this time, when she moved her arm forward, she released before the knife was aiming at the target.

Stunned, she stared at the tree. The hilt vibrated, and the

blade was stuck right in the center of the target.

"Woo-hoo!" she shouted and threw herself into his arms. He patted her on the back and released her as she danced around him in a jig. "I did it. I did it."

"Yes, you did. I told you that you could."

She ran to the target to retrieve the two knives and then hustled back to where he stood. "I want to do it again."

"Do it," he said. "Just calm down and concentrate."

She did as he said. She took a deep breath, straightened her shoulders, and looked at the target. Then pulling her arm back, she let the knife fly—right into the center.

"Thank the gods," she breathed. "I didn't think I was going to get it."

"Of course you would." He patted her on the shoulder. "Like you said, you've got great aim."

"And a great teacher." She went to him and looked him in the eye. "Truthfully, you are a great teacher."

"Tomorrow we switch. I want a shot at that bow."

49

A DAY LATER, TESSA AND Jax entered a coastal town.
"It smells funny here," Jax noted.
"I think it's the smell of all that water." They sat on
their horses on a hill overlooking the town. All the buildings
resembled each other, their wood worn and storm-beaten with
a gray cast. Fishing boats lined the shore. Farther out, larger
ships were anchored. Men clambered over them like ants.

"I've never seen anything like that."

Jax was staring at the expanse of water, so Tessa let her gaze
drift. The sea went all the way to the horizon. She had never
seen anything like it.

White birds called and swooped over the waves that moved
into the shoreline. Even from this distance, she heard men as
they called to each other, climbing over the rigging and decks.

The boats, even those anchored off the shore, looked so
small compared to the sea. Was that really what they would ride
on? Would that be all that would stand between them and a
deep, watery death? Just thinking of it, a small bead of sweat

ran down her back.

She looked again at Jax, and the eyes he turned to her reflected her own thoughts.

Fear. Plain and simple fear.

What would it be like to be out on that much water? Would she be able to see into it? Would she view the bottom like when in a lake? Could she see the fish? And how big were the fish in that much water? Just the thought of that had her heart racing.

She didn't look back at Jax again but gave her horse a nudge and started down the hill into town. After a moment, the sound of his horse's hooves on the gravel road came from behind her.

The nearer they got, the louder sounds became. It had been days since they'd been around so many people. Not since the tribe. Voices and animal noises closed in on her, making her tense. She pulled her horse up to walk alongside Jax.

The stopped a few blocks from the wharf at an inn called The Flying Fish. The hanging sign above the door had a weathered picture of a fish with large wings protruding from its body soaring over waves. Tessa dismounted and tied her horse to the post so she could study the sign. Jax stepped beside her, his eyes also on the sign.

"What?" he asked.

"Huh?" She looked at him, a small crease between her eyes.

"The sign." He tilted his head toward it. "What about it are you looking at?"

She shrugged.

With his hand on her arm, he climbed the stairs. They walked through the door together, the rise in volume stopping them both. Tessa took a couple quick blinks and then directed them around the tables to the counter where the proprietor stood.

When they stopped in front of him, he eyed them, a question on his face.

"Sir," Tessa began, "I'm wondering if you might have seen two people. A man and a woman."

"Lots of men and women around here." He returned to what he was doing.

"Um. Yes, sir."

He looked up again, his mouth pursed and eyes narrow.

"I'm looking for a particular man and woman. I believe if you've seen them you would remember them." She cleared her throat. "The woman has red hair and the man has dark skin."

"Nope." He looked down again. To his paper he said, "No one like that around."

"Okay. Thank you." She started to turn away but then turned back. "Sir?"

His expression darkened.

"Are there any other sleeping establishments in town?"

"Nope."

When he dismissed her again, Tessa turned to Jax and then toward the door.

"Let's go down to the dock," Jax said. "Maybe they didn't stay overnight. Maybe they went right on board."

"That's a good idea. Maybe they're on board a ship right now, just waiting to sail." Her face glowed at the thought, and she grabbed Jax's hand to pull him outside.

The doors drew shut and the volume fell away. Tessa hadn't realized how tense she'd become inside until they exited. She took a deep breath and marched to the end of the walkway. Standing on her toes, she looked at the water. Over the curve of the road, she saw the spars of fishing boats. A smile split her face and she hurried down the plank steps. She stopped in the street and waved Jax forward.

"Come on, Jax. Hurry up. I'm sure they're on board."

He had almost caught up to her when she took off down the street. He picked up his speed, trying to catch her.

"Tessa!" he yelled. "Wait up."

Over her shoulder she hollered, "Hurry up. I don't want to miss them."

Tessa stopped on the edge of the dock, looking left and right. "Keep an eye out for them. I'm sure they're here."

"Tessa," Jax began. "You know, they might not be here."

"What?" She glanced at him then looked away. "Of course, they are." She grabbed his arm and pulled him toward the dock. "Come on. I don't want to talk about it. Let's find them."

Jax allowed her to pull him. He'd wait and see. Maybe she was right.

50

TESSA STRODE THROUGH THE CROWDS at the dock, her chin high. She just knew her mother and Sentinel were here. She would find them. She was tired of being an adult. Tired of having to deal with all the responsibilities. She wanted her mother.

They made it to the end of the dock and were circling around when she realized the two they looked for could already be aboard a ship.

"Jax," she said, excitement in her voice. "Do you see a building that might house the shipping business?" He scanned the area. "I bet someone there could tell us what ship they're on."

"Um. Well maybe that one over there." He pointed to a building where men entered and exited. Above the door a sign read *BlackJack Shipping*.

"Yes." She was practically jumping up and down with excitement. "I bet they'll know immediately where we should go."

She hustled away. Pushing through the door, Tessa glanced up when a bell jingled. She moved toward the rear where a man studied charts and papers behind a desk. When she rushed to him, he glanced at her and then returned his attention to the papers.

"Sir," she said, "can you tell me if a particular person is aboard a ship?"

Again, he looked up at her. "Now you just run along, young lady. I have work to do here."

When she didn't leave, he stood and looked down his nose at her. Tessa confronted him with a direct gaze, which he broke to look at Jax. Jax did nothing.

"Didn't you hear me, little girl? This is a business. Men are working here. You need to leave."

"Sir," she began, "I'm looking for someone I believe is on board one of the ships out there." She pointed out to the bay. "I just need to know which ship she is on."

The man sat back down and crossed his hands over the maps. "There's only one ship that takes passengers, so if the person you seek is on board, they would be on that ship."

Tessa sighed in thanksgiving. "And which ship would that be?"

The man stood again and pointed a long finger out toward the door. "The *Windjammer*. She's loading right now. Her captain plans on setting sail before sunset. In fact, he told me he planned on catching the set."

"Tell me how I can tell if someone is on the *Windjammer*."

"Little lady," he began, "you are a mite impertinent."

Jax shifted Tessa behind him. "Sir, please excuse my friend. She's searching for her mother and, in the way of women, is highly excitable." He stumbled forward a step with the punch Tessa laid on his lower back. "If we could locate her mother, I'm sure she would cease to disturb you."

The man looked from Jax to Tessa, who stayed back and quiet. With a nod, he pulled a book from a drawer in his desk.

"What is her mother's name?" he asked, flipping the book open to a page.

Jax looked toward Tessa, his eyebrow raised.

Tessa jumped forward. "Maya. Maya Singh."

The man stared at her for a moment as though assessing her, and then he glanced at the page. He ran his finger down a list and, snapping it closed, placed it back in his desk. "No one on the *Windjammer* by that name."

Tessa didn't know what to say. The man sat back down and again began looking over his papers. Blinking, her thoughts in disarray, she turned from the man, Jax following her. Partway to the door, she stopped and returned to the desk.

"What do you mean she's not on the *Windjammer*? She must be on that ship."

The man sighed and placed his hands on his thighs, again standing. "Perhaps the woman you seek is on another ship, in another port."

"Another port . . ." Tessa repeated softly.

"Yes. There are any number of shipping ports along this coast. *This* port is one of many."

Tessa stared. One of many. How was she ever to find her

mother?

"Is there anything else I can help you with, young lady?" The man's voice led her to believe he really didn't want to help her. There was one other thing she had to know.

"Does the *Windjammer* go to the city of Berth?"

The man gave her a long look, and then with a sigh, he found a sheet of paper under some others and scanned it with a finger. "Yes. It appears it does, though it makes port a few times before reaching Berth."

Tessa grabbed Jax's arm. She was bouncing on the balls of her feet again.

"We would like to go on that ship."

He looked down his nose at her. "You would like to book passage on the *Windjammer* for the city of Berth?"

"Yes."

"And do you have any money?"

Tessa looked at Jax, her eyes wide. The boy stepped forward. "How much will it cost for the two of us to sail to Berth?"

The man did a quick computation and quoted him an amount.

Jax nodded. "We'll be back."

He turned from the man, taking Tessa's arm and pulling her toward the exit.

"But we don't have any money."

"Come on, Tessa. Let's step outside for a minute." When he opened the door to the sound of a bell, she stepped out with him right behind her. She didn't take more than a couple steps before turning.

"What, Jax? What can we do with no money?"

He put a hand on her shoulder and maneuvered her down the street. Leaning in, he told her, "The horses. We have the horses. I bet we could sell them for at least the amount we need to book passage on the *Windjammer*."

Tessa stopped again. A smile broke across her face. "I hadn't considered the horses. They're not ours, but I guess it's like they are."

Jax nodded. "Who else would they belong to?"

They hurried down the street back to the inn where they'd left the horses. They found them where they'd left them, packs tied to their backs. They untied the reins and headed toward the stables.

* * * * *

WITHIN THE HOUR, TESSA AND Jax found themselves back in front of the shipping offices. They were no longer in possession of two horses but now had ample money to make the transaction.

They carried their packs and weapons as they once again entered the office. The desk where they'd talked to the man was now empty, but another man worked at a desk one over. Tessa and Jax looked at each other and then approached the man.

"We would like to get tickets on the *Windjammer* to the town of Berth," Tessa said.

The man filled out some paperwork, took their payment, and in no time, they were standing back on the walkway. Tessa looked at the water. When Jax caught her eye, she broke into a large smile.

"Soon." She patted him on the shoulder and headed toward the port. "Soon, we'll be with my mother."

51

MOVING THROUGH THE AREA, TECK turned to make a final pass by the old cabin. Even after all this time, when the wind blew just right, he thought he caught a whiff of smoke. Remembering that night, when he thought Maya dead, his heart pounded painfully. He thought the only way to feel truly normal again was to find her. So why was he standing here?

He'd just talked himself into walking away when a sparkle caught his eye in the light of high noon. He squinted and moved closer to the ruins. Everywhere there were plants, green and flowering. Each twined their way over and around charred lumber and the stone pile of the chimney.

Stepping over the obstructions, he moved to the interior of the shell. The ground here was spongy with years of rot and growth. He moved where he thought he'd seen something reflecting and looked around, scraping his boots on the land.

Compelled, he squatted and dug into the dirt. Rich and loamy, the scents of soil ballooned around him. With the hot sun on his back and the cool dirt sliding between his fingers, he dug deeper. He didn't understand it, but he knew he saw something.

When he felt it, he had a moment of wonder and confusion. How could this have been what reflected the light, buried so deep? He pulled it from its bed of dirt. It was hard and cool. Vibrant blue burst forth. Every shade and hue. It reminded him of looking deep into the ocean.

He moved from the skeleton of the cabin, his attention focused on the object in his hand.

A rock maybe. A gem?

He pulled his shirttail and cleaned the remainder of the dirt from its surface, once again fascinated by the swirls of colors and light. When he turned it over, on its side he saw an etching. The figure didn't appear to be scratched inside but rather a natural occurrence.

Three equal lines joined at their ends. Simple, yet beautiful.

THE SUN WAS SETTING WHEN Teck put the treasure in his pocket. The day had passed without him being aware of it. Now, glancing into the darkening sky, he turned his back on the cabin and looked forward to the future.

52

TECK WAS AWARE OF THE group before they showed themselves.

"Hallo to the campfire."

Teck looked up as the three men entered the fire's glow, his hand on the hilt of his sword. He watched the three, making no overt moves.

"Mind if we share your fire?" the one in front asked. They circled the fire. "Thanks, mister," he said without waiting for an answer. "Cold night." He kept his eyes on Teck as he squatted to the flames. He reached out to the kettle over the fire and, without breaking eye contact, took the spoon and tasted Teck's meal.

"Rabbit stew?" He took another bite. "Could use some seasoning." He dropped the spoon back in the kettle.

"We're travelin' inland. Maybe to one of the cities." When Teck didn't reply, he asked, "You?"

Teck nodded and sat up straighter, his hand remaining on his sword. "Yes, heading to the cities."

"You know, there's safety in numbers. Maybe we could travel together."

Teck preferred to stay away from these sorts of men. He recognized them—knew their ilk. He also knew to deny them would end his night in violence. He nodded slowly at the man then allowed his gaze to rest on the other two, one by one.

"You're all welcome to share the fire's warmth."

Seeming to know when not to push his luck, the leader nodded to the other two men. They were quick to join him by the fire.

Teck took his hand from his sword but didn't relax. Crossing his arms, he brushed the end of his long knife. He offered a portion of his stew to the strangers. Soon after, they rolled into blankets and soft snores filled the site.

Teck stared at the flames, knowing he'd get no sleep this night. When he glanced at the leader, he was not surprised to see his eyes reflecting the light.

The man held Teck's gaze for a moment and then his lips quirked. "What's your business in the city?"

Teck sat forward and, after stirring the fire, placed more fuel on it. As the flame caught and leaped, Teck watched its light fall over the stranger.

"Just looking for work. See what I can see," he finally answered.

The stranger nodded as though this were a commonplace situation, and Teck guessed it probably was.

"Yep," the man said. "Always on the lookout for opportunities."

"Yes," Teck said and returned his hand to the hilt of his knife.

The man didn't add any more, and after a moment he turned over and slept.

* * * * *

THE CALLS OF MORNING BIRDS roused Teck. He didn't recall falling asleep, and as he woke, he was aware of the sounds around him.

Deep, even breathing surrounded him. Without shifting, Teck concentrated on pinpointing the location of the three men. Two distinct breaths came to him, but he couldn't hear the third.

He waited a moment and then, opening his eyes, rolled over.

Two of the men still slept by the fire's embers, but the third was nowhere in sight.

Teck studied his belongings. They didn't appear to be disturbed. Standing, he made his way to the edge of the camp to relieve himself. When he turned back, he saw the third man returning.

He gave Teck a nod and kicked his companions. "Wake up, the two of you."

They popped up like he'd touched them with a hot poker. Neither complained as they bundled their gear and got ready to leave.

Pack ready, sword strapped on, Teck waited for the three to precede him and then fell in behind them. Within a few steps, the leader dropped back to walk alongside him.

"Name's Maxyt."

"Teck."

"Thanks for lettin' us tag along."

Teck acknowledged his words with an inclination of his head but didn't speak. He kept the man in his periphery.

Around midday, one of the men walked into the woods to return a bit later with two game hens strapped to his belt.

THE SUN WAS DIPPING IN the sky when Maxyt whistled and gestured off the road. The two followed him and, with an inner shrug, Teck followed.

The two made short work of starting a fire and getting the birds roasting.

Warm and fed, Teck thought perhaps there would be a benefit to traveling with the trio.

WHEN HE WOKE TO A blade at his neck and the grinning face of Maxyt above him, Teck kicked himself. A little comfort and food and all his instincts deserted him.

He lay still, glaring up at the leader. Wanting just a moment—just a second—and he'd turn this situation around.

"Sorry Teck. But a guy's gotta take what he can, when he can."

He heard the words, smelled the breath, and everything went black.

TECK ROLLED TO HIS HANDS and knees, a low moan escaping his

lips. He rose to his heels and touched the back of his head, his fingers coming away wet with blood.

Stupid. He'd been so stupid.

He squinted in the sunlight, pain lancing through his skull. Through the slit of his lids, he scanned the area. Empty but for the smoking remains of the campfire.

Resigned, he pushed to his feet and studied the ground — pacing in expanding circles until he found what he looked for.

Footprints.

Three sets of footprints. One larger, heavier than the others.

He envisioned what was to come. With an easy trot, ignoring the spike of pain each footfall caused, he followed his prey.

53

TESSA STOOD AT THE SHIP'S rail looking toward the horizon. She saw blue in every direction.

The first day at sea, she'd felt near panic. After the first hour or so, when all land disappeared, tension tightened her chest. The motion of the ship rolling with the waves and the scent of the sea air were so foreign to her she felt as though she were dreaming. Even now, days later, she had to discipline her mind not to think of the enormity of water under her feet.

When she and Jax had first come on board, with Striker on her arm and both of them weighed down in gear, the crew had stared. They were directed to separate large staterooms. Women shared one and men were in the other.

Two women, a mother and daughter, had already claimed an area against one wall. Tessa put her things next to a small cot in one corner. She looked around, happy to see the open rafters above her area. It would be a good spot for Striker to roost.

"Ma'am?"

When Tessa turned, the small girl was standing behind her.

The child looked to be about ten years old but small for her age. She had two blonde braids, and her nose was covered in freckles. The girl looked at Striker with a mixture of fascination and fear.

"Yes?" Tessa glanced at the mother who was busy with their belongings.

"Can I see your bird?" The girl's gaze was locked on the hawk, and he, likewise, had his gaze on her. His head bobbed back and forth as if testing his distance from her.

Tessa sat on her bed and rested her forearm on her leg. She gestured the girl forward and ran a hand down the bird's back and wings.

"His name is Striker, and he's a friend of mine."

When the girl hesitated, Tessa nodded. "It's okay. You can pet him, but you want to be gentle."

With a feather-soft touch, the youngster ran a finger over the soft feathers on the bird's chest. He tilted his head, his bright eyes intent on her. When she touched his foot, he picked it up to shift on Tessa's arm.

"You're tickling his toes," Tessa told her with a smile.

The girl gave a peal of laughter, drawing her mother's attention.

"No, Pennie," the mother shouted and rushed across the room, grabbing the child's arm to pull her away. Her motion pulled the girl right off her feet and caused Tessa to lean back on the bed. Striker flared his wings and made a sharp noise of displeasure. The mother hustled the girl across the room and bent over her, berating her the whole way.

With another flap, the bird righted himself and calmed.

Tessa ran a hand over his back. "That's a good boy. Don't let that grumpy old woman bother you. You're a good bird." At her crooning, Striker mouthed her hand with his beak. Made for rending and tearing, he was still gentle with Tessa.

When a knock sounded on the door, Tessa looked up. The woman moved to open it, keeping a keen eye on Tessa and her bird. She opened the door and there stood Jax.

"Hey, Tess. Wanna come up on deck and watch as we pull out of the harbor?"

At this point, Tessa would be interested in doing anything to get out of the room. She nodded and moved toward the door. The closer she got with the hawk, the farther back the woman stepped. At one point, she grabbed her daughter and shoved her behind her ample frame. Tessa shook her head at the woman. How could she be so silly?

The fresh air that filtered down the hall revived Tessa's flailing senses. It was good to be out in the wind and spray. Different but oddly refreshing.

The anchor was pulled, and slowly the ship moved out of port. Tessa stood with her back to the wall of the dining area and stared at the slowly diminishing land. Soon the people looked like ants running to and fro.

Tessa leaned toward Jax. "I wonder how far ahead of us my mother and Sentinel are."

"Oh, I wouldn't think too far."

"I'm going to let Striker stretch his wings for a bit. He's going to have to be inside quite a lot of this trip."

Jax nodded, and she walked toward the rail, lifting her arm. With an extension of his wings, the bird projected himself into the air. Workmen in their vicinity stopped to watch the majestic animal soar off the ship.

Tessa longed to go with him, to be free of the sea. Had she been alone, she would have soared alongside him. This situation, however, didn't allow for that type of freedom. She watched for another moment then stepped back to stand with Jax and watch the shoreline shrink.

With a sidelong glance at him, she asked, "Have you ever been on a ship before?"

"Yes. I sailed here. Long ago. But I was young and don't remember it."

Tessa realized she didn't know hardly anything about Jax. It was odd to feel so strongly that she could trust him, with her life if necessary, and yet not know what motivated him. What situations he had been through in his short life.

"Where are you from, Jax?"

His lips turned up in a small smile, but he didn't look her way. "Just a small village far from here."

"What brought you here?"

Now he did look at her. His soft, brown eyes held sadness. "Does it matter?"

She shook her head slowly and laid a hand on his arm. "No. No, it doesn't matter at all."

He looked down at her hand and then returned his gaze to the departing shoreline. Just a rim showed on the horizon, and above it, a large golden bird glided.

THAT NIGHT WHEN JAX LEFT Tessa at the cabin, she quietly opened the door and stepped inside. The room was now full of women. Each bed was taken, and belongings were stacked along each wall.

Some of the women were already asleep, their backs turned to the lanterns hanging in the room, but most of the women sat together in groups. The sounds of their muted conversations reminded Tessa of sitting on the porch at the Hampshires' farm and listening to her mother and Anna visit. The cool evening, lying next to her mother, covered in a quilt. Her mother's long fingers raking through her hair. She'd be in that place in between sleeping and wakefulness. Floating on the ease and comfort of her mother's voice.

Hearing these women now made Tessa's heart break with longing for her mother and easier times.

She slipped onto her cot, Striker quiet on her arm. No one seemed to notice her unusual companion.

She wanted to fall asleep to the hum of the voices. She stood on her bed and lifted her arm, inviting Striker to step to a rafter.

Stripping out of her boots and jacket, she lay on top of her blanket. Above her she watched Striker shift and get comfortable. The humming took her back.

54

HER STOMACH ROLLED WITH THE motion of the sea, the waves hitting the ship's hull.

It had been days, and Tessa didn't think she would ever get used to not being on dry land. The constant ebb and flow was just something she wasn't cut out for. One of the best ways she could combat the sickness was to sit on the deck, keeping her eyes below the level of the rail. She didn't know if she really couldn't perceive the movement or if it truly wasn't as obvious. Either way, she felt more like herself.

That was where Jax found her. When he walked up to flop beside her, she was studying the strange rock she'd been given.

"What's that?" he asked.

She held it out, the sunlight glinting off its surface. "Pretty, huh?"

"Where'd you get it?"

She pulled it back in to examine it closer. "The chief in the village gave it to me."

"What?" Jax slid up to his knees, facing her. He tried to grab the rock, but she evaded him and pulled it into her chest. "What do you mean the chief?"

"When we were leaving the arena. He took it off the top of his staff and gave it to me." She held it out again, letting the light filter through it. "I think it's pretty."

He held out his hand. "Can I see it?"

She squinted at him, assessing his interest. When he looked at her, eyes wide, empty of guile, she placed it in his hand.

Most of it was almost clear, a true cream color. Shot through the interior were shards of greens, pinks, and purples. He turned it over. On the reverse side was a symbol. He ran his finger over it, feeling for the rough edges, but there was no indentation where the symbol ran. Tessa had done the same thing. He held it closer.

He looked at it for a moment more and then dropped it back in her waiting hand.

"I think you should throw it over the side." His eyebrows drew together.

"No." She held it between her forefinger and thumb. She dropped it into her palm and scanned the deck then stood and walked to one of the crew. She spoke to him, and the man nodded and handed her twine. Tessa returned and sat back down beside him.

"What did you get?" Jax asked.

She held up the length of twine. "I'm going to make a cage for it to rest in. That way I can wear it like a necklace."

Soon she had a necklace that she tied around her neck. The stone in its webbing rested between her breasts, flashing in the noon sun.

* * * * *

DAYS PASSED WITHOUT TIME. THE sameness of each day, the never-ending blue.

Tessa took to standing at the rail, looking toward the horizon. Her mind stretched to infinity. The captain assured them they would reach land within a couple of days, but Jax had difficulty believing that. It all just seemed so unending.

Under Jax's hands, the rough wood of the rail cut into his palm. Aged with weather, salt, and wind, its spikes reared to punish the unwary.

Today, the sun's warmth and light were hidden behind a blanket of gray clouds. They rumbled their discontent with the threat of rain, but except for a light mist, Tessa and Jax remained dry.

The wind, gusting off and on, whipped Tessa's hair around her body and across her face.

When the motion began on the water, Jax stepped forward beside her. First one, then a gathering of many. All sorts and ilk of sea creature rose from the depths. Legs, tentacles, misshaped bodies, some bursting as they crested the waves, victim to the ravages of pressure and air. They seemed to be surging toward the ship. Wanting it, even needing it. Killing themselves to get to it.

Drawn by the spectacle, his breath caught in wonder, Jax's gaze fixed on the watery dance of bodies. He didn't at first notice Tessa's rigid body until she didn't react to the strangeness below them.

Her head was thrown back out of its natural position, and when Jax moved to the front of her, he saw her eyes were once again white—just as they were that day in his room. The stone that she'd tied around her neck glowed with a warm interior light.

"Tessa," he said softly, afraid of startling her.

She didn't answer or move. She was barely breathing.

He moved closer, unsure if he should touch her. Behind him, the animals continued to rise, some to die. They buffeted the sides of the ship, their calls of want and death the thing of dreams—or nightmares.

The animals and their sounds drew others to the deck. Voices blended with the beasts' cries. Jax looked around. The deck was filling fast. He needed to do something.

Not sure if Tessa would be safe, he grasped her by the arm and shook her. "Tessa."

He was just about to give her a harder jerk when an ear-splitting cry pierced the day. He ducked. When he looked toward the cry, he saw Striker coming in low and fast. Barely skimming above the undulating bodies in the sea, he soared straight at Jax.

When the raptor swooped over his head, the boy dropped to one knee, sure he was going to come away bloody. The bird winged into the rail, dropping directly in front of the girl. Again, he voiced a scream, causing Jax to cover his ears. The stampede of people fell back from where he and the girl stood.

Tessa took a step back, and when Jax looked up, it was to see her looking down. Her eyes were a normal green once again.

"Tessa," he breathed and stood, taking her arm, although this time his touch was gentle.

She seemed to be coming out of a dream. She looked around. The commotion on the ship caught her attention and she moved forward to stare at the rapidly calming sea.

The creatures were drifting below the surface. An occasional thrash or flail of limb occurred, but the excitement was over.

"Wha—What happened?"

Jax tried to catch her eye. When she wouldn't look at him, his interest was caught by the stone at her throat. It lay, inert, without any internal fire. His gaze moved to the bird who still stood on the rail. Calmly, he flared his wings and then settled.

When Tessa swayed, he put an arm around her and led her back to a seat near the cabin. She dropped her head into her hands. Jax sat beside her, anxious about her well-being.

After a moment, she scanned the area. Most of the people had continued about their business now that the excitement was done.

"Tessa," he said, and she glanced at him. "What was that?"

With a sigh, she leaned back, her head resting on the wall behind them. Not looking him in the eye, she said, "I've always had a bit of magic."

She blinked and glanced his way, barely making eye contact before again looking up. He didn't say anything. "My family . . . Well, I come from a family with magic. My mother and grandmother, I'm told, could do certain things." She dropped her head back into her hands as though exhausted and rubbed hard at the back of her neck.

"For me" — he had to lean in to hear her — "I've had a way with animals. Not just Striker, he's different." She peeked at him again. "I'll tell you about him someday."

With another sigh, she sat, pulling her legs up to wrap her arms around them. "I've never done anything like that before. I'm not sure where it came from."

"The stone," he interrupted her, causing her to look at him. "The stone was glowing."

She stared into his eyes for a moment and then looked down at the stone, lifting it from her chest. After studying it, she let it drop.

"I don't understand, but perhaps it amplified my abilities." She shrugged.

"Do you know what you were doing or thinking before you went into that trance?"

"A trance?" She stared off in the distance, thinking. "I guess it is like that—huh. That's what happens whenever I link with Striker." She peeked back at him and then looked away. "I can link with my bird."

"I knew you could—at least I knew you did something that involved the hawk. I saw you that night in my room, remember?" Jax was glad to be talking about this with her. He hadn't asked again, afraid of driving her away. Now she was freely giving him information, and it made him feel important. Someone she trusted.

She nodded. "I didn't know what you saw."

He turned his body from her and looked out at the deck. "What more can you tell me? Did this time feel different?"

"Yes." She nodded. "Though it's hard to remember. It was busy."

"Busy?"

"Yes. Usually it's calm, peaceful. Just me and Striker. Quiet. This wasn't like that. There were many . . . voices? I'm not really sure how to explain it."

"Well, they sure all wanted to come to you. They were willing to tear themselves apart, and maybe tear this boat apart, too."

"It could have been dangerous. I could have capsized the ship."

"So, what started it?"

"I was looking for Striker. I can communicate with him without truly linking minds. I opened myself to him, and suddenly, I was drowning in them. They were all around me."

"You need to be more careful."

She nodded slowly.

"And maybe you shouldn't be wearing that rock." He pointed to the stone strung around her neck.

"No. I think wearing it is exactly what I'm supposed to be doing."

"What do you mean?"

"I'm not sure, but I'm working on it. When I have an answer, I'll let you know."

55

SENTINEL WATCHED MAYA. SOMETHING WAS different. He couldn't place what it was, but within the last couple days—after exiting the caves—Maya had changed.

She was never secretive with him. And now, she would sneak away. Spend time alone in the woods.

The night before, he'd gone looking for her. He tracked her through the trees. She sat by the stream, hunched over, and he would swear he heard her whispering.

He moved closer, careful of where he stepped. He had tried to catch the words. Nearer, the tone of her voice came to him and the hackles on the back of his neck stood on end.

Intent on Maya, he had missed a step, sending a small stone down the hill. The woman's head jerked up. Whatever had been happening was over. She fumbled, righting herself and gathering her things. He'd been seen, so leaving subterfuge behind, he stepped from the trees and approached her.

"Sentinel," she had greeted him as if glad to see him. He knew better and kept a keen eye on her. "Come," she said and passed him to head back to the camp.

Sentinel turned with her, and for a moment it seemed as if she were a stranger.

"Maya." When she turned to lift an eyebrow at him, she was again his girl. The woman he'd known for years. The closest thing to family he would ever know.

She waited for him to come even with her. When he placed a palm upon her cheek, she scowled at him in confusion. "What is it, Sentinel? Is there something wrong?"

He studied her, looking again for the shadow, but it was gone. It was gone, and she was here.

"No," he had said and dropped his hand.

"Well, let's get back to camp and make some supper. I'm starved." She walked from him, and for just a moment more, he watched her before following.

56

FOR DAYS MAYA WRESTLED WITH the urges. Sometimes they were so strong, she had to go off by herself just to get her head right again. She thought about confiding in Sentinel, but she was afraid. Never had she felt so out of control.

She'd known last night that he knew something was different. Now, watching his back in front of her, she knew she would need his help. Her mind was fracturing. She heard voices calling her. At first, it was during her dreams, but now it was also during the light of day. Others would joke and tell stories around the campfire, but all she heard were the whispers.

It was the stone. After coming out of the caves, she'd dreamed it then found it in her pocket. It whispered secrets she could never quite remember, and when she held it, it glowed. She thought, if she could just recall the things it said, she would be okay. Each day she pushed herself to remember, but still only fog clouded her mind.

So, she would talk to Sentinel. He was the one. He had been with her the longest, knew her the best. They had fought together many times. They would fight this, too.

When they stopped to camp that night, she waited until everyone was settled down. Dinner was cooking over the fire, bedrolls were laid out, and Inger and his men relaxed.

When she moved away, Sentinel followed her. If she'd needed any confirmation that he knew something was wrong, he'd just given it. Walking to the edge of the clearing, out of the fire's glow, she turned to wait for him.

When he was within a couple feet, she said, "I'm going to need your help."

"I wondered how long it would take you to ask."

She nodded, her eyes misting. He knew. If nothing else, his words helped her to relax. Everything would be all right. When they were together, everything was always all right.

She made herself comfortable on a fallen log, and he squatted in front of her.

"Tell me, my girl. What is making you so afraid?"

Maya stared at Sentinel for a moment and then, reaching into her vest, pulled out the greenish stone.

"What is it?"

"After we were in the caves, I dreamed of this stone. Then, it came to be."

"What does it do?"

"It speaks to me." Her voice fell to a whisper. He leaned in closer to her.

"Maya, what does it say?"

She broke their eye contact. When she stood, Sentinel followed. He shifted his gaze to the stone. Pulling her hands toward her mouth, she whispered something, and within the rock a small flame ignited.

Sentinel stepped back, his eyes wide, mouth slack. He looked from the stone to Maya. Her eyes filled with a blue illumination as the flame inside the rock glowed brighter.

Behind him, Sentinel heard the men shifting, some of them rising. He glanced over his shoulder. Some of their group were coming forward. He shook his head at them, gesturing to stay back. He couldn't be sure they would be safe or that their intervention wouldn't cause harm to Maya.

When she grasped his upper arms, Sentinel returned his attention to the woman. She was staring at him, blue eyes blazing. She no longer held the stone. It glowed on the grass between them, its glow intensifying.

"The coming," Maya muttered. "The Three . . ."

But it wasn't her voice. This one was deeper, harsher. He scanned her features for a sign of pain or fear. His body flushed, but he wasn't sure if it was the contact with her, or fear for her.

"You must hurry. Tessa. Sylvan. The Three and Three will become One. The time is nigh."

As she uttered the last syllable, Maya's body convulsed. Her grip tightened, drawing blood. Her back arched, and she threw back her head and screamed into the night.

Plants burst from the ground all around them. Leaves, roots, and soil rained down.

Sentinel locked his arms around her, the only protection he could give. No sword or knife would battle this. He felt the pull of the plants. Vines, bushes, all sorts of foliage folded around them. Hemming them in. Sealing them together. Sentinel closed his eyes, bowed his head to rest his face against her shoulder, and hung on.

* * * * *

INGER AND HIS MEN STOOD in silence. The tower of greenery had appeared so quickly they couldn't react. Now it undulated, weaving within itself, shifting and pulsing.

The only sounds were the crackle of the fire and the whispers of the plants as they moved against each other.

"Are they dead?"

Inger looked at the speaker and then back at the column. He shook his head.

As the mass continued to move, Inger took a step closer. His men moved up behind him. He turned only to find his men clustered behind him. He inched toward the spectacle.

Clouds moved, and the light of a three-quarter moon fell upon the tableau. The number of plants continued to grow, the circumference of the column expanding. Leaves unraveled, and flowers bloomed.

Inger stooped to rest on one knee, his elbow on his thigh, chin to his palm, eyes on the tower. Behind him, the men followed his example. They waited.

57

SENTINEL DIDN'T KNOW HOW MUCH time passed when the plants moving across his back began to drop away. First, breathing became easier. As the vines unraveled, Maya's weight started to drop, but he tightened his hold on her.

When they all fell away, he leaned her unconscious body across one of his arms and slid the other arm under her knees to lift her from the mound of green. Stepping carefully, he turned with her and waded through the plants back to the campfire. When he passed their traveling companions, the men moved to the side to allow him through.

At the fire, he laid Maya by its warmth. She remained unconscious, her breathing shallow, her skin cold.

"Is she alive?"

Sentinel ignored the men. He took Maya's hands in his, one by one, and rubbed them vigorously. When she stirred, shifting her legs and rolling her head, he turned to Inger.

"Water."

The man hustled over to their packs, stepping over and

even on one of his men who fell over getting out of his way. He brought back a bladder of water.

When he looked over Sentinel's shoulder, Maya had her eyes open. Sentinel laid a palm on the girl's cheek, his thumb rubbing her skin.

Inger handed the water container over Sentinel's shoulder. Opening the flask, Sentinel put a hand behind Maya's neck and helped her sit. When she reached for the drink, her hands shook, and he helped her to steady it. She sipped, took a deep breath, then sipped again.

The men gathered around the trio, their curiosity almost tangible.

"What was that?" one of them asked.

Inger squatted next to them. "We would have attacked the plants had we known we wouldn't be injuring the two of you."

"No," Sentinel said and looked to the men. "The plants are Maya's. They are her magic. They would not harm her."

Inger scowled. "It appeared as if they were attacking her."

"No. Never. They were reacting to the stone."

When Maya reached for his hand, he returned his attention to her.

"The stone," she whispered.

All the men looked toward the mounding vegetation. "It is in the plants, where you dropped it."

"I need it."

Sentinel's face hardened, his mouth pursing. "I think we should throw it in the river. Get rid of it."

"No, I need it. Please, bring it to me."

Sentinel shook his head. "It is evil."

"No, Sentinel," she said. "It is powerful. Very powerful, but not evil." She struggled to sit up, and the man placed a hand behind her back to assist her. When she was comfortable and once again sipping water, she looked him in the eye. "You must bring me the stone."

Sentinel nodded. When he stood, the group of men fell back.

Sentinel moved some of the plants aside with his foot, looking for the grass beneath it. Finally, he had to get down on his knees and pull and shove at the vines. Inger and two of his men helped him. With the four of them working together, they were able to shift enough of the growth to clear the area. The stone sat, unscathed, on the grass.

No longer glowing, it still gave off a vibrant greenish hue.

Sentinel hesitated then glanced at Inger, who shrugged.

Sentinel held it, waiting to see if anything would happen. When nothing did, he returned to Maya. She reached for it and he placed it gingerly in her palm.

She didn't look away from it until Sentinel kneeled beside her.

"I know now. I finally understand."

"What do you understand?" he asked.

"What I must do."

Sentinel took the hand without the stone. "In your trance, you mentioned your mother. And Tessa."

She seemed to think for a moment. "My mother is beyond us, and Tessa is safe. Thank the gods."

She closed her eyes and lay back for a moment. When she opened them again, it was to squeeze Sentinel's hand.

"We need to hurry. We must be there when they arrive."

Sentinel shook his head at her. "I don't understand. When who arrives?"

"The Three. We must be there if we are to save everything."

58

TECK WATCHED THE CAMP FROM the tree line. The trio was sound asleep, or at least it appeared so. He'd been watching them for hours and would soon move in to retake his belongings. He studied the men and saw no watch to ensure their safety. He had one thought.

Arrogant.

After a few more moments of careful monitoring, Teck made his way into the camp. The night wasn't truly silent—none were—but with animal calls, flapping of night birds' wings, whistling of the wind through the trees, and crackling of the fire, the sound of a big man light on his feet would just be another sound.

Teck took his time. He kept his eyes trained on the men by the fire.

He'd run to get here, to catch them. They were moving fast, seeming to know exactly where they were going. His heartbeat had calmed, his breath regulated. Now, his body functioned like a machine. Fluid. Calm. His lids were heavy, almost languid, but his mind was alert.

When he got within reach of the first man, he stopped. He'd like to have a weapon. Since they took all his, he'd just have to borrow one of theirs.

Teck squatted beside the man, listening to his soft snoring. Looking down the length of his body, he identified a knife near his hand, partially hidden under a light blanket. As he felt the hilt slide into his palm, the man began to stir. Perhaps something of the figure lurking over him finally got through to his subconscious.

Teck covered the man's mouth with his other hand, pressing down with all his weight. The man's eyes flew open, wide and alarmed, seconds before Teck slammed the blade into his chest cavity.

The man died instantly. Almost no blood came from the crater in his chest. Teck looked at the man for another moment then took his hand from the quickly cooling body, turning to the other men.

Maxyt was the farthest from Teck, and it felt fitting that he would be the last to die.

Teck made short work of the second man. In the time he'd spent with them, neither of them had stood out in his mind. He didn't even know their names, and now he never would.

When he made his way to where Maxyt slept, he kicked him in the thigh. The man jumped up, a knife in his fist. Teck had to admit, his reflexes were sharp.

Maxyt stared at him as if not believing he could possibly be there. Then, keeping Teck in his sights, he looked at his men.

"Guess we picked the wrong traveler to rob, huh?"

Teck didn't care to get into it with the man.

"Why'd you wake me?"

Teck's brow furrowed. Why had he awakened him? He could have killed him as he slept, like the other two. He'd always prided himself on keeping a cool head, but this one felt personal. Maybe because it was. Always in the past, Teck had done work for someone else. But this was all about him. His belongings, his time, his payback.

He'd decided even before he found them that he would engage the leader. Not to give the other man the option of living—Teck was confident that wouldn't happen—but to allow Teck to ease some of his anger. He'd been stupid, and he was angry at them and at himself.

Taking a step back, Teck gestured with the knife. A spark came to Maxyt's eyes, and he grinned. Maxyt tossed his knife from one hand to the other. Teck bent his knees, loosened his grip on the knife, and waited.

It didn't take long for Maxyt to tire of his antics and rush into the fight. Teck sidestepped, evading the man's wild thrust, then ran his blade down his back.

Maxyt bellowed and grabbed at his back. He looked at his hand in disbelief. His jaw set, he wiped his hand down his pants leg and circled Teck.

Teck pivoted. He watched his body, legs, and arms for indicators of his next action.

Maxyt raised the knife over his head, gave a guttural yell, and plunged forward. Teck waited a second and then, with a twist, he sidestepped the man's rush. Bringing his hand up from hip height, he rammed the knife in the man's gut to the hilt. Maxyt's forward motion came to an abrupt halt.

He bent over Teck's arm, his breath coming in pants. His knife fell to the ground. He grasped Teck's arm and looked up at him, eyes already fading.

Putting his hand on Maxyt's shoulder, Teck pushed him back and off the blade. The man crumbled, blood seeping through his shirt to pool around him and soak into the dirt. He had his hands laced and pressed to his guts. His eyes closed tightly. Leaning down, Teck wiped the blade and his hand on the end of the man's shirt. Standing, he pushed his blade into his waistband.

He didn't spare Maxyt another glance. One by one, he went through the men's belongings. When he found something of his, he put it in one pile, and when he found something that he could use, he put it in another.

When he found his sword tossed in a bag with other items, he stood and looked toward the crumpled form. He thought about stabbing him again.

He untied a bandana and dumped the contents. A blue stone winked at him. He looked at it and then lifted his head to stare off to the tree line. He'd forgotten he had that.

Reaching for the stone, he ran a finger over its surface. Scanning the clearing, he listened intently. When nothing occurred, he picked up the stone, stood, and dropped it in his pocket.

Teck walked back to the piles and began repacking his

things, strapping his sword on, placing his belongings in his pack, and putting it on. He took weapons, food, and any valuables he found off the men. Most of it he left with the bodies. There was no reason to become weighed down with a bunch of unnecessary items.

Picking up a small sack, he took one last look around the area and walked away.

59

TESSA STEPPED FROM THE GANGPLANK to the land of her mother's birth. She thought she would have a more profound feeling, but she didn't. She was just glad to be off the boat.

Still confused, her mind still consumed by the happening with the sea creatures, she tried to tap into her senses, tried to know what to do.

She'd thought they would sail straight to Berth, but she had learned the ship wasn't making that trip. She and Jax were disembarking as close as they could. They would have to travel across the country, but she was still confident she would find her mother and Sentinel.

She looked over the docks. For a moment she studied the strange people. She'd never seen such clothes. Even their mannerisms were different from the people she knew. Streets stretched out of sight into the town. If they were to get to Berth, they would need to get directions and supplies.

Jax touched her arm. "I bet there's a general store farther in town. We can get some goods and information."

Tessa looked up as Striker passed overhead. She nodded and moved through people on the dock. Tessa stepped up on the plank walkway to the store and pushed open the door to enter. It was a bit more all-purpose than she was used to. One side had goods like flour, eggs, and potatoes, while the other liquor. Some tables and chairs were laid out through the middle of the room. Women wandered the store side with baskets on their arms, and men sat on the other, drinking.

She shrugged. Maybe it kept the men occupied while the women spent money.

She and Jax had very few funds left with the purchase of their tickets on the ship, but she thought they would be able to afford some basics.

Taking a basket by the door, she began to wander through the bins and shelves. Jax trailed her, pointing out something he wanted when he saw it.

* * * * *

TECK LOOKED UP WHEN THE door opened, and two people came in. He was already dismissing them when the girl caught his attention.

Something about the girl struck a chord, as if he'd met her before. He'd been gone from this land for the better part of his life, though. And she was young, barely more than a child. He couldn't have met her before. She and the boy with her were packed down with their belongings. The only weapons they carried were long knives in their belts, and the girl had a case that he thought might be a bow.

He realized he'd been too obvious in his curiosity when the boy saw him. Aggression.

Teck dropped his head back to his beer and hid a smile. *Young love.*

Could he even remember what it was like to feel that deeply? To burn with that overpowering need to have, to protect.

His smile faded when he realized that, yes, he could remember it. He remembered, and he wished to feel it again.

Teck had just finished his beer and signaled for another when the girl stepped up to the counter. She laid her basket on it and scanned the room, her eyes resting for a moment on Teck.

Again, he had that sense of recognition.

Damn.

After setting Teck's beer in front of him, the proprietor stepped behind the counter and began to empty the items out of the girl's basket. Teck watched her over the rim of his mug, feigning disinterest.

"This everything?"

"Um." She looked at the boy behind her. He nodded and gestured to the shop owner.

"We're traveling to Berth. We were wondering if you might be able to give us directions."

At the word *Berth*, Teck's spine straightened and his ears practically perked up. Now what were the odds that they would be going where he was going?

"Yes, sir." Teck had missed the question, but her answer fixed that. "No. We don't have enough money to purchase horses. We'll walk."

The owner said something else Teck couldn't catch—it would be nice if he'd quit mumbling—and then the girl was nodding and looking at the boy again.

"All right. Thank you."

She took the bag with their purchases and followed the boy to the door. At the last minute, her eyes flickered, and Teck realized she was staring right at him.

The boy took her arm and she turned. Then they were out the door and gone.

60

THE CREATURE WHO ONCE WAS Sylvan Bathsar wandered the dank, dark cave. She still had memories of her other life—she knew of the other woman. The Other.

But that life was unimportant. In this life, she was important. The children. The death of the land. These were all means to an end. Nav-lys was the vessel who would bring triumph to Cassandra.

She couldn't kill the Other, for to do so would be to kill her, but she could keep her so deeply buried that she might as well be dead. She would never see the light of day again. Never control this body. Never feel the touch of another.

She paced and waited. Her lord was a hungry lord, and the cycle turned. The time would soon be upon them for Nav-lys to serve.

61

TESSA AND JAX HAD WALKED for miles before the boy leaned in to whisper, "We're being followed."

"Followed?" she said and stopped.

He grabbed her arm, pulled her forward, and hissed, "Keep walking."

She moved with him, glancing over her shoulder. When they dropped down an incline, Jax pulled her behind a stand of trees. He put a finger to his lips and motioned for her to crouch. He joined her, and they peered out at the trail to wait.

They didn't have to wait long before the sound of footfalls came to them. Tessa leaned forward, her hand on Jax's shoulder. When the man came down the trail, she scowled. It was the stranger from the store. He'd just passed them when she jumped out from the bushes.

"Hey! What do you think you're doing?"

The man turned to look at her as Jax stepped from the thicket.

"You two following me?" Teck gestured at Tessa.

"Us following you?" She pointed at her chest and then thrust a finger at Teck. "You're following us."

"Look, little girl, I'm just walking here. You two are the ones harassing me."

"You're not fooling anyone." She put her hands on her hips. "We know you were following us, and I want to know why."

Mirroring her, he put his hands on his hips. "I'm on my way to Berth. I don't know what you're doing."

Tessa opened her mouth to say something else when Jax grabbed her arm and pulled her away. She watched the man while listening to Jax and shaking her head. As Jax continued to talk, she began to nod and look down. With a final nod, she again turned to Teck.

"We're on our way to Berth, too," she said and stepped to him.

"That's nice."

"Well. We were wondering . . ." She glanced at Jax. "Maybe it would be a good idea if we could all travel together."

Teck's eyebrows shot up.

"It's just, safety in numbers, you know?"

Teck looked at her for so long, she fidgeted, moving her feet back and forth. "I'm thinking, there's nothing in this for me."

Tessa took a step back, squinting. When she put her hand on the hilt of her knife, Teck put his hands up.

"Wait," he said. "That's not what I'm saying."

"Well then, mister. What exactly are you saying?"

Teck couldn't figure it out, but for some reason he liked this girl. She was ornery and feisty. He'd hate to see her come to a bad end—the two of them alone on the trail.

"Just wondering if there would be any pay in it. Wages for protection and showing you the way."

At that, Jax stepped forward. "We know where we're going."

Teck nodded. "Sure, I bet you do."

Tessa looked from one man to the other, not sure what the right decision was but knowing it felt better to be in a bigger group.

"We don't have any money. We spent the last of it on supplies." When no one added anything, she said, "But we're meeting up with my family. I'm sure I can get you some payment from them. They'd be grateful . . . if you help us get safely to Berth."

Teck nodded and offered a hand. Tessa stared at it, unwilling to take it, even if it was to seal their deal. With a shrug, Teck dropped his hand and turned to head down the trail.

Tessa and Jax shared a look and then hurried to keep up with the large man's stride.

* * * * *

TECK LEANED BACK, EXTENDING HIS feet to the warmth of the fire, his hand on a full belly. They'd located an out-of-the-way spot to spend the night, and he had first watch. His traveling companions stared into the fire, everyone deep in their own thoughts.

Tired of the quiet, Teck sat up straight and threw a log on an already blazing fire. "So, where do you come from?"

The girl continued to make him think he'd met her before, and the fact that he couldn't place her was like a thorn in his thumb.

"Not here," the boy answered.

Teck sent him a look. He really didn't care for the kid.

"What's taking you to Berth?"

Before Jax could answer, Tessa jumped in. "Like I said, I'm meeting my family."

Teck nodded slowly, staring into the fire. "Yep. You said. Just can't figure out what two children are doing traveling by themselves."

Jax practically jumped up at his words. Once again, Tessa stepped in to answer for them. "We're not children."

The corners of Teck's lips curved at her tone. It might just be interesting traveling with these two. "How'd you come to be together? You brother and sister?"

Jax did make it to his feet. Tessa stood and blocked him from Teck. He heard her whispering to him. When the boy shook his head and went to step around her, she placed a hand on his arm and threw a look over her shoulder.

Teck was fascinated. And amused. The boy was so easy to goad. When Jax looked at him, Teck caught his eye and smiled.

Jax erupted. He pushed Tessa to the side, causing her to trip and almost fall.

With a raise of his eyebrows, Teck watched the boy advance on him. Under his amusement was curiosity. What did this kid really think he could do?

Before Jax reached him, Tessa intercepted him. She stepped between them, grabbed Jax's arm, and pulled him to the side and around to face her.

"Jax. Look at me. Quit this right now."

The boy's chest heaved with his breaths. He gave a sideways glance at Teck then, dropping his head, walked away. Tessa let him go. She watched as he moved out of the firelight and stepped among the trees.

Tessa sighed then returned to her spot at the fire.

"Boy's got a real chip— "

"I don't want to hear your opinion of my friend."

Tessa stared at Teck for a full minute. Then, as if tired of looking at him, she turned to her bedroll. Climbing in, she pulled the blanket up over her ears.

62

THE THUNDER OF HORSE HOOVES echoed through the canyon, and a cloud of dust plumed.

Maya kept a hand buried in her mount's mane and legs tight on its body. They needed to get to Berth. She saw the image in her mind. The throne room in the temple. Back to where they started.

Sentinel rode beside her, and behind them, Patrick's men tried to keep up.

After she'd regained her composure from the interaction with the stone, she'd been insistent they hurry. They were losing time. She could hear it ticking down in her head.

When her horse stumbled, she slowly reined it to the side of the road, the others following. The horses had been moving for most of the day. They were lathered and wheezing. If they didn't stop or switch animals, they were going to have dead animals. Her horse dropped its head, its large body expanding with deep breaths.

"There's a small settlement a couple of miles ahead of us."

Inger walked his horse up to her. "We might be able to change out the horses for fresh."

"Let's do that. We can walk them the next few miles."

Maya swung a leg off her mount and dropped to the dust. She didn't wait for the others, but with her horse's reins in hand, she began to walk, her mind in turmoil.

When Sentinel walked up beside her, she glanced at him and then back down the road.

"We will get there in time."

"We must." She picked up her pace.

WHEN THEY ENTERED THE HAMLET, Maya wasn't sure what stock would be available for them to exchange or purchase. It was more a carriage stop with a single home and barn.

They walked into the yard, and two large dogs ran out barking to greet them. They circled them curiously. On their heels, a woman stepped out on the porch. She was wiping her hands on an apron.

"Help you folks?"

Inger stepped up. "Yes, ma'am. Might you have mounts we could exchange ours for? We are in a hurry and ours are quite spent."

She looked the horses over. "I see that. Not a good way to treat your animals."

"Yes," he agreed. "As I stated, we are in a hurry."

The woman nodded, dropped her apron hem, and came down the stairs. She gestured for them to follow her and moved around to the back of the building. Next to the barn was a corral full of horses. Maya figured people must exchange the carriage horses at this weigh station.

The woman turned and gestured. "Take what you need, keep track, and let me know what you take and what you leave."

"Thank you, ma'am." Inger lowered his head and then turned to his men. "Get in there. Get what we need. We must be off."

His men filtered in among the stock, looking for the strongest. They stripped tack from their mounts and led them to the corral then transferred everything to the new horses. In no time they were leading the fresh horses back around to the front of the building. Inger climbed the stairs and knocked at the door. When the woman opened it, she glanced at the group, took a sheet of parchment from Inger, and closed the door.

"Well," Maya said to Sentinel, "that was odd."

"Yes," he agreed. "Not the most pleasant of women."

After Inger mounted his horse, they were again on their way.

63

SYLVAN FLOATED IN A SEA of warmth and forgetfulness. An age had passed since she had tried to surface. Her existence wasn't so much an attempt to forget, as not knowing there was anything to remember.

When the illumination of thought pierced the blackness of her world, she blinked against the brightness and closed her eyes tightly, but the intruder would not let her be. She opened her eyes, squinted, and tried to determine what was happening and where she was.

The darkness of oblivion lured her in with its soft words and promises. She almost succumbed to it. If not for the image of a small red-haired girl running and laughing in the sunlight, chased by a gray pup, she would have allowed herself to sleep again.

She pushed up, determined to regain something of herself. Almost awake, almost free, the blackness pursued her. Icy claws pulled her below the surface of its dreams.

She flailed, kicking for the surface. Breaking above the

façade, she gasped, swallowing oily blackness, but she felt something solid beneath her. Violent coughs brought up the lies.

On her hands and knees, she gulped in reality. A sharp pain speared her temple, and she grasped her head, crying out. The faint sound echoed in the chamber.

She sat back on her heels and scanned the area. The black liquid splashed around as though still seeking her. Her nostrils flared in a breath, but no scent came to tell her where she might be.

"Hello," she called, but this too echoed back. Mocking her. She closed her eyes. Deep within her mind she pushed. The image of the child came back to her, this time as a young woman.

Sylvan's eyes flew open. "Maya."

How could she have forgotten about her child? How long had she slept?

She needed to get out of here.

* * * * *

NAV-LYS FELT THE OTHER, AND her eyes narrowed. The stirrings itched under her skin. She twitched and then got up to pace.

"My love." The moist, wispy tones of Orson came to her from the back of the room. She'd forgotten he was even there. She whipped about, her gown billowing behind her. "You appear restless. Is there anything I can do for you?"

She stared at him for so long, he dropped his gaze to her

feet. His submissiveness made her feel more in control, made it easier to ignore the feeling of bugs crawling on her skin.

"When will the offerings be here?"

"Soon, Nav-lys. We will begin the ceremony soon."

* * * * *

SYLVAN HEARD THE VOICES. THEY were faint, just a hum. She couldn't understand what was said but recognized the tones as coming from a man and a woman.

She cocked her head, listening intently. If she could figure out from which direction they came, perhaps they would help her escape.

"Hello," she called again, only to once more have her voice reverberate back to her. "Hello!"

The voices were quiet. Again, she was alone.

64

MAYA'S GROUP THUNDERED INTO THE port city of Fairspeak, drawing stares.

They drove their mounts right through town, straight to the barn at the end of the main road. Above the large double doors that stood open was a sign that read *Livery*.

With a swing of one leg, Maya dropped from her horse.

"Get them sold, Inger. I'll book passage."

She'd already turned to walk away when he nodded. Sentinel handed his reins to one of the men, gave the horse a pat on its broad neck, and hurried after her.

In town, people stared. Sentinel was used to their curiosity. Everywhere they went he was exotic and unusual. "Why are you in such a hurry?"

"Our time is running short. I feel it in my bones, like they're burning."

"What are we to do?"

Maya shook her head. "All I know is we must be at the temple, at the correct time. I don't know exactly how long we have, just that the clock is ticking." She scanned the street as she continued. "If we're not there at the designated time, all will be lost."

Continuing at her side, he nodded as if understanding what she didn't. But he was with her, always with her. His loyalty was never in question.

Midway down the street, the offices of the shipping line came into view. She pointed with her chin and they entered the building.

A clamor of chaos greeted them. Men strode through the front room, yelling at one another. Some gestured at papers, arguing a point Maya didn't understand. She and Sentinel stood just within the doorway, and not a minute later, a man walked to them.

"Well," he said, "what do you two want?"

Maya felt her hair bristle at his tone, but she wasn't here to fight. "We're in need of passage to the city of Berth."

"The two of you?"

"There will be seven of us."

"Seven?" The man stepped back and looked them up and down.

"Yes." She mimicked his movement with her own gaze. "Seven."

"You got enough money to pay for that? We don't take trade here at Munson Shipping."

Maya nodded, and perhaps something in her eyes made him hesitate. He went behind the desk and readied the paperwork they needed. He was just finishing when the door opened and Inger stepped in. Seeing Maya and Sentinel across the room, he hurried to them. He handed her a packet.

He smiled. "We got a good price for the horses and tack."

She acknowledged his words with a nod, and when the man approached with the passages to board the ship, she was ready with payment.

THEY LEFT THE SHIP LINE offices not only with their tickets but with a fair amount of money still in the packet. Maya was in a positive mood. She was sure they would get to Berth in plenty of time to stop whatever calamity was coming. She was saying as much to the men, her head turned to continue the conversation, when she ran into something. A man grabbed her arm, steadying her.

"Whoa there, little lady." His stale breath blew into her face.

On reflex she pulled her arm out of his grasp, stepping back against Sentinel.

"Excuse us. I didn't mean to run into you."

"Well, now," he said, "you runnin' into me is one of the more pleasant happenings I've had." He locked onto the hilts of her swords above her shoulders. "Well, well. What have we here?" His eyes gleamed and he reached toward her weapons.

Fast as a snake, she slapped his hand down, earning her a dark look.

"That's not real neighborly, missy."

Stepping around him, she said, "Excuse us." Sentinel and Inger followed her, and she didn't look back though she could feel the man's eyes on them.

"I think we should board the ship just as soon as we're able," Inger said. "This town might be getting unfriendly really quick."

Maya nodded in agreement. "Let's get our things and the other men and head to the wharf."

MAYA STOOD AT THE RAIL on board and watched the sunset. They hadn't encountered any problems, hadn't even seen the man again.

The men were bedded down in a communal room. Because she was the only woman on board, she had a private room for their trip. She admitted that she was glad for some privacy. She hadn't been truly alone for weeks.

The captain told them that they'd be casting off before the sun rose in the morning. Until then, they would have patrols on board to ensure the cargo stayed safe.

With a deep breath of the cool, salty air, Maya told herself to relax. They would be on their way; she couldn't get to Berth any quicker than by sea. The urge to hurry prodded at her. She would just have to get used to it for the time being.

With one last look at the seaside town, she went to her cabin. She would try to get some rest.

65

AT THE CALL FROM THE crow's nest, Maya looked up. She couldn't understand what the boy said, but he was gesturing off the port side. When she looked where he pointed, she saw another ship on the horizon. All around her, a flurry of activity exploded.

Maya watched the crew for a moment then walked to the captain on the top deck.

"What is it?" The captain turned when she spoke to him. When he didn't answer her, she asked again, "What is it? What has the crew so excited?"

The captain studied the ship that had moved closer. When he looked back at her, he sighed.

"Pirates."

A shiver ran down her spine. She squinted at the approaching ship. "Can we outrun them?"

The captain gave another sigh and shook his head. "No. Their ship is leaner and swifter than this one. Theirs is made to be fast."

"What are you carrying? Is it the cargo they're after?"

"Probably. We don't carry anything of great value. Just happen to be here and vulnerable."

"I didn't know there were pirates in these waters."

"Yes, though not usually this far north. They usually work the southern trade routes. Those ships carry silks and gold. Better pickings."

"What are we to do?"

"It's unusual for them to harm anyone on board." He eyed her and added, "Being the only female here, I suggest you lock yourself in your cabin. Stay out of sight."

"I appreciate your concern, Captain, but I will not lock myself in my cabin."

The man looked her over again and shrugged. "Suit yourself."

OVER THE NEXT FEW HOURS, the pirates closed the distance between the two ships. Maya and Sentinel stood at the rail and watched its steady approach.

"I feel so useless. It's horrible having to stand here and watch them get nearer."

"Come with me, Maya," Sentinel said. "We should not be standing here."

"Yes, let's fall back. Assess the situation as it occurs."

When Maya and Sentinel moved to the front of the ship, Inger and his men went with them. It was even harder to wait here than at the rear of the ship.

When the shouts of men and the sound of grappling hooks

came to them, Maya pulled a blade. Sentinel followed suit. They would not meet this threat unarmed. Her back to the cabin's outer wall, Maya slid forward to see what was happening. She could hear men's voices but didn't know what they should or shouldn't do.

When she peeked around the corner, bodies littered the deck. They were still, and blood pooled around them. So much for the captain's assurances that the pirates would not hurt anyone.

Pulling her eyes from the bodies, she saw a group of men huddled in a corner, the captain among them. In front were five or six well-armed men with their backs to her. They had long swords, and a couple carried knives. They spoke to the group, but she couldn't hear what was being said.

With a flourish of a hand that held a long knife, one man spun to scan the ship. Maya dropped back, her heart in her throat.

"It's the man from the street. The one outside the shipping house," she whispered to Sentinel.

His eyes showed he understood who she meant. Inger stepped forward as if to look, but Maya grabbed his arm.

"This feels very bad."

Sentinel watched her. "He is here for you, Maya."

On the heels of his words, a man's voice came from the other side of the wall.

"You can come out. I know you're on board. You won't be harmed."

Maya and the men waited silently, not willing to reveal

themselves. She'd never been in a situation where flight wasn't one of her options. She really didn't want to end this day with people dead, but she would do that if it became necessary. There were larger things happening than this one man's desires.

She wondered if she could make him see reason. He would have to be intelligent to have led his bunch to overtake this ship. She had some coins left. Maybe he could be bought.

Letting actions guide her, she slid her weapon back into its housing. When she stepped toward the rear of the ship, Sentinel just missed grabbing her arm.

"Maya," he hissed.

She glanced at him. "I must try."

When she stepped around the corner of the cabin, the man from the street was facing her across the deck. His face brightened into a gaping smile and he spread his hands wide.

"Ah. There she is."

Maya stopped. When he stepped toward her, she stepped back. His smile widened. "Little girls shouldn't walk around with big ole weapons. Makes a man wanna take 'em."

"They're not for sale," she said, her voice steady.

"Well, now. I don't remember offering to buy them."

She looked behind him, gesturing to the group. "You and your men need to leave. There's nothing for you here."

He gave a little chuckle and rubbed his nose with a finger, looking at her from the corner of his eye. "We're not going anywhere, and there's plenty here for all."

"I thought we could talk about this."

"You can talk, girlie. I like the sound of your voice." He

again took a step toward her. She took a step back.

"I'm trying to save lives here. If you and your men would just leave, we'll all make it through this day. I don't want to kill anyone."

The man threw back his head and laughed, the men behind him chuckling. "Oh, you are gonna be fun to break."

Maya decided she was finished. Maybe killing today wouldn't be such a bad idea after all. Her arms crossing over her head, she grasped the hilts of her swords and pulled them from their scabbards. The men's laughter died in the hiss of steel.

Maya saw a shadow of doubt on the man's face. She stepped forward, spinning one sword in a circle. "Let's do this then," she said. "I always did want my own ship."

The man scowled, and with a yell, he rushed her, knife thrust forward. When he got close, she sidestepped and cut his upper thigh. He gave a howl of pain and grasped the bleeding wound.

With him and his men separated, she moved to the side to keep them both within her sights. Spinning first one sword and then the other, she bent her knees and waited for another rush. But the man was having none of that. He limped back a couple steps and yelled to his men.

"What are you waiting for? Get her!"

When one moved, Maya shifted her stance to face them. They came en masse. The first went down with a cut across his neck and chest. Blood sprayed from it in an arch. The slick fluid tripped the next two men who went down on their own.

Sidestepping again, she kept the entire deck in her sights. With a thrust and a spin of her wrist, the next two men were out of commission.

The remaining men slowed, assessing her. She crouched slightly, her weapons ready, her eyes steady.

"Well? What are you waiting for?" The man from the street limped forward, blood flowing between his fingers on his thigh.

She gave him another glance, surprised he was still on his feet. By her figuring, he'd soon be dead. The flow of blood from his wound was fatal.

Sentinel, Inger, and his men stepped behind him. When the pirates saw them, they mumbled to each other and backed up. Not realizing he had men behind him, the leader screamed at his men. For a moment, they appeared confused. When their leader fell to his knees and then on his face, the pirates turned and fled over the rail, shinnying back to their ship.

They cut the ropes holding the grappling hooks, and within moments the two ships separated.

Maya walked to the pirate leader and turned him to his back with her foot. He stared, and she thought he was dead, but then he blinked. She squatted and leaned into his line of sight.

"Not all things are yours for the taking."

She watched until his eyes dulled, and she was sure the life had left him. Killing a man was never rewarding, but occasionally, it was necessary.

66

PATRICK HAD TAKEN TO DAILY walks. He'd roam farther each day, observing the rot in the land. Sometimes he'd think it really wasn't too bad, but then he'd look again. It was spreading.

Yesterday, he'd come across a small clearing littered with bird carcasses. What if Maya didn't come? Soon there would be nothing they could do to save themselves. He thought, by being out, that he would hasten her return. He could meet them and hurry them along.

He fantasized about seeing her and Sentinel. After all this time, would they look the same? He'd changed over the near two decades they'd been apart. Would they know him?

As he took in the remaining beauty, he often thought of Caleb. Every day he prayed, but still no Caleb.

Making his way through a particularly beautiful valley, the call of crows had him studying the sky. They were circling something, then landing and taking off again. Their calls echoed.

As he neared, he saw a black, shiny mound of birds. The motion of their mass made it appear as if they were boiling up from the ground.

He took another step, and the birds shied at his closeness. As one, they rose into the air, leaving the carcass bare. Even from afar, Patrick could tell it was a large deer. Parts of it had been picked clean by the flock, but enough remained for him to see the rot.

He stepped up to the body. A lot of the black rot covered the animal. Thick on its legs and face, tracing back and up like stripes, it was obvious the rot had started when the animal was still alive. Possibly while grazing. It would not be a pleasant way to die.

This was the first evidence the priest had of a larger life form succumbing to the rot. A finger of fear snaked down his spine and had him stepping back from the carcass.

After a few more steps back, the crows again swarmed on the deer. As he watched them moving around the bloated body, tearing bits to eat, he wondered how much of it they were spreading in their travels.

67

ECK, TESSA, AND JAX TRAVELED in almost complete silence for three days, their relationship contentious. They watched out for each other, but other than that, they could have been alone. Now at the end of the third day, they sat, eating and staring at the fire.

Teck decided as the oldest, he should be the wisest and end the silence. "We need to decide what will happen when we reach Berth tomorrow."

"Easy," Jax said. "We'll go our way and you'll go yours." The men looked at each other for a moment and Jax added, "All you were was a means to an end. We needed to get to Berth and you knew the way."

Teck gazed at Tessa. "Is that how you see it?"

Tessa was exhausted by the men's need to have this separation among themselves. She didn't know how to fix it. Jax was her friend. They'd been through so much together. Why couldn't he get along with Teck? They could use his expertise and wisdom when they reached the city.

She opened her mouth to comment when a man stepped from the woods. He had a bow and arrow, the bow drawn, the arrow aimed at them.

She and Jax jumped up, rounding the fire to put it between the man and them. Teck stood slowly, staying where he was.

"Who are you?" the stranger asked.

Teck put his hands up, palms forward. "We're no threat. Just staying here for the night."

"You're on my land."

"Our mistake, mister. We can move on. No problem." Teck stepped closer to the man, so his eye and arrow were pointed at him.

The man had blond hair, almost white. His bright gray gaze shifted to her when she stepped sideways, closer to her knives. Jax already had a blade palmed.

"Really, mister. You can put the bow down. We don't mean you any harm and didn't know we were on anyone's property."

"What are you doing here?" The man was twitchy, his gaze jumping between the three of them.

Teck stepped closer, drawing the man's eyes back to him. "We're just heading to Berth. Stopped here for the night."

"What's your business in Berth?"

Teck dropped his hands. "Well now, why is that any of your business?"

"These days, Berth isn't a safe place to be."

Teck looked at Tessa, a question in his gaze. She stepped around the fire and took a step toward the man. "We have business in the city. We would appreciate being able to stay here for the night, but if you'd rather, we can move on."

The man stared at her for a minute, then his gaze returned to Teck and Jax. When he dropped the arrow to aim at the ground, Tessa expelled a breath she didn't know she'd been holding.

His tone apologetic, the man said, "Can't be too careful these days. Strange happenings."

"We understand," Tessa said. "We have no desire to cause you any problems."

The man nodded and released the tension in his bow.

"Then you are welcome to stay here tonight. If I were you, I'd leave someone on watch."

Tessa nodded in agreement. "Thank you. That's wise advice."

Seeming to think about it, the stranger added, "Perhaps, tomorrow you might stop at my cabin to break your fast before continuing to the city. I fear you're going to need all the strength you can get."

THE SUN WAS JUST PEEKING over the hills when the trio made their way down the lane to the small cabin. Birds flittered around small feeders. A horse and cow shared a paddock off the end of the lane, and the cabin, though small, had a welcoming air about it. Tessa liked the place. Flowers grew next to the stairs, and an aged rocking chair sat on the porch where a large black dog slept. When they neared, its head lifted, and it stood and gave a mighty bark.

They were almost at the cabin when the door opened and

the man stepped out. Letting the door shut behind him, he placed a hand on the dog's head and made his way down the stairs. The dog followed him, still growling under its breath.

Tessa liked the man. She didn't know why, but she liked him. He filled her with brightness, and she wanted to know him. She walked right up to him, unafraid of him or his dog. When he greeted her with a smile, she thought perhaps he wanted to get to know her, too. He turned from her to lean over the large dog, and she heard him whispering to the animal. When he stood the dog sat, now quiet, but watchful.

"Good morning," Tessa greeted him, her hand outstretched. "We never did introduce ourselves in the confusion of last night."

He grasped her hand. "I'm Tessa." She turned slightly to include her companions, seeing they both wore slight frowns. "This is Jax." She indicated the boy. "And this is Teck."

"My name is Wyliam. It's a pleasure to meet you all." He nodded at the men and kept Tessa's hand in his. "I'm sorry about last night. There have been more and more strange happenings in the land the last few years."

"We understand." She included the two men with a gesture. "We never meant to intrude."

"It's no problem." Indicating the dog, he added, "This is Sam. He's nice. Just big and noisy."

"He's good. I love animals." She released Wyliam's hand to squat next to the dog, her face near his. Teck took a step forward, but Jax put out a hand, halting him.

Tessa was still for a minute, then she reached out to scratch behind the big dog's ears. He leaned into her, rubbing his head on her arm, almost toppling her over. She giggled, stood, and patted him on the head.

"You certainly have a way with animals. I've never seen him take to someone so quickly." Wyliam said.

"Like I said, I love animals."

He nodded and, placing his hand around her waist, directed her to the house. "Come in now and let's have a meal."

Teck looked at Jax, and for once they seemed to agree. Each for their own reasons, neither liked this development.

* * * * *

INSIDE THE CABIN, WYLIAM HAD a table set. Though his plates and utensils were mismatched, the overall feeling was one of welcome. He led Tessa to a chair at the end of the table and pulled it back, assisting her to sit and scoot up to the serving area. Smiling at her, he turned to sit, only to see her companions had taken the chairs on either side of her.

For a moment he seemed lost, but then he straightened himself and loaded the table with food. He pulled a pot filled with hearty porridge from the fire. Bread came from the sideboard, still warm. He placed a pitcher of cool water on the table. Lastly, moving to Tessa's side of the table, he set down a small basket of fresh berries.

"Oh, berries!" she exclaimed. Wyliam straightened a little more. "Thank you, Wyliam. This is really too much." When she smiled at him, he reached toward her only to pull his hand back.

With a dip of his head, he moved to the remaining chair. At first, he'd been upset that he'd been thwarted from sitting beside her, but now he realized the men had done him a favor. From his chair, he had an unobstructed view of her.

In the morning light, her dark hair gleamed with health and vitality. Her skin, smooth with a slight tan, made his fingers itch with want. And when she laughed at something the young man said, Wyliam's gut clenched.

"Wyliam, aren't you going to eat anything?" He blinked and saw she was looking right at him. He'd been watching her eat. Watching her interact with her friends. Watching her in his home, looking like she was right where she belonged.

Now she sat, a steaming roll in one hand, and eyed him, her brows raised. He nodded and dipped his head to take a bite of his porridge. It tasted bland today; the only nourishment he wanted was the sound of her voice, the flash of her eyes.

The meal finished much too quickly for him, and Wyliam cleared the table while listening to the three discuss their plans. They would be leaving soon. He turned, took a deep breath, and walked to the trio.

"Tessa, could I speak with you for a moment?" When they all looked at him, he added, "Privately?"

"Of course, Wyliam. Let's step outside." And she headed toward the door.

When he followed her out, Sam jumped up and walked with her down the stairs. It looked like someone else was caught in her spell.

Wyliam followed her across the yard to the corral. The

horse and cow came to the fence, pressed their heads through, and nuzzled the girl. He stood behind her and watched in awe.

It was uncanny. The three of them acted as if they'd known her forever. Even now, Sam was leaning against her leg, tongue hanging out, waiting for her touch.

She gave the horse and cow each a kiss between their eyes, and with her hand on Sam's head, she turned to look at Wyliam.

When he didn't say anything, she prompted, "You wanted to speak with me?"

"Yes." He cleared his throat and then plunged in. "I'd like you to stay here with me." As the words came out, he realized how they sounded, and he backtracked. "You could have the cabin, of course. I would sleep in the barn."

"Wyliam," she began, "you don't even know me."

"I want to know you."

She dropped her head and shook it. "I have to go to Berth."

"Why? You don't realize how dangerous the city has become. It's not even safe this far from it. And the danger keeps growing."

"I have to find my mother. She'll be in Berth."

"Your mother? Why would she be going to Berth? Nothing good can come from her going there."

"That's just more of a reason for me to get there and find her. She may need my help."

"Find her? So, you don't even know where she is? Berth is a large city. You could search for weeks and not locate her."

The girl's cheeks reddened, and she turned to walk away from him. He followed her, afraid she was going to leave without him convincing her to stay. When she spun to face him, he stopped so suddenly he swayed for a moment. Her color rode high on her cheeks, and her eyes sparkled. For a second, she just gestured with her finger.

"I don't need you to tell me my mother is in danger," she blurted. "You have no idea what I've been through just to get to this point."

He put out his hands in an attempt to pacify her, almost touching her shoulders, but she jerked from him. As he started to speak, he heard a whistling sound and looked up to see a large bird heading for him like an arrow. He ducked, and the bird swooped by. It altered its flight to circle back around the girl. He was reaching up to pull her down, to cover her, when the raptor landed on the top rail.

He stared up, the girl afire with anger, the bird behind her. It spread its wings and opened its beak to release a scream. Wyliam cringed. The horse and cow startled. They turned and ran from the fence where the bird sat. Sam whined and rolled on the ground, rubbing his ears.

Behind him, he barely heard the door slam and the sound of stomping feet. The next thing he knew, Jax was putting his arm around the girl and pulling her away from him.

He turned with them, shuffling away from the bird.

When he got to the bottom of the stairs, Teck blocked his ascent. Jax and Tessa went into the house. He met the man's eyes, and the first island of calm showed in the confusion of the past couple of minutes.

He took deep breaths. When sufficient time had passed,

Wyliam risked a peek at the hawk, which had vanished. He surveyed the area but could not locate it.

Turning back to the man, he said, "What was that?"

Teck shrugged.

"Is she all right?"

Again, he shrugged.

"I need to see her." He put a hand on Teck's shoulder to move him aside.

"Yeah. That's not going to happen." He didn't budge under Wyliam's force.

"But— " He stepped to the side, his face up to the window of the cabin. "Tessa!" he yelled.

Teck stepped in his way, once again an immovable barrier. "Why don't we just give her a bit to calm down. I'm sure she'll talk to you before we leave."

Wyliam stared at the man, unable to process his words. "Why did she get so upset?"

Teck blinked slowly and once again shrugged.

"Don't you know anything?" He was near to yelling.

"I know we should wait."

"Wait," he said under his breath. Turning away, he went to find his dog.

68

TESSA SAT IN THE CABIN feeling ashamed. She'd lost control. She'd never done that before.

The anger, and mixed with it—driving it—was fear. What if she didn't find her mother? What if something had happened to her? She'd been through so much. What if it were all for nothing?

"I feel stupid."

"There's no reason for that." Jax sat next to her, his hand on her knee. "We all lose it at some point."

"I'm sure I've scared him away."

"That's okay. You've got me."

She glanced at the boy beside her, noting his hand on her leg. For the first time, she realized his feelings for her were different than what she felt for him. He was a good friend. A great friend. She'd come to trust him above anyone other than her mother and Sentinel.

"Um, Jax . . ." she began, but he interrupted her.

"I think we should leave here. We need to continue on with

our plan."

"Yes. I agree. It is time we were leaving."

"Great. I'll get our stuff."

Tessa walked to the window overlooking the yard. Teck sat on the bottom step leading to the porch. She looked around and finally saw Wyliam near the corral. He sat on the ground, his arm around Sam. He stared off toward the road and scratched at the dog's neck.

He suddenly looked her way. She almost stepped back from the window but didn't. She still wanted to know the man better. She liked him. She was sorry she'd gotten so angry.

When he walked toward Teck, his gaze on her, she stepped back and moved to the door.

"Where are you going?" Jax called, setting their things on the bed.

"Go ahead and get us packed up. I'll be right back."

She heard him say something behind her, but she was already opening the door and stepping out. Teck moved back as she came down to their level.

"Tessa." Wyliam reached for her hand, but Teck grabbed his hand and pushed it away.

"Teck," she said. "Could you give us some privacy?"

He looked at her and then, as if deciding, nodded. He turned and walked up the stairs and into the cabin, closing the door behind him.

"Tessa," Wyliam said again, but this time he didn't reach for her.

She was staring at her boots and looked up from under her

brows. He looked so worried, so earnest, when all the time, it was she who needed to make amends.

"Can we walk?" When she headed toward the timberline, he fell into step beside her. "I wanted to thank you for the offer to stay with you." When he started to say something, she said, "But like I said, I have to find my mother." After another step or two, she turned to face him. "I'm sorry I got so angry. I'm not sure where it came from. It was just there."

"You don't have to apologize to me. I didn't mean to make you angry."

She smiled and turned him to walk with her in the field. Wyliam laid a hand over hers where it curved around his arm.

"Look at the two of us," she said. "Neither of us doing much of anything, and both of us feeling responsible."

"Can I ask," he began, "what was the hawk? Is he yours?"

She chuckled. "Yes. That's Striker. I'll have to explain him to you someday."

"So." He turned her to face him, keeping his hand on hers. "You're going to Berth."

"Yes, I must."

He nodded and took one of her hands in both of his. "I understand. I'd like to go with you. Like to make sure you stay safe and find your mother."

"You can't just leave your place."

"Actually, I can. On the way to town, we'll pass my neighbor. I can stop and have him care for the animals. Except for Sam—I'll bring him with me."

"Really, Wyliam. You don't have— "

"I want to. Tessa, listen to me. I want to. I don't know how to explain this, but I think this is just what I've been waiting for."

She shifted her hand, grasping one of his. "What do you mean?"

He stared over her shoulder, his eyes not really focusing on anything. "I've been here for so long, alone. Once, I thought I would be part of something bigger than myself, but then my life just evened out. This is a good place. It's been good to me, but I remember wanting something different."

She shifted until she was in his line of sight. When he focused on her, she gave him a small smile. "What do you want?"

"I want to go with you. I want to help you find your mother. Then, when you have what you need, maybe we can see if we still want to get to know each other."

She laid her other hand on his cheek. "I think you should pack some things. And maybe a bone for Sam."

When her words penetrated, his smile shone like the midday sun.

"I'll hurry. I won't keep you waiting." He hurried back to the cabin. Seconds after he entered the dwelling, Jax came bounding out. She stood by the corral and waited for him.

"What do you mean by telling that farmer he can come with us?" He shook, and in his anger, his eyes welled with tears.

"Jax," she said, "he needs this. He wants to come with us."

"He wants you, is what you mean." The boy's voice rose and broke with his emotions. "You know that. You know what that means, but still you'll have him come with us."

She didn't know how to calm the boy; she realized she was tired. She turned from him to walk back to the cabin. When he didn't follow her, she faced him. He stood in the grass, his breath coming in big gulps.

"Let's just get to Berth, okay?"

Jax wiped his fist under his nose then nodded. "Okay." He walked with her to the cabin.

* * * * *

WHEN THE FOUR OF THEM headed down the road to Berth, one was ecstatic, two were confused, and one was amused.

Tessa was talking nonstop and rushing the others along. Wyliam had told them that Berth was within two days' walk. If they hurried, she might be with her mother again soon.

Tessa and Jax led the way, their conversations drifting back to the other men. Teck and Wyliam walked together, Sam trailing them.

"We're going to have to get her to slow down," Wyliam said. "Rushing is only going to cause trouble." Teck didn't add anything. "There are many things in this land that are dangerous."

"There are many things in every land that are dangerous."

Wyliam took his words in. With a nod of agreement, he put his mind to getting to Berth.

It wasn't two hours later when they ran into the priest.

69

PATRICK WANDERED FARTHER AND FARTHER each day. This last evening, he'd been so far that the idea of returning to the keep seemed like too much work.

When he grew too tired, he stopped by a stream. After drinking his fill, he lay down to sleep. His rest was troubled, filled with images of what had been and what could yet be.

WHEN HE STIRRED THE NEXT morning, it was to startle a doe from her morning drink. She bounded across the water, splashing droplets on his cloak.

Such a vision of nature was a welcome image to wake to, and with a lighter heart, Patrick readied himself for his day. In his mind was the thought that if he kept going, kept looking, he would come across Maya. If not her, perhaps another solution would present itself.

A COUPLE HOURS LATER, PATRICK saw five figures in the distance. It was plain, even from this distance, that one of the figures was a dog. A large dog.

As they drew together, it became evident by the walk and something in her bearing that one of the figures was a woman. Patrick's heart quickened for a moment before he realized this could not be Maya. Even with the passage of time, Maya was never this tall, and this woman's black hair shone in the sunlight. A far cry from Maya's rich red.

When they were too close for shouting but still too far for speaking, Patrick halted. He would wait here for them to come to him.

Closer they came and then the dog began to bark. He had a large bark, and Patrick hoped he was not about to succumb to a vicious animal.

He heard one of the men speak under his breath, and the dog quieted, though he still walked with his legs stiff and his tail curled up and over his back, his head held high. Patrick was certain he was not yet in the clear from this one.

"Good morning," the woman called, and Patrick realized she was more of a girl than a woman. When she approached him, one of the men—tall with hair as black as the girl's—held her back. She gave him a quizzical look and then scanned the others in her company.

The man caught Patrick's attention. He knew him. And he knew the man knew him. Teck. Patrick remembered Teck from their time in the tunnels of the resistance. Was there a reason the large man chose not to acknowledge him? Did it have something to do with Maya? It had been years since they'd seen each other, but Patrick was sure Teck recognized him, too. If he could get Teck alone, maybe he'd learn something of Maya.

Patrick put his immediate confusion aside and spoke to the girl.

"Good morning to you, miss," Patrick called, sure to make his voice as calm and welcoming as he could. "I am no harm to you all. I'm not even armed." He added, "I'm a simple priest out for a morning walk."

"Where do you hail from, priest?" This time the blond man, the one who'd spoken to the dog, spoke to him.

He shifted to better face him. "I live in a keep not far from here. I'm on the road waiting for friends."

The younger man stepped forward. "You shouldn't be out here alone. You're not safe."

"Thank you, lad." Patrick smiled and turned toward him. "I am as safe as the gods will keep me, whether I am with someone or alone."

"We're heading to Berth," the girl offered. Her companions turned to look at her, their faces a mixture of surprise and disapproval.

The priest took a step in her direction. As soon as he moved, all three of the men—and the dog—stepped toward him. She was obviously under their protection.

"My name is Patrick."

Tessa stepped up to him amid the complaints and moans of the men. "I'm Tessa. I'm pleased to meet you, Patrick." She put out a hand.

He took her forearm in his hand, allowing her to grasp his arm the same way in the universal greeting. "I'm very pleased to meet you, too, Tessa."

"You're welcome to walk with us a way." She pointed with her chin down the road. "Perhaps you'll find your friends."

Patrick assessed what he knew to be true. He was probably fooling himself to think he would meet up with Maya and her group by simply walking along the road. He didn't even know from which direction they would be coming, if they were coming.

Here, right in front of him, was Teck. The last time he'd seen the man, he'd been in the company of Maya. Surely, he knew something.

"Thank you, miss. I'd like to come along with you and your friends."

"Great." She turned a brilliant smile on the others. "The more of us there are, the better off we are."

The girl continued down the lane, waving him along. As the men passed him, he nodded at each until it was just Teck.

When the black-haired man passed, Patrick heard him say, "Priest," low in his throat.

Patrick lowered his head in acknowledgment and uttered, "Teck," before following the group.

70

MAYA AND HER COMRADES HUSTLED down the plank to the dock. The port area was almost deserted and had a haunting feeling. No one else disembarked. As soon as the last of Inger's men stepped from the plank, it was pulled back.

Maya looked across the narrow expanse of water at the captain. They weren't separating under the best of circumstances. He made it clear that he thought it her fault the pirates had targeted them. Giving her no credit for saving their lives, he insisted that the dead sailors' positions be filled with some of their men. Maya disagreed.

For the rest of the journey to Berth, Maya and her men had done what they could to assist with the sailing of the ship, but with the understanding that they were volunteering and none would be staying when they reached their destination.

Now, as the remaining sailors cast off, the captain stared at her with hate in his eyes. She didn't know why he was so upset and thought that perhaps it was because she was a woman and she dared to defy him. And having defied him, she was strong enough to back it up.

With a small inner shrug, Maya turned from the departing ship to again assess the town.

Berth was a far different place now than when she had left.

Then, a thriving vibrant city, it now resembled a large, dead animal stripped to its bones. A person scuttled across her line of vision occasionally, but for the most part, the streets were deserted. To add to the overall feeling of inhospitality, a low wind blew debris through the streets. The mournful howl of it drew a shiver down her spine.

With a deep breath, she straightened and stepped up to the street. They would do what they came here to do, and to begin that, she would need to locate the priest.

71

WHEN MAYA STEPPED INTO THE city, Nav-lys felt the reverberation run up her frame. She stopped pacing and sniffed the air.

The child had returned. The time was nigh. They needed to hurry.

The Other's stirrings continued to gain in strength. The only way she knew she could triumph was to have her god—Cassandra—burn the Other out of existence. To do that, she would need to bring her god to her. The only way she knew how to do that was to have a sufficient offering to draw the deity to the ceremony.

Nav-lys had it all planned, all ready.

The offerings were here, the land ripe for cultivating. She had been promised an existence past this world. Now, with the child back, the Other would strengthen. The nearness of the child calling to the mother. They would have to act before the Other regained her full strength—before the Other could break the bonds she had placed upon her so many years ago.

Nav-lys paced, the train of her gown dragging behind her. She was unable to sit still, unable to find rest. The stirrings from within scratched at her. She was bloodied from the inside out. This body ravaged by the brutalities and degradations heaped upon it.

From the edges of the candlelight, her servant, Orson, watched. His eyes reflected in the light. She knew he desired her, was compelled to be with her. Coveted her power. He saw her as a means to an end, and if he could have her, too, that would please him.

She was the stronger of the two. She had her god's attention, not him. She would be the one to last this day. This day and the next.

She paused, an idea coming to her. A sacrifice. Something small, just enough to whet the appetite. Just brutal enough to drive the Other back into hiding. Cause her to pull the covers back over her head.

A smile split her face, a glint in her black eyes. She did so like it when the Other cried out in horror and shame. It had been so long. Maybe she had been wrong to hide her so deep.

If she played this game right, she could be one with Cassandra and have the Other gone. She could have it all.

72

ECK SAT BY THE FIRE and watched the priest. He needed to find a private moment with him. If anyone knew where he could locate Eldred Bathsar, it would be Father Patrick. But he had no intention of having the rest of their little party privy to his personal business.

He was certain the priest knew he was staring, but the fool ignored him. He'd spent the evening with Tessa. And for her part, the girl seemed to be enjoying the priest's company.

Now, something in their conversation caught his attention.

"Oh, how horrible," Tessa said, laying a hand on the priest's forearm. "Well, you've adjusted very well. I didn't even realize at first that you were missing it."

Saying something under his breath, the priest patted the hand on his arm.

Unlike most, Tessa didn't seem at all put off by the man's missing appendage. He'd seen her reach for him multiple times throughout the day and evening, often taking the arm without a hand. Never once had she pulled back from him.

For some reason Teck couldn't figure out, he felt pride in her. Her parents were lucky to have her. She was quite a girl and promised to make an even greater woman. She came across as exactly who she was. Honest. Fair. Intelligent and friendly. He found he liked her more every day. And he still enjoyed her feisty, ornery side.

Teck smiled and looked down at a stick with which he was digging at the edge of the fire. Maybe he'd relax and enjoy the evening. He'd find time to speak with Patrick tomorrow.

"Well, no . . . I don't think the bow would be too easy for you with one hand . . . Maybe with a special bow that strapped to your wrist . . . but a throwing knife. That's something you could master."

Teck's attention was again caught by the conversation. The priest was smiling at the girl and patting her hand in a pacifying manner.

"No really. I'm telling you the truth. I could show you. Of course, Jax is the real expert when it comes to knife throwing. He's been teaching me." When she stood, she grasped the priest by his good hand and pulled him to his feet. "Come on. I'll show you."

Teck watched them wander to the tree line where Tessa took a small knife from her belt. She untied a sash from around her throat and, with the knife, stuck it to a stump. She pulled the priest back from it a few feet and then went about explaining to him how to throw another knife she produced. Teck wondered how many knives she had on her person.

When the two of them started to laugh, bending over at the

waist and holding on to each other, he moved closer to them. He still couldn't understand what they thought was so funny, but soon Tessa straightened and called to the boy.

"Jax. Hey, come over here and help me."

Jax jumped up from the fire and went to her aid. A true trainer, the boy got serious very quickly, his instruction to the priest precise and exact. At first, Patrick seemed embarrassed to give the knife throwing a try, but under Jax's steady tutelage, he was soon hefting the blades.

The first few didn't even make it to the tree, but after a while, one or two even hit the scarf.

"Yeah!" Tessa jumped up and down and clapped for the priest's accomplishments.

"Now, Tessa. If Jax has been so accommodating to teach you the art of knife throwing, what have you taught him?" Patrick asked, once again heaving a blade.

"Oh. We thought it was only fair that I teach him how to shoot a bow."

The priest stopped mid-throw. "Yes, I saw your case. Are you good with a bow?"

"Good with a bow?" Jax asked, his tone incredulous. "She's amazing."

The priest looked about at the other people in the clearing, each man now approaching the area. "I'm sure we'd all like a demonstration."

"Yeah, Tessa." Jax smacked her on the shoulder. "Show 'em what you've got."

Tessa looked at the men's faces, and they were all smiling

and nodding at her.

"Well, okay," she said. "If you'd like."

With a whoop, Jax ran back to the fire and packs and grabbed her bow case and quiver.

* * * * *

TESSA TOOK THE QUIVER AND slung it over her torso. Taking the case, she walked back toward the fire. She would need more distance for the bow than for the knives. The four men dropped back with her, clearing the path to the target.

Tessa turned, fiddling with her case. When she reached in and grasped the bow, the case pooled by her foot. With a small flick of her toe, she moved it out of her way. She stepped on the foot of her bow to pull the cord to the notch. As it slipped into place, she took a long cleansing breath. Her bow reminded her of her mother and reasserted her goal in her mind.

The wood felt as though she had come home. Her heart felt lighter, her hands firmer, her eye keener. The hum of the men's conversation behind her was on the outside of her consciousness. Not a distraction, not an encouragement.

When she pulled an arrow, drew it, and let it fly, she thought her essence flew with it—so light did she feel. Close on the first, she let loose a second and then a third.

THE THREE THUMPS STARTLED THE men into silence. Each stared at the tree, the ends of the arrows still quivering, each arrow stuck in the same hole.

Jax gave a whoop and, like a pup after a ball, ran to the tree. Teck stood with the other two, stunned. He turned to look at her, taking in her glowing face and proud stance. His gaze dropped to the bow in her hand, its end set on the ground, and he froze.

His eyes glued to the weapon, he heard the congratulations Wyliam heaped upon her. Ripping his eyes from the bow, he glanced again at her face and then at Patrick. The priest looked stupefied. Brows drawn, lips pursed. When he met Teck's gaze, his smoothed out and he gave a small shake of his head.

"Where did you get that bow?" Teck's voice was rough as he rounded on the girl.

Tessa halted her conversation with the blond man. She looked around him, drawn by the tone of Teck's voice.

"It's mine. What do you mean?"

"Yours?" he bellowed. "It can't be yours."

Her anger rising to meet his, she stepped around Wyliam and stomped up to Teck. Jax slowed on his return trip with the arrows, his gaze skimming over the group.

Patrick moved to Teck and placed a hand on his shoulder. "Now, Teck. I'm sure there's an explanation."

Teck shrugged off the priest's hand and stepped up to Tessa. They stood nose to nose, two bulls in a field.

"Of course it can be mine. What are you trying to do? Claim it for yourself?"

"Well, it's more mine than yours." He practically bumped her with his chest, causing her to step back.

Tessa moved back to her former position. Now the group

circled around them, not sure how to stop the argument.

"Ha!" she shouted. "I've had this bow for years. It was a gift from my mother."

"Liar."

"Liar?" she hissed. "I'm no liar, you big ox."

"I know exactly where that bow came from and to who it— " Teck dropped his head and took a step back, blinking fiercely.

Tessa squinted, chest rising with her breath. She scanned the other men, but no one offered any insight. Everyone watched as Teck took another step back from the fray.

*　*　*　*　*

"TECK." PATRICK AGAIN WENT TO him, though this time he didn't touch the big man.

Teck stared with glassy eyes. Then slowly, his gaze moved to the girl. How could he have missed it? The shape of her eyes and face, her black hair, her height. The bow was simply confirmation of something he must have known deep inside.

"Tessa," he whispered and stepped forward.

"What's wrong with you?" she said.

He took another step, coming within range of her. When he reached out to run a hand down her arm, she flinched as though expecting a blow. Grasping her by the upper arm, he pulled her forward and encircled her in a fierce hug.

She stiffened, not fighting his hug but not participating in it. Confusion colored her face, and from within the circle of his frame, she stared at Jax.

When he released her, she stumbled and only his grip kept her from tripping.

Lifting his head, he looked at her with tears in his eyes.

"Are you all right?" she whispered.

With a deep breath, he released her arms and walked away from them. When he passed the fire and kept going, she took a step in his direction. The priest stopped her, and she looked at him. "Wait, my dear. Let's give him some time. I'll check on him in a bit."

"Is he okay?"

"Yes. Yes, I'm certain he'll be fine."

73

WHEN TECK CAME BACK INTO the clearing, Tessa was the only one sitting by the fire. Jax and Patrick were rolled in their blankets, if not asleep—at least making a good pretense of it. Wyliam and Sam were off at the tree line on first watch.

Tessa saw him coming, and without subterfuge, she watched him come. She didn't know him well but knew he'd been acting out of character. Something was bothering him, and she'd know what it was before the night ended.

He stopped next to her. "We need to talk."

His expression was serious. He held out a hand. Staring at him for a moment longer, she reached out. When his palm closed around hers, she relaxed. It no longer mattered what this was about—good or bad—she realized she trusted him. With a small smile, she allowed him to pull her to her feet. He kept her hand in his as they wandered to the tree line.

They walked for a few minutes over fallen stumps and clumps of grass. When Teck stepped over a large log and indicated for her to sit, she did. He straddled it, facing her.

Neither of them said anything. The full moon illuminated his expression, but she couldn't read it. When another full minute passed and he didn't speak, she swung a leg over the log to face him. He didn't even look up at her.

"Are you all right?"

He lifted his gaze. Again, his eyes pooled and she thought he was going to break down. She'd never seen a man cry, hardly even seen her mother cry. Beginning to panic, she searched her mind for what she should do.

"Yes. I'm better than all right. I'm fantastic."

Well that was good, she thought. "What did you want to talk about?"

"I'd like to tell you a story." She nodded. "When I was a boy, about nineteen summers, I loved a girl. She was a special girl. Strong. Smart. Capable. And beautiful. Like you."

Tessa liked the timbre of his voice—a calming force. She settled in and listened.

"I'd known her for years before she became mine, but I'd always wanted her. Just when we were beginning to find each other, a tragedy struck, and she had to go away. I decided I didn't want to stay where I was, not without her, so I followed her." He stared at the log.

"We traveled. We had adventures. We loved each other." When his breath caught, Tessa laid a hand on his. He held it, and she felt the slight tremble in his frame.

"I was stupid. Now I can say I was young, but even knowing that, I was stupid." He nodded in agreement with himself. "I left her. I was jealous—without reason to be. I wanted to be her whole world, and when I wasn't, I left." Shaking his head, he muttered, "Stupid."

She squeezed his hand, gaining his attention. "Like you said, you were young." She tilted her head. "What happened?"

"When this girl had her sixteenth Names Day, I gave her a special gift. Something I had spent a lot of time on. Something I had put my heart into."

Tessa nodded, both in understanding and so he would continue.

"She's why I'm back in this land now. I came back to find her."

"We'll help you. All of us will help you. We won't stop until we find her for you." Tessa's voice came out forceful, impassioned. The need to help him burned deep within her. Even if she couldn't make a commitment for the rest of their group, she wouldn't give up until Teck and his love were reunited. Her heart swelled with the romance of it.

"In a way, you already are."

Her eyes opened widely. "Well, good. That's good that we're going in the right direction."

"Tessa," he said and then scooted forward just a bit more. Taking both of her hands in his, he looked deep into her eyes. "The item I made for the girl, the special gift for her Names Day . . ."

"Yes," she prodded.

"It was a bow. Carved and etched with vines and leaves."

"What?" Her brow furrowed and she shifted back. When

she tried to pull her hands from his, his grip tightened. "What did you say?"

"I made it for a beautiful red-haired girl. For Maya. The girl I gave it to, the girl I left home for, the girl I loved — still love — is your mother."

Tessa pulled her hands from his with a strength that surprised them both. She swung off the log, standing so fast she stumbled backward a step. Teck was right behind her, moving with her, his eyes intent on her face.

"Tessa. Do you hear what I'm saying? Do you know what that means?"

"My father left my mother and me." Her voice came out in a whisper that he could hardly catch. "She wasn't on her own, but she was devastated. Her heart broken."

She took two steps from him and then swung back to face him. As her passion grew, her voice got louder. She'd never cared to know her father. She barely even thought of the idea. "She never told me of her heartache — she would never do that — but I knew." She pointed to her chest. "I knew every time she looked at me."

She stomped away from him and he followed her. Suddenly, she swung back around, her voice breaking. When he saw the tears on her cheeks, Teck stumbled back.

"I know my mother loves me. I *know* it, but looking at me broke something in her just the same." She shook her head, her breath hitching. "Thanks, *Father*. Now I know why that is." Tessa took off for the camp, and Teck let her go.

✴ ✴ ✴ ✴ ✴

WHEN TECK AND TESSA HEADED into the woods, Wyliam almost went after them. Jealousy surfaced so fast and strong he laid a fist on his chest. He told himself she wasn't his to tell what to do and not do. She could do as she wanted, but he still had to hold himself back from following and slamming his fist into Teck's face.

When Tessa ran from the woods, tears streaming down her face, Wyliam thought his heart would stop. He flew across the clearing, intercepting her before she could get to the fire. Wrapping her in his arms, he spun to look toward the woods.

"What happened?" He held her at arm's length, scanning her for evidence of violence. "Are you all right? What the hell happened?"

When all she could do was bend over, sobbing, he cursed under his breath and started for the forest. Teck stepped from the cover of the woods.

Wyliam lost all sense. He broke into a run, heading toward the larger man. Tessa yelled his name, and the other men woke, jumped up, and headed in Tessa's direction.

Patrick and Jax reached her, shouting questions just as Wyliam reached Teck. The older man put up his hands in a pacifying gesture, but Wyliam plowed through them, planting his fist into Teck's jaw.

Teck was knocked to the side but kept his feet. He evaded a second punch and shoved the boy back.

"Now just a minute!" he yelled.

"You bastard. What did you do to her?"

"I didn't do anything." Teck tried to explain, but Wyliam rushed him.

Confusion reigned in the clearing. Everyone was yelling, Sam was barking, Wyliam was punching, and Teck was evading.

When two sets of hands grabbed Wyliam and hauled him back, he fought them. His vision red, all he wanted was Teck. His mind spun with what he thought the man may have done.

"Wyliam." The priest's soft voice broke into his rage. "Calm down, Wyliam. Let's discuss this."

"Discuss?" the young man spat. "You want to *discuss* this?" Wrenching his arms from their hold, he returned to Tessa. He led her toward the warmth of the fire.

Patrick watched them walk away and then turned to Teck, who was rubbing his chin.

"Kid's got a great hook."

"You want to talk about it?" Patrick asked.

"Not really."

Jax looked from the departing duo back to the priest and Teck. "What happened?"

"Nothing." The priest approached the boy and gave his shoulder a pat. "Everything's going to be all right. There's just some confusion. We'll work it out. Why don't you go back to sleep now? We'll be leaving early in the morning for the city."

Jax headed back to the fire. Patrick saw him stop and speak with Tessa. She shook her head and said something. When he answered her, she touched his hand and responded. Looking at

Patrick and Teck, the boy returned to his bedroll.

Patrick studied Teck. The man still fingered his jaw.

"Looks like you're going to be sporting a bruise tomorrow."

"Yeah." He nodded. "I'm thinking I've earned it."

"So you told her?"

Teck looked from the couple at the fire to the priest. "That I'm her father? That I left her mother out of selfishness?" Nodding, he said, "Yeah. I told her."

"You might be being too hard on yourself."

"I don't think she would agree with you. Seems like right now, I'm the lowest of the low." When Teck's head came up, Patrick turned to see what was happening.

Tessa had climbed into her bedroll. Wyliam pulled the blanket up around her shoulders then brushed her hair back and kissed her on the forehead. Standing, he threw a look at the two who watched and then pulled his bedroll near Tessa.

"I'll take the watch for the remainder of the night," Teck said. "There's no way I'll be getting any sleep anyway."

"Okay," Patrick agreed. "If you get sleepy, just wake me," and he walked toward the fire.

Teck watched him until he too was wrapped in his blanket, and then he made a circuit of the clearing, his ears and eyes open for anything unusual. Everything was quiet, and he made his way to the tree line. Sitting against a tree, he stretched his legs out. A moment later, Sam approached him and lay with his head on Teck's lap. Teck rubbed the dog's head, watching his daughter's silhouette through the night.

74

THOUGH THE SUN HADN'T YET peeked over the mountains, Tessa knew it to be morning by the low singing of the birds.

For a moment, she thought the drama of the past evening had been just a dream. The knowledge of its truth, however, came to her quickly with the soreness in her body, the swollen feeling of her eyes, and a slight ache that knocked in her head.

Her anger was swamped by embarrassment. She allowed her feelings to get the better of her. Again. Never had she been as vulnerable to her emotions as she'd been on this journey. The magnitude of her angst showed her how much it had bothered her over the years when her mother's looks of love had turned somehow inward and dark.

She had no idea she so resembled the father who left them. Knowing she could have done nothing about it, maybe understanding it would have lent her some comfort.

Only the dying embers of last night's fire offered illumination, but she sensed Wyliam next to her. He'd been so wonderful, so careful with her. He'd been understanding without even knowing what was happening. She'd told him nothing, just that Teck had done nothing. That he had no reason to enact vengeance.

Rolling to her side, her face almost touched Wyliam's hand, which he had anchored to her blanket. She needed some privacy. Her soul longed to fly with Striker, something she hadn't been able to do while in such a large group. Now, though, in the soft light of early morning, she could steal a few moments.

Pushing to her feet, she froze when the man next to her shifted, his breathing catching for a moment. When he relaxed and sank into slumber once again, she stepped from her bedroll.

After relieving her bladder, she moved farther into the woods. She would be quick, taking just a few moments of peace with her pedagogue.

She located a large tree, its canopy wide. Sitting cross-legged at the trunk, she took a cleansing breath. She thought of the bird, and her body relaxed.

As she flew, her head touched the bark behind her, and her open eyes turned white.

75

TECK WATCHED THE GIRL. HE'D spent the night by the tree line, most of it with the dog's company.

When Tessa first shifted, he thought she was just turning over in her sleep, but then she rose and walked away from the camp. Certain she was just looking for her morning privacy, he didn't at first react. When she didn't return, he moved toward the forest.

Her prints on the dewy land were child's play to follow. He sensed her before seeing her and slowed. When he located her under the large tree, for a moment he thought she was asleep, so still did she sit. Her eyes made him freeze, and then adrenaline pushed him forward, thinking she must be injured.

Teck scanned her and saw she didn't seem in any distress, her breathing deep and even, and no visible wounds. He decided to wait, so he sat under a nearby tree.

THE SUN HAD CLIMBED STEADILY into the sky when the girl moved. Teck sat forward. When her head dropped, she blinked.

He shifted, and her green gaze met his.

"Your mother had magic."

She didn't so much as blink at him, sitting like a statue.

"Not that I saw much of it, but I knew it was there."

"If you'd have hung around, you might have seen more of it."

Teck nodded, dropping his gaze. "Yes. I am well aware of the magnitude of my errors concerning your mother." They sat for a few minutes, his eyes soft, hers hostile. "Where do you go? When you're like that."

Tessa sighed deeply and shifted her gaze to a point over his shoulder. When she again looked at him, she said, "I suppose it doesn't matter if you know. I'm with Striker—my hawk."

"You're able to link with him?"

"Yes. But it's deeper than that. I can't really explain it, but we're part of each other. He came to me when I turned sixteen summers."

"Ah . . ." Teck breathed. "Like Sentinel to your mother."

Tessa's brows furrowed. "You know Sentinel?"

Teck nodded. "Yes. It was he who I was jealous of. Your mother and I were together before his coming, and sharing her to such a degree after having had her all to myself . . . well, it was more than I could do."

"I understand that."

"You do?"

"Yes. I have had times when her relationship with Sentinel was something I was jealous of. When I've wanted more of her attention."

She relaxed against the tree. "I'm sorry," she said.

"You're sorry? You don't have anything to be sorry about."

"I do. I judged you. I judged you unfairly."

Teck didn't agree with her, but he felt humbled. He'd judged himself over the years, and he didn't think she'd been harsh enough.

"I'd like to get past this if possible," he said and leaned toward her. "I'd like to have a place in your life."

"I'd like that, too." She gave him a small smile.

Teck stood and offered a hand. Eagerly, she slipped hers into it and he pulled her from the ground. When they stood face to face, he seemed about to say something but hesitated.

Tessa wrapped her arms around his waist. After a blink of surprise, Teck hugged her. They stood like this for a time, the morning aging around them.

When she pulled back, he let her go, but his arms felt empty without her. Looking down at her, he mourned for the years he'd missed.

"Ready to head back?" he asked.

"Yep. The others are probably frantic by now."

"It'll be okay to have a later start today. We should be in Berth before the sun sets."

"I'm excited to see my mother." She looked at him through the corner of her eyes. "I suppose you are, too."

Teck smiled. Slinging an arm around her shoulders, he said, "I'm just hoping her welcome is less angry than yours."

"Good luck."

76

MAYA LED HER PARTY INTO the broken-down temple. So many years had passed, and yet, it felt like just yesterday that she and Sentinel had run for their lives from this place.

Could it be true? Could her mother be alive? She'd missed her so terribly.

Maya thought back to the last time she'd seen Sylvan. Swirling with her magic, crazed and scary.

And let's not forget her trying to kill me.

Now, moving through the halls, that long-ago day came back to her. She remembered the battle with the guards before they even reached the throne room. Her hand moved, hoping to feel Rory's head. Some days, she missed him so much. He had saved her life over and over.

Looking over her shoulder at Sentinel, she caught his eye and a feeling passed between them. This place, lying in ruin, seemed empty. Harmless. But she knew better. In this town nowhere was safe. They would be on their guard even more than before.

She approached the gap where the golden door used to be. That day, they'd been fleeing. She had looked back to see the door thrown into the hall, its weight bashed against the far wall. Now no door rested there. Nothing of the opulence remained.

When she stepped in, she somehow expected the chaos of before. Now, the room was vacant of people. Plants filled it. Her magic catalyzed it all. Even with her gone, it had continued to live, to thrive. Even more than before, the flora overtook the room. It grew up from the cracked tile and in from the smashed glass dome. Today, sun shone in. If it weren't for her memories, she might even consider the room to be welcoming, full of plants, sunshine, and life. But she couldn't quite put her memories away.

She stood on the dais, pivoting to scan the entire room. Along the edges, Sentinel, Inger, and his men searched the room with a diligence she could appreciate.

Maya reached into her pocket and pulled out the greenish stone she'd received while in the tunnels. It twinkled in the sunlight, winking as if they shared a secret that she wasn't privy to.

At least not yet.

When Sentinel walked to her, she stopped studying the stone. Resigned to not yet understand, she slid the rock back into her pocket.

"Anything?"

"No," he said. "There is evidence that someone was here not long ago, but it could have been a scrounger looking for something to sell."

"Inger," she called. He walked to her. "Do you know where we are supposed to meet Patrick? Where is he?"

"There is a keep outside of town. Most often that is where he is found."

"All right then." With a final look, she stepped from the dais. "Let's head there. We need to find out what he thought I could solve."

Inger brightened and headed toward the exit. "He will be gladdened to see you."

"Let's hope so."

77

WHEN MAYA SAW THE GROUP coming down the road to the keep, she couldn't believe her eyes.

Her group had arrived at the keep late last night. It was full of townspeople, all of whom were excited to see them, but no Patrick. Some of the men said he'd been wandering afar, and a few days ago he hadn't returned from his walk.

She hadn't known what to do with that information. What was she supposed to do without his direction? She'd slept fitfully and spent the day wandering the halls of the old castle wondering if they should head out and search for the priest.

Now, looking out a small upper window, she saw a group of five coming to the keep.

One was Tessa.

Maya blinked and looked again. How could Tessa be here? She was supposed to be safe at the Hampshires'. Her eyes locked on her daughter for another moment, then she bolted down the stairs and outside.

The first of them was just coming into the courtyard when Maya flew out the door.

"Tessa!" she yelled and launched herself at the girl.

"Mama."

Maya wrapped herself around the girl, still certain her eyes were deceiving her. She pulled back, gave her a good look, and then hugged her again. Pulling back once again, she grasped the girl's face between her palms, wiping tears from her daughter's cheeks.

"What are you doing here?"

"I'm so glad to see you. I've been searching for you."

Both women spoke at the same time, talking over each other. They stopped, wanting to give the other a chance to speak. Looking at each other in silence, they broke into laughter. Maya thought her heart would shatter with happiness having Tessa near her again. Fear for her daughter peeked its head, but she pushed the unwanted emotion aside. For now, she would enjoy this reunion.

"Is Sentinel here with you?"

"Yes. Come inside. You must be tired. We've been waiting for someone who hasn't returned." Maya took Tessa's arm in hers and walked toward the door of the keep.

"Maya." She turned at her name, and Patrick stood in front of her. Older, but still the same man, she couldn't believe how familiar he looked. How wonderful it was to see him again.

"Patrick." She shook her head and walked toward him. "You and Tessa are together? How did that happen?"

"I met her on the road while I was searching for you."

She stepped to the priest, placing her hands on his upper arms and looking him in the eye. "It's good to see you. I thought you'd died that day in the temple."

He nodded and leaned down, kissing one cheek. "It is good to see you as well. Good that you have come back."

Behind him, other people moved into the courtyard, drawing her attention. She glanced over the priest's shoulder and then back to him. For just a second, time froze, and she really had to pay attention to the newcomers. Only one of the three held her attention. Large, black hair, and still as good-looking as she remembered. He was just finishing saying something to one of the men he walked beside and was turning her way, a smile on his face. He stopped walking and shifted when a body hit him. But he didn't move forward. All conversation around them stopped.

"Maya," he said.

Turning, she moved past everyone to get to the keep door. Sentinel was just coming out as she pushed her way by him. Startled, he stepped out of her way and then looked out at the group. Seeing Teck, his gaze spun back to follow Maya.

"Mama!" Tessa called. Starting after her mother, Tessa looked over her shoulder at Teck and then continued after Maya.

78

TECK NEEDED TO SIT DOWN. Seeing her, being so near her after all this time—it felt like a dream.

He smiled and put a hand on a bench so he could lower himself. He didn't even care if she was angry with him. Didn't care if she didn't want to see him. He was here now, with her. They could work out any difficulties.

People filtered away, some going into the keep. Wyliam and Jax followed a man. Teck heard something about food and getting settled. He would need to go in soon to take his punches from Maya like a man, but for now, he just needed to sit.

His legs were shaking. With a small laugh, he rubbed his palms on his thighs and looked up at the blue sky.

When Patrick sat next to him, Teck regarded him.

"It is good to all be together again," the priest said.

"Yes," Teck breathed.

"I fear you may be in trouble."

"Yes," he agreed again.

"Such strong-willed women. Thank the gods, as they will

save us all."

Teck turned at his words, his brows drawn. "Do you know what is to happen, priest?"

"No." He shook his head. "Not really, but I have my faith."

For a while, the two sat in silence, each contemplating the future in their own way. After a bit, Teck again looked at Patrick. "What now?"

"Now? Now we prepare."

79

SYLVAN STRETCHED HER MIND WITHIN the confines of her prison. It felt as though she were moving through mud, but she could also flex her muscles. Her body wasn't completely in her control—muscles atrophied, in need of nourishment—yet, it was good. She wanted more.

In all the time that had passed, her captor thought of her as gone—asleep. And for much of the time she had been. She'd learned how to stay hidden, how to watch and learn.

Within the bursts of her jailer's magic, Sylvan had been practicing her own. Hidden. Secret. And she was becoming stronger. Every day she found more of herself. Remembered more of herself.

She watched her jailer. Knew her to be called Nav-lys. Knew her for the evil she was. And not only her, not only the small man. There was another. Sylvan had witnessed the interaction between Nav-lys and what she thought of as her god.

Cassandra. They called her Cassandra.

When she first saw what they were doing together, in her horror, she almost gave herself away. Luck kept her presence unknown. Since then, she had become smarter and harder. It had been difficult, but she'd had to inure herself to the suffering of others. The suffering of children. She could do nothing to help them, not yet.

But soon. Soon.

She didn't know how, but she had faith that somehow, she would triumph. Getting stronger, Sylvan was able to influence the body in different ways. When she saw the spark of their magic, she studied it. Where before it had been a ball of pure light, now the scope and range of darkness varied. Grays darkening into the blackest of ebony. At first, getting near the power caused her pain. When she continued to push—to try to reach it, she finally succeeded. With her own thoughts of past loves, needs, and happiness, she found she was able to stifle the colors, allowing the pure white to shine through.

Staring at the spark, she knew she couldn't stop Nav-lys from using their magic, but she could ensure its strength was limited.

80

TECK SAT THROUGH THE MEAL, but he was unable to eat. Across the table and down, Maya visited with Patrick. She had yet to acknowledge him.

Earlier, when they'd crossed paths, she'd stepped around him and kept walking. She acted as though he wasn't even there. He allowed that she was mad at him. He'd known she would be. He should be glad she hadn't met him with her swords.

When Maya laughed at something Patrick said, Teck clenched his jaw. Was she doing it on purpose? What was it going to take to get a moment of her time? He was sure if they talked, everything could be worked out.

* * * * *

MAYA WAS MORE THAN AWARE of the man sitting at the end of the table. She didn't look at or acknowledge him, but every time she glanced that direction, he was still staring.

What did he think? That they were going to jump right back in where they left off? Just act like nothing had happened? That he hadn't left her alone and pregnant?

Okay, she thought. She hadn't been totally alone. And maybe he didn't know she was pregnant. Maybe she'd been more involved with Sentinel and all she was learning. Involved with her new powers. Maybe, just maybe, she'd been young and selfish.

It didn't matter, though. His leaving her was a cowardly thing to do. He could just pack his stuff up and head back to whatever life he'd made.

She glanced at him again, taking in the memory of what they'd once had, and her heart constricted.

Probably has himself a wife and ten kids back wherever he's been.

You sound jealous.

I am not jealous.

She rested her elbow on the table and rubbed between her eyes. All the thoughts in her head were making it ache.

"Mama."

She shifted to see Tessa standing behind her. Swinging her legs off the bench, she stood up to hug her daughter to her. It was so wonderful to have her here, yet so terrible. But with all that had happened this day, she chose to relish her daughter's presence.

"How are you? What can I do for you?" Maya asked.

"I think I'm going to turn in. It's been a long time since I've got to sleep in a real bed, and I'm looking forward to a good night's sleep."

"Of course. You know which room you've been given?"

"Yes. I put my things in it earlier."

"And Striker?"

"He's with me. Patrick gave me a room at the top of the keep. It has a wonderful window that Striker can come and go through."

Maya and Tessa had just pulled back from another hug when the blond man walked up. At first Maya couldn't remember his name, and then it came to her. Wyliam. He touched Tessa's hand and curled his around it.

Oh, she thought. This would bear watching. But looking into her daughter's face, she could see how happy she was. And the young man was obviously captivated by Tessa.

Suddenly, she felt very old and remembered her mother's affection for Teck. Again, she glanced at the dark-haired man. Maybe she should have stayed away from him. But, no. Then there would never have been a Tessa, and nothing would be worth that.

She finished her good nights to her daughter, and giving Wyliam a long look, she watched them walk out of the dining room, hand in hand.

Maya gave one final glance at Teck. He was visiting with some of the men at the table. She was tired. The emotions of this day had her worn out. She walked out of the room, leaving the sounds of male voices behind her.

* * * * *

WHEN MAYA LEFT THE DINING hall, Teck's gaze followed her. He excused himself from the conversation and pushed back his chair to follow her.

He didn't see her right away and thought she headed to her room, so he started up the steps. A blast of cool air blew down the hall, a closing door cutting off the current. He headed toward the sound.

Walking through the outer door, he saw Maya in the courtyard. A set of torches at the gate illuminated her, the light splashing her frame, shifting as the breeze moved the flames, her hair flickering among them.

When he pulled the door shut, she glanced over her shoulder and then returned her gaze to the night. Walking up behind her, he shared her view. For some moments, neither of them spoke.

Unable to help himself, Teck wound a tendril of her hair around his finger. Rubbing it between his thumb and finger, he leaned forward to bury his nose in the curls by her ear. She smelled the same. Sweet. Warm. Like home.

"I'm sorry," he whispered, his heart in his words.

She leaned backward into him. Taking her action as forgiveness, he pulled her into him. The two of them stood like that for some time. Finally, Maya turned toward the keep. She took his hand in hers and led him in.

81

TESSA PUSHED OPEN THE DOOR to her mother's room. It was early, but her mother had always been an early riser. This morning, however, she was still in bed. Tessa moved closer to the bed, taking in its rumpled appearance. Maya was on her stomach and the blanket was pulled up to cover her lower half. Tessa was surprised to see she appeared nude.

Just as she was getting ready to wake her, the door to the balcony opened and her father walked in. He had on trousers but no shirt or shoes, and he slung a linen towel around his neck.

Tessa looked from him to her mother and back again. The realization of what had transpired made its way into her mind.

When Teck saw her, he put a finger to his lips and hurried around the bed to usher her out of the room.

"Let her sleep. She's exhausted herself in the last few weeks."

Tessa gawked. "You stayed with her last night?"

"Yes." He moved back a step and looked at her. "I'd like your blessing, Tessa, but with or without it, I plan on being part of your mother's life."

She nodded but said, "I'd like to speak with my mother about this first."

"Of course. But let's let her rest for now, all right?"

She nodded again and began to make her way down the hall, a stunned look on her face.

Teck watched her go, waiting a minute before reentering the room. Maya still slept, and he walked to the bed. A small smile crossed his lips, and a lightness lifted his heart. Tossing the towel aside, he stripped off his trousers and climbed back into bed.

Maya stirred when he pulled her into his embrace but soon settled down and snuggled in. He remembered; she was a cuddler. He remembered that first night in the rocks, him with dislocated fingers, them fleeing captivity. He'd felt heavenly.

Now, given the chance to spend time with her, he planned on taking full advantage of it. If he had his way, they'd stay in bed all day.

Teck wrapped both arms around Maya and snuggled her head under his chin. His nostrils filled with the scent of her hair, green growing things, a spring breeze. Holding her closely, he closed his eyes and realized he had, indeed, gone to heaven.

82

PATRICK CALLED A MEETING. HE was amazed that after waiting so long, he now had almost everyone together. Sylvan, he felt, was lost to them.

When each came into the dining room, taking seats around the table, he scrutinized them. Trying not to be too obvious, he assessed each for strengths and weaknesses.

Maya and Teck came in first. Patrick was quick to notice their joined hands. He was happy for them and hoped that this time, if they all lived beyond the next few days, they would have a happier go of it. It was good to find happiness where one could.

Sentinel came in right on their heels as if he'd been visiting with them in the hallway. He sat next to Maya but leaned over her to say something to Teck.

Tessa wandered in next, Wyliam close behind her. She stopped by her mother and, placing a hand on her shoulder, whispered something in the older woman's ear. Maya nodded, and Tessa moved on to sit farther down the table. Wyliam sat next to her and then Jax came in. He stopped when he saw Tessa and Wyliam, moving to the other end of the table.

Inger came in and walked directly to Patrick.

"I know my work is done, but I was wondering if I could sit in on the meeting."

Patrick placed a hand on his shoulder. "Of course. Your help has been invaluable. Stay. I value your opinion."

With a nod of appreciation, Inger took a seat.

Looking from one end to the other, Patrick thought for a moment before he spoke. "I'm warmed and heartened to see everyone. This has been a long time coming, and I'm positive in our outcome by the fact that we are all here. What are the odds of that? That Inger would locate Maya, and Teck would be here when she arrived." They all looked at each other, perhaps for the first time seeing fate in their being together.

"The last time we faced this evil, we became aware that Maya's mother, Sylvan, had somehow been turned." Tessa looked at her mother, who scowled.

"I'm sorry, my dear," he said to her. "It seems you haven't been brought up to date, but we'll take care of that. Let's get through this first, shall we?" Tessa nodded and he continued.

"We all believed Sylvan had perished in that altercation, but it was not to be." He paced in front of the table. "I've recently been given information that soldiers are amassing at the temple in Berth. We haven't seen soldiers in this area since Mikel Bathsar's time."

Maya spoke up. "We were in the temple. There's nothing there. Why would soldiers be at the temple when there's nothing to protect?"

"They are preparing, fortifying. We believe there may soon be something to protect. The gossip is of a large celebration. Some ceremony for Nav-lys."

A babble of conversation ran around the table.

"The rot is spreading. More people are dying or simply disappearing. We can't fool ourselves any longer or hope for things to get better. Something is coming, and we need to be prepared to fight. Time has run out."

Maya stood. "I too have felt that we are running out of time. For the entire journey, it has burned in me."

"Do you know where the feeling comes from or what it means?" Teck asked.

"No," she said with a shake of her head and sat back down. "Just that I needed to hurry."

Teck took her hand in both of his and placed a kiss upon her fingers. When she looked at him, he gave her a small smile.

"So, Patrick," he said, turning to the priest, "what are we to do?"

"We must get a spy into the temple. Someone who can come and go and tell us what is happening. When the ceremony, if that is what they are preparing for, will be performed."

Inger stood, his head bowed. When he looked at Patrick and then around the room, his gaze was intense. "Allow me to do this for you. I've been gone from the land, so no one will know I'm with you. I could get a job as a laborer."

Patrick stared at the man. "Are you certain you wish to do this? You've only just come home. You should spend time with your family." Unsaid was the risk. If Inger didn't see his loved ones now, he never might.

"I am prepared to do this. I believe in this cause."

Dropping his head, Patrick said, "So be it. Inger will be our eyes and ears. He will let us know when the time is right. We will need to strike hard and quick."

He walked to Maya, squatted before her, and took her hands in his.

"You know what will be required of you?" When she nodded, he added, "And you are prepared for this?"

She thought for a moment, holding his gaze. "My mother died years ago. This creature that inhabits her body . . . I don't know who or even what this is, but it's not my mother."

He nodded and stood. Speaking to the entire room, he said, "She is right. Nav-lys is a servant of pure evil. This evil has a name. She calls herself Cassandra."

He had their attention now. Each individual stared right at him, waiting for his next words.

"When I was a boy, alone on the streets of the city, eating garbage and hiding from the clutches of people who would harm me, a man . . . no not a man. He was a being. A deity perhaps. He told me that this time would come. That I needed to prepare. I would need to find the ones who would help triumph over this evil. I have spent my life working toward this goal."

From the folds of his cloak, he pulled an old parchment. It crinkled as he moved it, the corners crumbled and curled.

"In a time of strife, in a world of fear,
age will come for three of the blood.
When the core is joined,
Three and Three become One,
and darkness will be consumed by light."

Placing the text back within his cloak, Patrick again faced them. "We are here to do more than just save our town or our land. This evil will consume everything. Everything we know and love will be gone. We must not fail."

Tessa spoke up. "What does it mean, 'three of the blood'?"

Patrick walked to her but then looked around the room to include them all. "I don't know. What I think, is that it will take three of us to combat this evil. We must be prepared to do whatever we must."

When he finished, the assembled people looked at each other. Some had seen the evil and some had not, but each believed him.

* * * * *

OUTSIDE THE ROOM, TESSA STOPPED next to Maya. She watched as the others filed out.

"Mama, can we speak?"

"Of course, love. Let's step outside."

Out in the courtyard, the two women sat on a bench. They enjoyed a moment of the calm, sunlit day before Tessa turned.

Maya said, "I suppose you're curious about your father and

me."

"Well, yes. I meant to ask you about that."

Maya shrugged. "I'm happy. I was always happy when I was with him."

Tessa opened her mouth to speak but Maya interrupted her. "I know he broke my heart. And he assures me that he's here to stay. I'm not going to hold him to that. I'm older now. I'll take what I can get."

"And you'll be happy with that?"

"For now. None of us know what our futures will be. I'd be a fool to push away happiness when I might be dead tomorrow."

Tessa nodded. "Tell me about your mother."

Taking her daughter's hand in hers, Maya told her of her mother. She spoke of the mother who cooked wonderful meals. The mother who taught her how to make a quilt. The mother of laughter and sunshine. When she got to the kidnapping, Tessa had questions.

"I'm sorry, I don't know much about who took her or where she went. I only know the next time I saw her, she was a crazed, vengeful being. She would have killed me had my father not sacrificed his life to save mine."

"My grandfather?"

"Yes." She patted Tessa's hand. "I'd only just found him, and to lose him so soon . . ." She bowed her head and gave Tessa's hand a gentle squeeze. Looking again at her daughter, she said, "There were many emotional misfortunes so near each other. By then, I knew about you, and it was this knowledge that kept me going. Sentinel and I left the land, found our home on another. Left this all behind. I had you and we were happy."

"You've always been a wonderful mother."

Maya slid over and wrapped Tessa in a tight hug. "I love you."

"And I love you, Mama."

* * * * *

TECK STOOD IN THE WINDOW and watched the two women. They were the most important people in his life now, and he would do anything to keep them safe.

Patrick made it sound like Maya would be in the front of the danger, but Teck didn't know if that was true. Maybe he could do what needed to be done. If this Nav-lys needed to be killed, maybe he could just kill her. Patrick was all about the ceremony and the words on that old paper, but Teck didn't see it that way. Nav-lys needed to die, right? So, she'd die.

His mind working around a plan, Teck at first didn't notice Jax, who stood on the other side of the courtyard, partially hidden by a flowering hedge. He, too, was watching the women, but something about his manner unnerved Teck. After a moment, Jax backed away and disappeared.

Teck was looking for him when the outer door opened, and his women stepped in.

He put his arms around each of their shoulders, pulling them closer. First, he planted a kiss on Tessa's forehead and then, tilting Maya's chin up, he kissed her on the mouth.

"Inger headed into town," he said. "We should hear something back from him by tonight. With more information, we'll be able to set up a plan."

Maya nodded. "Good. I'm ready to finish this."

* * * * *

JAX WALKED FROM THE KEEP. His emotions seared through him. He'd tried to control them, tried to make excuses for her, but finally, he released the ties. The pain of betrayal. And hate. He thought they were a team, but she threw him away for another.

Jax was closer to town than the keep when he saw the rider sitting on the side of the road. He slowed but kept walking. Even on the horse he could see the man was short. His stirrups were pulled up so far, he would have to have assistance to mount the horse.

"Hello, Jax." His voice had a nasally quality that Jax didn't like.

"Do I know you?" The boy stopped on the far side of the road from the rider. He squinted at him, trying to remember if he'd ever met him before.

"Not yet you don't. But I think you and I are going to be great friends."

"What do you mean?" Fighting the pull of the rider and losing, Jax took a step toward him. When the boy stepped within a few feet of the horse, the man reached out his hand.

"Shake with me, Jax. Shake and be one."

In a fog the boy reached out, sliding his hand along the

man's. A shiver of revulsion crawled down his spine at the feeling. Cold, moist, and it seemed to wriggle in his palm. When the man pulled back, Jax dropped his hand to the side.

JAX BLINKED. HE WAS SURPRISED to find himself standing in the middle of the road. He remembered leaving the keep, remembered being upset, but didn't know how he'd gotten here.

Spinning in a circle, the boy looked for anything that would give him a clue, but he was alone. He held out his arms and looked down at himself, but he seemed fine. When he grabbed his belt to hike up his pants, he hissed and peered at his hand. The palm looked bruised, almost burned. Jax tried to remember what he could have done, but nothing came to mind.

He turned toward the keep. He was hungry and wondered if he could find something to eat in that kitchen.

83

SYLVAN FLEXED HER MUSCLES AGAIN. She continued to get stronger every day. Stronger in body and in mind. She remembered everything now.

The creation of Nav-lys was something she blamed herself for. If she'd just been stronger. Surviving the torture in that place, she'd cracked, and out of the dark places had oozed Nav-lys.

Some days, she forgave herself, remembering the pain, the fear. Other days, she berated herself. This was her fault. She would need to be the one to fix it. She'd begun to try something new. Putting all her effort into it, she could control the body. Just small things, a finger moving, eye ticking. Each success was an achievement. She was getting stronger and stronger.

When the time came, she would be ready.

* * * * *

WHEN NAV-LYS STEPPED THROUGH THE entry into the large,

dimly lit cavern, the cat lifted his head.

For two decades he had watched and waited. Now the time was at hand. He could smell his girl within the creature. She was strong and getting stronger.

The tips of his ears twitched when she walked by, never knowing he was there. He'd found her quickly those many years ago, but he'd realized she was more than just the woman he looked for. The creature was strong within her. And the creature's master was even stronger.

He stayed close. At first, he thought his girl was gone for good. Then one day, he'd scented her, faint and far away. Nothing had changed, not for the longest time.

He'd seen the atrocities her master was capable of. Had seen Nav-lys become stronger. For the longest time, he'd thought all was lost. But that small scent, that elusive quick essence of his Sylvan and he'd had hope that she would come back to him.

Then, one day, while the sun was high and bright, his Sylvan appeared. It had been for the briefest of moments—Nav-lys was weakest at that part of the day. He'd been lucky to be there when she'd surfaced. They hadn't talked, but he'd seen her, and he'd known she'd seen him. It wasn't much, but it was enough to keep going.

84

INGER CAME TO THE KEEP four days after he'd left. He snuck in through the back, meeting Patrick in the kitchen.

"Inger," Patrick said and clasped the other man's forearm, "we expected you before this."

The other man grasped the priest and gave him a hug. "It is good to see you, Father. These past days have been busy and harrowing. But I have information."

"Let us gather everyone so we may hear it all at once. Come, be at rest." Turning toward the woman kneading bread, he said, "Breva, bring food and drink to the dining area. Enough for all."

Patrick led Inger to the dining hall. Along the way he saw a young servant boy who he sent to gather everyone.

By the time the whole household had gathered, Inger was just finishing his meal. He leaned back, one hand on his stomach, the other wrapped around a mug. As each person came in, they eyed the man but took a seat.

Finally, all were gathered, sitting in much the same places as the last time they met. Patrick once again stood before them and addressed the entire room.

"As you see, Inger is back, and he has brought information. I've asked us all to be here to hear this information so we may discuss it." He indicated to Inger and sat next to Jax.

Inger stood, seeming a bit uncomfortable being the focus of everyone's attention. "Um. Well, the temple is swarming with soldiers. It reminds me back to the time of Mikel Bathsar."

WHEN THE DOOR OPENED HOURS later, participants began filtering out. Conversation hushed between them. They had a plan. Now to put it into motion.

* * * * *

JAX LOOKED AT HIS HANDS, studying them in the dusk light. Everything confused him anymore. His hands did things he couldn't control, things he barely remembered.

He looked from his open palms to the body lying against the wall.

Did I do this?

He could almost remember it, like a distant thought. Why would he kill the stable boy? There was no reason for it. The last thing he remembered was leaving the meeting with everyone else. They'd talked about getting something celebratory to drink. Then he'd had this idea to go to the stables.

He never went to the stables, he thought. Really didn't care for horses. Too big. But here he was, in the stables.

What was he going to do with the body?

His joints were stiff and painful. Trying not to look at the boy's face, Jax grabbed him by the wrists and pulled him to the back of the barn. Moving him along the far wall, he piled bales of hay over the corpse. On his way back to the door, Jax used his foot to brush stray straw over the drag marks on the floor.

The boy already forgotten, Jax walked out of the stable once again thinking about food.

85

AT SUNSET THE NEXT DAY, Maya, Tessa, and Teck sat in the courtyard. They watched the sun sink below the hills, each in their own thoughts.

Tomorrow was the day. Tomorrow they would make their way into the temple. Live or die, they were committed to ending the reign of Nav-lys and her master.

Their daughter between them, Maya and Teck had discussed privately that they would do whatever it took to see her safely through tomorrow. Maya wrapped an arm around Tessa's shoulders, her hand landing on Teck's arm. At her touch, he gave her fingers a gentle kiss.

How could he have just found them only to possibly be losing them?

Teck would have taken his woman and child and left this land. But they would have no part in that. Maya argued if Nav-lys wasn't halted here, soon no land would be safe. This was the best chance they would ever have. If she got stronger, the evil that fueled her would never be stopped. Life would end.

She was noble. He loved her for that.

So tomorrow they would go, and he would go with them. He would never leave them again.

* * * * *

HOW HAS IT COME DOWN *to this?*

Maya soaked in the sun's warmth. Enjoying her daughter next to her and her man close to them, she softly rubbed Teck's shoulder, the feeling a balm to her nerves.

She was going to stop this Nav-lys and the evil that fueled her, but her greatest concern would be getting Tessa out of the temple. She would tell her she couldn't go, but knowing her daughter, that wouldn't work. Having her stay at the Hampshires' didn't even go as planned.

So, she'd go with them tomorrow, but at least they would know where she was at every moment. At least they would be there to pull her out of trouble.

Tomorrow would finish this thing. Her life—this part of it— had begun so many years ago. That day, she'd been out with Rory. Her life had changed so profoundly, she barely remembered that young girl of that morning. Tomorrow she would get her life back.

* * * * *

TESSA SAT BETWEEN HER PARENTS, but her thoughts weren't on the following day. She looked around the courtyard waiting to see Wyliam. She wanted to discuss what lay after.

She enjoyed the closeness of sitting between her parents. This was like nothing she had ever before experienced. And her mother was more relaxed. She'd never seen her quite like this.

When Wyliam and Sam stepped from the keep, she could tell he was looking for her. His gaze was intense, and when he saw her, a smile lit his face. She jumped from the bench, but before she could get too far, she heard her father say her name.

"Yes?"

"Where are you off to?" Teck eyed the boy behind her.

"Tomorrow is an important day. I want to spend some time with Wyliam." As she finished and turned toward the boy, he came to her and placed an arm around her waist.

Teck looked at Maya with a raise of his eyebrows. She glanced from him to their daughter. "Be careful, Tess."

Tessa turned from her with a roll of her eyes but then had a vibrant smile for the blond man. Taking his hand from her waist, she led him out the gate and into the forest.

"Come on, Wyliam. I want to discuss something with you."

The man followed her willingly, Sam close on their heels. Moving deeper into the tangle of forest, Tessa selected a spot within a copse of trees. Sitting, she patted the area next to her.

"You know my relationship with Striker is special," she began as he sat. Wyliam nodded.

"I'm able to connect with him. Mind to mind."

Picking up her hand, he gave the fingers a gentle kiss. "I knew you were unique the first moment I met you."

Laying her other hand on his cheek, she looked him in the

eye. "I can also connect with other animals."

"What do you mean?"

Shaking her head, her gaze introspective, she tried to explain. "I can call to them. My mind can touch theirs." Laying a hand on the dog's head, she added, "That's how Sam and I became such good friends so quickly."

"I thought there was something else going on there. So why are you telling me this?"

"You know how we keep hearing how many soldiers there are at the temple? How a big problem is going to be we're undermanned?" Wyliam nodded. "Well, I have an idea of how we can even those odds."

* * * * *

PEERING AT THE COUPLE THROUGH the trees, Jax couldn't stop the hate that burned through him. How could she just throw him aside?

Jax watched for some time. The couple finished their conversation, and as the sun began to dip in the sky, their touching became more intimate.

Tears ran down his cheeks.

86

THE SUN, WHICH HAD SHONE brightly when the small party headed out, now hid its face behind a blanket of gray clouds.

Maya repeatedly checked behind, not only to ensure that Tessa was with her, but that all of them were coming along. A sad smile crossed her face to see Tessa and Wyliam walking, hands clasped. How long would this young couple have? Would today be the end of their beginning?

When the group split, it wasn't with good-byes or hugs. A raised chin here, a nod there, and a quick tightening of hands for Tessa and Wyliam, and then they were two groups. One moved toward the rear entrance of the temple and one, boldly, toward the front.

Patrick, Wyliam, Sentinel, and Jax moved into the crowd at the front of the temple. Cloaked and hooded, they blended with the mass. The stairs were full of spectators, soldiers moving among them, keeping them under control. According to Inger's intel, most of them would be parents from the city and outlying communities—come to collect their children, if they could.

The men separated and moved into the crowd, their aim to get to the throne room. They would place themselves at three different locations, surrounding the spectacle on the dais. There they would wait for Maya's signal. If they could take Nav-lys from all sides and kill her, her reign of terror would end.

Patrick knew Nav-lys was a means to an end for Cassandra, but without any information from Caleb, closing the door for his sister was the best he could hope for.

Patrick shifted and sidestepped people in his bid for the throne room. Closing his mind and heart to their suffering, he counseled himself to keep moving. The best thing he could do for them was to end Nav-lys.

When he glanced over heads and around people, Wyliam and Sentinel entered the throne room and moved to opposite sides. They shifted along the wall. Unable to find Jax in the crush of people, Patrick hoped he was moving to his assigned location.

* * * * *

WHEN TECK, MAYA, AND TESSA separated from the three men, Teck watched the others for a moment before turning to follow the women.

They moved like wraiths through the city streets, keeping a sharp eye out for soldiers. When they approached the rear of the temple, it was quiet—most of the population was at the front of the building. Back here, walls and doors were intact, making it hard to believe such destruction existed in the throne room.

Slipping in and down dark hallways, the trio kept quiet, each one's thoughts private.

They were armed and ready. Teck with his broadsword, Maya with her twin blades, and Tessa with an arrow notched and ready to fly. Teck couldn't remember when his emotions were so hot. Usually cool-headed, something akin to panic kept raising its unwanted head. Pushing such thoughts aside, he kept them moving. Through the outer housings, across the courtyard, to the back hallway leading to the throne room.

At first just a hum, the nearer they got to the main room, the louder the jumble of voices became. No words were discernable, just panic and anger. At the entrance to the throne room, Teck squatted, gesturing to the women to follow suit. There the three crouched just out of sight. With a quick motion, Teck peeked in the room, seeing no soldiers. He glanced at the two women and indicated for them to follow him.

They crouched and walked to a half wall a few feet within the open area. Ensuring they were all together, he again peeked at the spectacle.

When lightning flashed overhead, all three looked up. Through the shattered dome, the evening sky was plainly visible. Darkness had come early with the cloud cover, but now it appeared a storm was brewing.

Teck peered over the wall, hoping to locate his comrades. In the crowd, he saw Patrick and Wyliam. Sentinel stood back along another wall. Jax was nowhere to be found.

Sylvan paced in the center. No, he thought, not Sylvan—

Nav-lys. He'd hardly recognized her. Old, gray, walking with a hunched gait. For a moment, the image of her outside the cabin flashed. Teck sat next to Maya.

"They're in position," he whispered.

"What now?"

"Now, we wait."

87

J AX SAW THE WOMAN IN the center of the dais and couldn't draw his eyes away. He'd never seen her before, but it was as if he knew her. Her thoughts were in his head, and all other thoughts, ones of loyalty and friendship, paled to her directions.

Pushing through the crowd, he made his way to the front. Soldiers barred the path, weapons brandished. People yelled at them, calling for the children. Every so often, someone would become too forceful, too aggressive in their anger and a soldier would act. Fatally. Bodies littered the front of the room. A gruesome flesh barrier.

Jax didn't take notice of the parents, the soldiers, or the dam of bodies. His eyes were trained on the woman. Gray-haired and hunched, she ignored all the chaos.

The sky above her continued to darken and swirl. A great storm was building, and the backdrop only made her more formidable.

When lightning struck outside, the crowd gasped and fell

back from the dais.

As if a harbinger for what was to come, the storm increased in ferocity. Swirling masses of clouds were overhead, long arms of them reaching toward the land.

As Jax neared, the woman turned. Her eyes mimicked the storm in a swirling black.

88

CASSANDRA WANDERED THE MAIN ROOM in her castle. The time was almost nigh. Just the thought of feeding on this world had her mouth watering. All worlds she fed on sated her hunger, but this world had many feasts. It would keep her satisfied for longer than most. Perhaps even hundreds of years with all the youth saturating the lands.

She would wait no longer.

Muttering a few well-chosen words under her breath, the air became heavy. Draperies moved, and the rushes on the floor shifted as a whirlwind blew. Items rustled at the edges of the room as the current moved in, becoming stronger.

Cassandra stood in the middle where her storm would soon be the most powerful. She raised her arms, waiting for the climax of sensation. As it closed on her, her gown first swayed and then battered her body, caught in the typhoon of air.

Soon, she wasn't visible from without the tornado. The wall of wind grew ever tighter, pulling down on itself, until with an audible snap, it was gone.

The room was empty. As the wind calmed, a lone rush floated down to again lay upon the floor.

89

O NCE AGAIN, TECK PEEKED OVER the half wall into the main hall. They would need to act soon. The storm was gaining in volume and fury.

Catching Wyliam's eye, the men nodded at each other. Teck slid down behind the wall, looking from Maya to Tessa.

"Be careful." Maya grasped Tessa's forearm, her concern evident.

Tessa nodded, her eyes large in her pale face. Maya studied her daughter. Her breath was labored, and the tip of her arrow shook. Maybe they should have left the girl at the keep. When Teck stood, it was too late to second-guess their plan.

Close on Teck's heels, Maya followed, her attention divided between the man in front of her and the girl behind. Stepping from the protection of the wall, the trio was immediately noticed. Soldiers peeled off the front lines to intercept them. Maya and Teck took down the first men to come against them. As per the plan, Tessa slipped to the side and made her way to higher ground where her skill with a bow would be of the best use.

With half of the soldiers fighting Maya and Teck, Patrick, Wyliam, and Sentinel moved toward the front of the crowd. They pushed their way through, gaining ground near the soldiers. Attention was on the fight in the back of the room, and when Sentinel cut the first one down, followed closely by two more, a moment of panic shot through the crowd.

People fell back from the bodies of the soldiers, turning to flee the immediate area. One or two of the parents took this opportunity to rush the stage, slipping past soldiers more intent on the warrior than on parents. One even got a hand on their child, but with a screech, Nav-lys turned on him.

Raising her hands, a pulse of energy colored with a slight gray flung at the man. He flew back into broken hunks of wall. Stunned, but not dead, he shook his head and sat up.

All heads swiveled to the man. Everyone had seen Nav-lys's magic. All knew how deadly it was. Nav-lys stared at the man who regained his feet. Uncertainty colored her face. Looking toward her hands, she thrust them in front of her.

The man ducked, covering his head. When nothing happened, he peeked at her. The realization that she was not as deadly seemed to hit the mob at the same time. The man jumped at Nav-lys, earning another shock of her magic. Thrown even farther this time, he stayed down.

The crowd surged forward. The soldiers were thrust back, some keeping their feet, others swamped and forced down by the crowd. Clambering over the fallen bodies, some of the villagers went down, only to be trampled by their friends and neighbors. The level of noise increased as more were trampled. Some cried out, stopped by soldiers with deadly intent.

Some made it through, running the gauntlet of soldiers and citizens. Nearing Nav-lys, they slowed. So conditioned by their fear, they were now having second thoughts about facing her.

When the group around her continued to grow, Nav-lys took a step back. She'd never had them look upon her like this. This aggression. This lack of fear. She didn't know what had happened to her magic, how had it been subverted.

With this question came the knowledge.

The Other.

90

CUTTING THROUGH THE SOLDIERS, MAYA saw the altercation between the villagers and soldiers as the people surround Nav-lys. She was almost struck by a lucky swipe of a blade but jerked back just in time. She plunged a sword into the hapless soldier. Refocused, she placed herself back-to-back with Teck. The soldiers called in more troops. They flowed in through the side doors.

When the soldiers Maya battled fell with arrows buried in their backs and necks, she glanced up to see Tessa, firing one, two, and even three arrows at a time. In that brief moment before more foes engaged her, Maya noticed Wyliam was readily apparent, her eye drawn to his white-blond hair.

She locked eyes with Sentinel. He took the head off a soldier who stood in his way then stepped to her on the dais. With a nod at Teck, the three battled toward Nav-lys.

The woman stood amid the turmoil. Her head thrown back, arms raised, eyes glued on the coming storm. Soldiers barely held the villagers back from her and the children that encircled her, but she never flinched.

Maya couldn't look at her. Somewhere in there, her mother once resided. Where was she now? What had happened in those first few months to turn her loving mother into this monster? Battling forward, Maya focused on killing Nav-lys—setting her mother's spirit free.

So many soldiers stood with this evil, yet she and her friends were so few. A sense of despair washed over her, and she tried to push it away. The swirling storm clouds drew her gaze. Plants flowed in it, over the opening of the broken dome and through the floor.

"Cover me!" she yelled to the two men. Without question they stepped to defend her back. Nearing the plants, Maya sheathed her swords. She shoved her hands within the tangled mass, closed her eyes, and grasped her magic before she pushed it into the flora.

91

SYLVAN WAS NEAR TO HAVING control over the light. Like a flash of lightning in a darkened room, images of the world beyond came to her.

Nav-lys mostly kept her gaze rapt on the storm, but occasionally it flickered to the room. In these brief instances, briefer still with the flickering light, Sylvan oriented herself and those around her. When she saw red hair in the melee, she thought her heart would stop. Then, to her amazement, the woman threw back the marauders. They fell to her blades like ripe wheat to a scythe.

With the warrior woman two men fought. Sylvan's pulse leaped when she recognized Teck. Older, she realized, but still Teck—and still with her girl. The other man she didn't recognize, but his exotic, almost otherworldliness, gave her a good idea who he was. After all, her pedagogue was a cat. Seeing him with twin blades of his own, she had no doubt he taught her girl to fight.

She knew she'd slept for a long time, but she hadn't realized it had been years.

A battle was happening all around her. Others stood against Nav-lys. This was the time to act. Digging deeper than she'd ever gone, Sylvan reached for her magic.

92

TESSA GRABBED FOR ANOTHER ARROW. When she felt the empty rim of her quiver, she confirmed what her hand had conveyed.

Her mother and father still battled below, Sentinel with them. There were too many soldiers for them to triumph over, and the fighters just kept coming. Tessa dropped below the wall of the balcony. She was out of arrows, but that didn't mean all her options were gone.

Placing her back to the half wall, she closed her eyes and tried to relax.

The ringing of steel against steel almost broke her concentration, but she focused. Deep breaths, clearing her mind, reaching for Striker.

Wind. Sun. Silence.

For a second, she just enjoyed being with him. Being in the peace of the sky. Soaring.

Knowing time was of the essence, she opened her eyes to the distant horizon. Without conscious thought, she put an idea in the raptor's mind, and they were dipping to skim the land.

Once again, she closed her eyes from within the hawk. Concentrating, she reached for life forms—the panthers, wolves, and other raptors. Any animal big enough to fight. Armed by nature with fang and claw. She called to them, instilling her need. Telling them of the enemy. Showing them what their world would become if Nav-lys and the soldiers were to win.

Almost immediately, she felt them. Like a tidal wave, they moved toward the temple in the middle of the city.

93

AV-LYS STEPPED FORWARD AS THE clouds descended. Like a funnel from a tornado, the swirling mass aimed for the ground.

She knew who battled her soldiers, and she was glad. The magic-wielders were her ultimate gift to her god. Cassandra would be pleased. Everything was coming together perfectly.

Stepping to the center of the dais, where the storm's apex descended, Nav-lys raised her hands and dropped to her knees. Spells gushed from her lips, welcoming words to her god. Her voice rich and full, she called.

When she felt the itch, she ignored it. "The time is nigh."

When the itch became a burn, she paused in her spells. Her shoulders shifting, she attempted to dislodge the irritation. Gaining her feet, she stumbled forward, scanning the room. Her eyesight was fading, growing dark around the edges. At first, she thought it was her god, something Cassandra was doing, a draining of power to allow the entity access to this world. Then, something familiar tickled in the back of her brain.

"No! It cannot be." Wobbling backward, she put out a hand but fell to her knees. Within her, she could feel the Other rising. Grasping her hands in fists, she slammed them to the floor.

"No!" Getting a foot under her, she pushed from the ground. "I will not let this be."

* * * * *

SYLVAN PUSHED HERSELF TOWARD THE light. Behind her, the spark of their magic glowed. Again, almost a pure white, it filled her with warmth and hope.

She reached for Nav-lys, clawing up her back to grab her by the throat and push her down. At the last moment, a burst of energy came from the doppelganger, and then she sank.

* * * * *

THE BURST OF MAGIC HIT Jax as he wobbled and then fell to his knees.

He knew what he must do.

94

HEN THE PLANTS EXPLODED, MAYA remained safe within their boundaries. A fire filled her. In some form, she was with the plants and still standing in the temple. The floor beneath them hard, the air above them hot. Plants and roots moved through the ground, and she with them felt the dirt on her skin, the smell of it in her lungs. When they grasped and skewered the enemy, she felt the blood flow and the flesh break.

In an instant, she was back in herself. The fire still burned in her veins, and when it burned even hotter over her heart, she didn't think anything of it. Laying an open hand on her chest, she glanced down and saw light flowing between her fingers.

The stone from the cave shone brightly.

The clouds rumbled and shot down a finger to collide with the floor. The impact shook the ground, people falling or dropping to a knee. Maya grasped the vines on either side of her and barely stayed on her feet. Scanning the room, she saw Teck regaining his feet and Sentinel still on one knee, his fists, still grasping swords, maintaining his balance against the floor.

"Mama!" Maya turned. Tessa leaped the last two stairs from the balcony to run to her mother.

A stampede of animals flowed through the outer doors. Above them, with others of his kind, was Striker. The raptor swooped, voicing an ear-shattering scream. The animals engaged the soldiers with claws, teeth, and talons. Some ran from the attack, clearing the way for more.

The din blocked out all else. Screams, roars, and cries, the rending of the temple by the plants. The ferocious wind.

Maya wrapped her arms around her daughter, but Tessa pulled away.

"Look!" Tessa yelled above the commotion. "My stone is glowing." She pulled a stone from her shirt. It was wrapped in twine that hung around her neck.

"Where did you get that?"

"From a chief. Weeks ago. It did this before, when Jax and I were aboard that ship."

Maya lifted the blue stone from her pocket, showing Tessa. With the women so close and the stones close to each other, the colors fired, arcing through the room. The women fell back, eyes wide. The stones' lights dimmed.

Maya's mind spun. Scanning behind her, Maya took Tessa's arm and pulled her toward the men. An awful keening began and gained in volume. As a unit, the four looked at Nav-lys, who lay on the ground. Her hands were fisted in her hair, and she rocked side to side. The sound that issued from her made the hair stand on the back of Maya's neck.

"What's happening?" Tessa turned an urgent gaze to her mother.

Maya took a step closer as others drew back. The woman appeared to be in pain. She continued her wailing. "This may be it." Maya drew a blade and stepped toward the dais.

95

BLURRY IMAGES CAME TO SYLVAN like she looked through a pane covered in mist. Sounds reverberated in her space, bouncing and dissipating.

There were people around her. Rushing, shouting, clashing. She strained to clarify the images, but everything was moving too fast. And her vision was still too poor. Her mind struggled to process it all.

Back in her mind, she flailed as though swimming through mud, pushing her way forward. This was it, she realized. This was the day. The moment to take back her life.

When she cleared the mud-like pit and pulled herself to the far shore, she shook off the remnants of despondency and oppression and stood tall.

Her eyes widened to again see the room. Silently she mouthed, *Maya*.

Her girl was stomping toward her, red hair flaming, eyes blazing.

And she was drawing her sword.

96

MAYA STEPPED TOWARD THE WOMAN on the dais. The wailing had stopped. Now she looked up, eyes visible through hanks of stringy gray hair.

After a misstep, Maya paused. Something in the eyes, some element of recognition made her hesitate. With a shake of her head, she again started forward. She wouldn't be deceived by Nav-lys. Her mother was dead, and no amount of wanting would change that. She must strike and strike hard, now when the creature was weak.

Now was the time to end her reign of terror and death. Maya raised her sword as she drew near. As the strike's arch neared the woman, unable to bear it, Maya closed her eyes. The reverberation of steel on steel ran up her arm and her eyes snapped open.

"Oh no, my pet. It will not be that easy."

Spinning his weapon, the small man thrust Maya back from the woman crouched on the dais, the screech of metal loud in the room.

Maya stared, unable to move. The memories of this man, the imprisonment, the punishments, the running, the terror. All that she had lost at his hands.

When her control broke free, she screamed in pure fury. Pulling her second sword, she faced off with him. He would not keep her from killing Nav-lys, and if it meant killing him first, she was happy with that.

She was aware of others around them staying out of their way. Overhead the tempest raged, coming ever closer.

She would end this. She would end it now.

The ring of steel on steel focused her wrath, pulling it to a pinpoint. Within her was all the loss of a life that could have been. The heartbreak of a mother taken, never to return. And not just gone, but subverted. The girl she once was and could never be again. All these emotions, despairs, and grief filled her heart until she burned with hatred.

Catching a thrust with the edge of her sword, she pushed his weapon back. With her second sword, she swiped at him, leaving a gaping wound across his belly. The small man stumbled back, hand to the wound, blood running between his fingers.

The sight of his blood spurred her on, blades spinning. She was no longer his victim. Now he would see what she had become. The small man tried to deflect her attack. He kept his sword moving, but she was too much, her speed devastating.

When he tripped on the edge of the dais and went down, his body was covered with hundreds of small cuts, blood oozing to coat him in red. He lay on the floor, spreading fluid on the tiles. Dropping her blades, Maya straddled his limp form, wrenching her knife from her belt.

Her body rose and fell with her breaths, tears running down her face. Dropping to her knees, she plunged the blade into his chest, leaning into it with all her weight. Her face mere inches from his, a sob escaped her as the light left his eyes.

For a moment, she couldn't move, fixated on the death mask of the small man. When she heard a whisper of a sound, she swung around, her hands already reaching for the blades from the floor.

Nav-lys was trying to rise from the far edge of the dais, her motions stiff and disjointed.

Maya stood and stepped from the small man in one fluid motion. When she swung a blade in a circle, red drops splattered the wall. With slow, measured steps, she approached Nav-lys.

She was halfway across the dais, her focus on the woman, when the volume of the tempest overhead heightened. Caught by the sight, she froze while the whirlwind aimed for her.

Hit from behind, she was wrapped in strong arms. They rolled together to impact the side wall as another explosion of wind hit the center of the dais. Maya rolled to her side to see Teck lying beside her, his eyes looking her over.

"Are you all right?"

"What was that?" She rolled from him, gaining her feet. The wind buffeted her body, driving her back into the wall. Almost tripping over Teck, she sat down hard on him.

Teck slid out from under her to stand. Grabbing her upper

arms, he helped her upright against the wind. Her hair covered her view, but Maya wrenched the tendrils out of the way. A woman stood within the storm.

"Cassandra."

97

NATHANIEL SLINKED ALONG THE WALL, staying well back from the middle of the room. He'd been more aware of his girl for some time now. He could feel her in his bones, their lives tied together. Her nearness pulled at his core.

Inching around a corner, he watched the woman. She seemed weak, confused. Having trouble standing, she had just gained her feet when an explosion in the center of the dais threw her forward. She landed just feet from him. Air exploded from her with the impact. She coughed on the dust floating around her.

When she pushed to her hands and knees and brought the breath back into her lungs, she scanned the area, hair falling over her face.

Seeing the cat by the wall, her eyes locked on him.

"Nathaniel," she whispered.

Large, yellow eyes blinked slowly. Throwing a look over her shoulder, Sylvan crawled to the wall and the cat. Sitting beside him, she took a long, shaky breath. Her hand trembled when she pushed the hair from her face.

Back within the room, laughter began. Low but building, it had an edge of lunacy to it.

"Nathaniel, it's me. Sylvan." She placed the shaky hand on her chest.

"Where has the Other gone?" he asked, still not confident she was who she said.

"Down," she answered and looked out to study the room. "We need to get out of here."

Stumbling to her feet, Sylvan slipped around the side of the wall. When she checked behind her, the cat trailed.

98

TECK AND MAYA CIRCLED THE dais, keeping the woman in sight. When they reached the others, Maya stepped between the threat in the room and her daughter. Around them soldiers and townspeople froze, fear and uncertainty covering their faces.

"What is she doing? Why is she just standing there?"

Everyone was looking at the entity on the dais.

Maya's gaze raked the room. "Where is Nav-lys?"

Now everyone in their small party was searching.

"There!" Wyliam yelled, pointing to the back of the room. As they all looked, a portion of her gown disappeared behind a wall.

"We have to get her. Perhaps it will weaken Cassandra. We can't take her on like this."

With those words, everyone again looked at the deity on the stage. Around her, the tile was black—and the rot was growing.

"Come on," Maya said and headed after the woman.

The company moved after Nav-lys, trying not to draw

attention. When Maya reached the turn in the wall, she glanced back at Cassandra. The deity had a smile on her face, her head thrown back, and her eyes closed. A flush colored her cheeks. The stain of black slowly seeped from around her to darken the dais.

"We're going to need to hurry."

When they rounded the corner, the corridor was empty. Maya brandished her sword and stepped into the next doorway, Teck right behind her.

Beyond lay an empty room. Hurrying now, they rounded into another corridor. There, ahead of them, was Nav-lys. Her stumbling pace moved her slowly, and her hand trailed along the wall.

"Nav-lys!" Maya yelled. The woman turned, her eyes wide.

Fury filling every cell, Maya ran toward the vessel of her hatred. She would kill this woman. She would see her mother freed from her torment. As her weapon began its descent, the woman fell to the floor. Unintendedly, her foot kicked Maya's boot, throwing her weight off. Maya landed hard on her side and lost her blade. Undaunted, she grabbed for the handle of her knife at her belt, realizing she'd left the weapon buried in Orson. Scurrying forward, Maya grasped her sword. Then a large cat jumped upon the downed woman.

Tail straight and fluffed out, back hunched, Nathaniel hissed. Barely catching her swing, Maya stopped her thrust. She pushed back against a wall opposite the woman and the cat. Eyes wide, she stared at the feline.

There was a rush of bodies, the stampeding of feet, and the

babble of voices.

All sound was cut off when the woman sat up and took the feline into her arms.

"Nathaniel?" Maya muttered.

The cat squirmed, and the woman released him. He walked toward Maya. "Yes, Maya. After all this time, we are all together again."

Teck sat down hard next to Maya. When she looked at him, his gaze was locked on the cat.

"Teck?" she asked and placed a hand on his knee.

"Did he just talk?"

Maya breathed out a smile. She patted his leg and turned back to Nathaniel.

"What are you doing, Nathaniel? Why do you protect her?"

"Look, Maya. Truly look." He stepped back to the woman. Climbing into her lap, he was again wrapped in her embrace. His purr loud, he said, "Look, and see your mother."

Maya's gaze flew to the woman's face. She crawled closer. "Mother?"

"Maya."

"Mother!" Crawling to the woman, Maya studied her. The person looking out was her mother. Gentle, loving Sylvan. "Is it true? Are you here? How can this be?"

Sylvan gathered her daughter into her arms. Rocking gently, she hummed, her body trembling with the coming tears. Maya's breath caught as she choked out a sob. Burying her face in her mother's shoulder, she hung on.

All eyes turned from the reunion to a loud racket in the

throne room. On the tail of the commotion were screams.

"We need to get back in there. We need to finish this," Teck said.

Everyone hesitated. They'd thought by killing Nav-lys they would weaken Cassandra. Now no one knew where Nav-lys had gone.

Maya was helping her mother to stand, pulling one arm around her shoulders and wrapping her other around Sylvan's waist. The two women almost ran into Wyliam. He stood like a statue.

"Sylvan," he whispered.

Sylvan's brows scrunched and she blinked at the man. She started to shake her head, then a flicker of recognition gleamed in her eyes. "Wyliam? Wyliam?" She reached a hesitant hand to lay on his cheek.

Nodding, he looked from her to the cat at her feet.

"Nathaniel?"

In an echo of a former time, Nathaniel stepped forward. "Yes, Wyliam. It is me, Nathaniel."

Looking back to the woman, the blond man said, "I used to think you were a dream. Something I'd come up with after my parents were murdered."

"I'm sorry I left you." She squeezed his forearm. "I wouldn't have if I could have helped it."

Teck stepped up to the group, his voice abrupt. "I'm sorry to interrupt this reunion, but we have a being to kill in the other room." When all eyes turned toward him, he said, "Sylvan, where is Nav-lys? Do we need to fear her still?"

"For now, she has gone quiet."

Maya studied her mother. "Do you have any idea how we can defeat Cassandra?"

Sylvan shook her head, dropping it as if weary. "No. She's very powerful."

When the troop again turned toward the throne room, at the end of the hall stood a figure, backlit by the larger room.

Tessa leaned forward. "Jax?"

When he didn't answer, she stepped closer. Wyliam grabbed her arm. "Wait. Something's not right."

Jax leaped forward, and Tessa screamed. His eyes swirled with black. When he thrust a weapon forward, she screamed again, and blood flowed from Wyliam's side. Dropping the knife, the boy fled. Tessa spun to Wyliam and placed a hand over his wound.

Sentinel and Patrick grabbed for the man as he faltered, lowering him to the ground.

"Teck!" Maya shouted. "Take her." She handed Sylvan off to him. Stooping before Wyliam, Sentinel said, "He'll be all right. The wound is not deep."

Tessa gave Wyliam a kiss on the head then ran after Jax.

"Tessa!" Maya yelled. She ignored Teck's shout for her to wait and pursued her daughter.

When Maya rounded the corner into the throne room, the level of noise had a physical presence, and she was buffeted back from it. Much worse than when they left, she could barely stand in the force of the wind. Pushing her hair from her face, she saw Tessa approaching the dais. Jax was already making his way to Cassandra. The deity moved toward them, her arms open wide.

"Tessa!" Maya screamed, but the wind pulled her words away.

Maya stopped, her eyes wide, mouth open, when the boy and Cassandra reached each other. She wrapped him in her arms, his body turning black and swollen before melting into nothing but gray dust that quickly blew away in the wind.

Tessa fell to her knees, her mouth open in a seemingly silent scream.

Then Cassandra was there, reaching for the girl, gloating in her distress. Maya hurried, helpless to reach them as Cassandra attempted to seize her.

"Tessa!" Maya screamed, her voice raspy.

Near enough for Tessa to hear her, the girl turned toward her mother. Catching sight of Cassandra, she dropped to the ground, trying to melt into it. Just as Cassandra stepped within inches of Tessa, the jewel at the girl's throat gave off a brilliant light. Cassandra fell back, her arm over her eyes as a screech erupted into the gale.

Maya skidded to a halt next to Tessa, dragging her to the disputable safety of the far wall. She squinted as light from her stone burst from her pocket, blending with Tessa's.

A cry from the dais drew her attention. Cassandra was falling back in pain.

The stones, Maya thought.

"Come, Tessa. Get back from her."

Maya dragged Tessa backward, keeping her eyes on

Cassandra. When she came up against a body, she wrenched around, raising a fist, only to see it was Teck. A sigh collapsed her shoulders and she leaned into him.

Behind him, the others filled the space. Wyliam had a makeshift bandage around his waist, the blood slowly seeping through, but he was on his feet. Tessa broke from her mother to run to him, weeping.

Maya looked at Teck, her gaze intent. "The stones, Teck. Did you see how the light from the stones hurt her?"

Nodding, he pulled the group back farther.

"She's recovering quickly. And she looks angry."

Moving up to Tessa so she could be heard, Maya took the girl's arm. Tessa lifted her head from Wyliam's shoulder.

"Tessa, we can hurt her with the stones."

Sylvan limped to them. Putting a hand on each of the other women, she said, "My stone. I used to have one like yours, Tessa. I always thought it was magical."

Maya's mind spun. "I remember. It sat on the shelf in our cabin."

"Yes. I found it in the lake on the night I came to our valley."

"Look, Mother." Maya reached into her pocket to pull out her green stone. "My stone is different from Tessa's. I can't remember exactly what yours looked like. Was it like these?"

Sylvan laid a finger upon the stone in Maya's hand. "Yes, like these, but blue."

"Yes, blue. I remember now."

Sylvan's head fell in defeat. "If I only had my stone now."

Teck moved back to where the women whispered. His ears

perked at the mention of a blue stone. "A blue stone? From the cabin?"

"Yes." Sylvan nodded.

"I have your blue stone, Sylvan."

All eyes turned to him.

"What do you mean?" Sylvan looked at Maya. They both regarded Teck.

"I took it from the remains of your cabin. It's all a bit foggy, how I actually came to have it, but I do have it." Reaching in his pocket, Teck pulled out the blue stone with white flecks.

Sylvan put out her hand but drew back.

"What, Mother? What is it?"

Sylvan pulled her arms into her chest. Her eyes were haunted. "What if it brings back the Other?"

Maya took her mother's hands in hers, rubbing to warm them.

"All we know is the stones' power hurts Cassandra. I can't promise you, but if anything, it will most likely drive Nav-lys further away."

"But I'm not strong. My magic isn't strong. What use will it be to vanish from sight?"

Maya wrapped her arms around her mother. "You are the strongest person I know." When she pulled back, she looked her mother in the eyes. "You're with us now. You came *back* to us. We need you still. It will take all three of us."

Sylvan reached again for the stone in Teck's hand. As soon as she touched it, color shot into the corridor. Tessa's stone shone in response, and when Maya lifted hers, it too was glowing.

Patrick moved to the center of the group. Now he saw the answer to his questions. All of the pieces came together.

"And the foretelling has come to be. The stones, gifts from Caleb, will thwart her magic. He is Cassandra's brother but is not her champion. These stones, if used together with your natural magics, will defeat Cassandra. They will be the catalyst to bring the Three and Three together." Patrick reached out to touch hands and shoulders, drawing the group together.

"It will be difficult. She is very powerful, but you must remember, she is not unstoppable." Looking at each of them, he tried to infuse courage into the small group. They must be enough. "The core must be joined, then the Three and Three will become One and vanquish the evil from this land. With your belief it will be so."

99

WHEN THE WIND DEPOSITED CASSANDRA in the middle of noise and chaos, she was right where she wanted to be. Bounty surrounded her. Immediately, she began consuming this world's riches. The feeding filled her with such glee, she laughed out loud.

Her gaze rested upon the prone body of one of her lackeys. If the spreading stain around him was any indication, he was permanently out of the game.

With an inner shrug, she counted the life forms in this room alone. Many children surrounded the area, and beyond them were adults. Though the children's auras were richer, the adults were just as welcome.

Oh, how she loved humanity's propensity for procreation.

A young man stood to the side of the dais, and at first it was his direct stare that drew her attention. Then, she saw his eyes. They swirled, and his scent was familiar.

Now, where was her little follower?

The boy again caught her eye when he turned to run into a

back hall. Gone, but just for a moment, he flew back into the room and straight for her. As he neared, his feet sank into the gelatinous rot around her. Undaunted, he pushed through it to reach her.

Welcoming his sacrifice, love spreading through her, she opened her arms to receive him. As they embraced, a scream rang above the din in the room.

Ah, there are my magic-wielders, come late to the party.

Secure in her assumption they would soon come to her, Cassandra directed her attention on burrowing her hook deeper into the ground. This room, town, and land were just a small portion of this planet. The deeper she infested here, the easier the taking would be.

The noise didn't bother her. In fact, she reveled in the chaos. So long had she waited, alone in her castle, for this very moment. Every nuance filled her with a hunger like no other.

This world was special, and it whetted her appetite.

When she again regarded the room, it was to see the magic-wielders returning, Nav-lys with them. This was good. Cassandra was ready for their sacrifices. Nav-lys too would be a worthy consumption—the promise of an eternal life with Cassandra an easy lie. She wrestled with no ethics or morals, her life one of the pursuits of power. The cessation of her hunger.

Spinning to face the three women, Cassandra prepared to dine.

100

MAYA'S BACK STRAIGHTENED, AND HER shoulders rose as the woman on the dais faced them. The three of them had their stones hidden in their clothing. For now, the glows were camouflaged.

Once, in this building, she thought she had lost everything, but now, the loss of everything could be a truth. Taking her daughter's hand and with an arm around her mother's shoulders, Maya moved them forward. When Cassandra smiled, she faltered, but tightening her control around her courage, she continued to walk.

"Nav-lys." The voice of the deity reverberated around the room, quieting everything else.

Sylvan quaked in Maya's grip. Turning to face her mother, she whispered, "She thinks you're Nav-lys. We can use this to our advantage."

"I— " She had to clear her throat. "I don't know how to be Nav-lys."

Maya rubbed her hand down her mother's back, hiding the

move from Cassandra. "It's all right. You'll only have to be for a little while. Just to get us close enough."

Tessa watched them avidly and listened to everything they said.

"Nav-lys!" the woman boomed again. "Come to me. Bring your offerings."

Maya said, "Go now. Stay strong. We'll get her between us." She gave her mother a small push.

Sylvan looked toward the woman on the dais and then back toward her family. With a hard swallow, she sidestepped around the edge of the platform, drawing the deity's gaze with her. Out of the corner of her eye, Maya and Tessa moved away from them.

When Cassandra took a step in her direction, Sylvan caught her toe and tripped, barely catching herself.

"Why do you hesitate?"

Sylvan cringed at the volume of Cassandra's voice, fighting the urge to draw inward. How could she pretend to be Nav-lys? She'd never even heard the Other's voice—her world had been one of silence.

She continued to move around the side of the platform, drawing Cassandra farther from the other two women.

Doubt clouded her mind. Fear filled her heart.

When she reached Cassandra, Maya and Tessa separated. Before Sylvan could fear an early discovery, they had Cassandra surrounded.

101

MAYA KEPT AN EYE ON her mother and Cassandra. When the woman had her back to them, she squeezed Tessa's hand and gestured for her to stay before she moved on a bit more.

When they had Cassandra centered between the three of them, she glanced at the doorway they'd come through. Teck, Sentinel, Patrick, Nathaniel, and Wyliam watched. Each of the men held a weapon, but she knew conventional weaponry would do them no good. This battle would be fought with magic and belief in that magic.

Cassandra was speaking to Sylvan, but Maya couldn't hear her mother's response. She saw her shake her head, and when Cassandra gestured to Sylvan, the woman took a step back. Sylvan's eyes were large, and her gaze shifted from Cassandra to the area around them.

Cassandra would soon be suspicious if she wasn't already.

Just when Maya gestured to Tessa to get ready, Cassandra reached across the distance between her and Sylvan and grabbed the smaller woman by the arm. The deity pulled her into the circle of rot and right up to face her.

* * * * *

WHEN SYLVAN ENTERED THE CIRCLE, she thought she'd faint. It was all too much—the smells, sounds, motions. How long had she lived in an isolated world of silence?

Inadvertently inhaling the noxious fumes, Sylvan choked out a weak, "No."

Fingers like claws, the invader shook her. Sylvan's head snapped, her arms flailing. When she reached for the stone within a fold of her gown, she missed. Pushing at Cassandra's hand, Sylvan tried to free herself, but the larger woman was stronger.

Her world a kaleidoscope of colors as her view shifted with each shake, Sylvan saw Tessa start across the dais toward her. Scooping up a bow and arrows from a dead soldier, she loosed arrows as she came, hitting Cassandra's head and shoulders, but none of the arrows penetrated the woman.

Dragging Sylvan with her, Cassandra spun toward the new threat.

"What is this?" her voice boomed across the expanse. "A little girl come to play?"

Tessa planted her feet.

"Tessa!" Maya yelled. The girl started toward her mother just as Cassandra lobbed a bolt of pure energy straight at the girl. Hitting the ground where she'd stood seconds before, tiles and rock flew into the air.

Cassandra again aimed for the girl. Maya's heart in her throat, she screamed with fear and rage. Vines lanced forward, encircling Cassandra's arms. Cassandra released her hold on Sylvan. She inhaled, and the air around her ballooned, causing the brambles to shatter.

The plants were quick to re-grasp the woman's arms and legs. More foliage burst through the room to swamp Cassandra as vines tightened around her.

Next came the animals. Big cats, wolves, and large ferocious rodents. They rushed the stage, taking down soldiers who thought to stand in their way. They grasped parts of Cassandra, who grappled while she fought. Some she fought off, but others hung on, biting down in desperation. If caught in the rot, those thrown sank below its surface, their dying screams an echo.

Birds of all sorts divebombed the woman, leaving blood running down her face to pool in the bodice of her gown. Cassandra seized an animal, but it disappeared, only to reappear again elsewhere. She cried her rage when she fought for another, and yet again, the creature evaded her grasp like a ghost.

Maya's gaze flew to her mother. Sylvan stood, eyes closed, head thrown back. She had her hands over her bosom, and a bright blue light seeped between her fingers.

This was it, Maya thought. The stone was amplifying her mother's magic.

Maya's gaze flew between her mother, Cassandra, and Tessa, who watched, stupefied.

Cassandra continued to throw off animals and brambles, but as quickly as she reacted to them, they were replaced.

Seeing their chance, Maya yelled at Tessa. The girl swung from the spectacle to face her mother. Maya pulled her stone from within her breast pocket. Immediately, green light streaked through the room.

Cassandra screamed and threw an arm over her eyes. When the green met the blue, a rainbow prism spiraled up through the broken dome.

"Tessa, now!"

Fumbling, Tessa reached in the neckline of her shirt to pull the stone free. She hadn't even cleared the cloth before yellow light burst into the room. The girl stared as the remnants of her makeshift necklace fell away, scorched by the stone's light.

Its promises made good, the storm overhead relinquished control. As rain fell, the torrent soaked everything it touched, leaving water and debris to wash across the dais and over the floor. The lights arcing through the spray of water took on an otherworldly appearance. Softened, the women appeared to be floating through a lake, their sights set on the serpent in the center.

Cassandra still fought. She spun to throw the flora and fauna from her, but they could not be breached. When the women neared the invader, the light increased in brilliance. Cassandra shrank back, pulling into herself. All around her, the black rot receded.

Soldiers attempted to rush the women. Teck, Wyliam, and Patrick defended their backs. Among their allies, the animals and plants kept up a steady barrage.

Lightning cracked overhead, and within the illumination, a witness stood on the perimeter of the room. A man cloaked and shrouded in shadow. His eyes glistened.

Closer still the women moved, Cassandra effectively trapped within the stones' brilliance.

When Maya felt a tingling sensation from the crown of her head to the bottoms of her feet, she glanced at her mother and daughter. They too scanned the area, brows drawn.

As if sensing their inattentiveness, Cassandra once again gained her feet. Towering over the assembly, she screamed, "Caleb!" and took a step forward.

The tingling intensified, and Maya thought perhaps they would not be able to hold her.

*　*　*　*　*

FIGHTING BESIDE HIM, TECK SAW Sentinel twitch. His skin rolled. It moved and shifted like it wanted to come free.

Throwing a soldier back, Teck reached out to touch the man, but the heat radiating off him forced Teck's hand back. Sentinel looked over his shoulder.

"Are you all right?" Teck asked.

In response, Sentinel performed a full body shake and cut down another soldier.

Then his body stiffened, his eyes glazed over. Just before Teck reached him, Sentinel dashed toward Maya. With a glance at Wyliam and Patrick, Teck broke from the front line and took off after the guardian.

WITHIN THE SHEETS OF RAIN and lightning, the three women were visible. The illumination of their stones splashed the area with colors. Not just the three colors of the stones themselves, but the colors they created.

Bearing down, Maya pushed her magic into the stone and stepped forward.

Tessa and then Sylvan stepped forward, too. As the three women neared, the intensity of the lights increased. The tingling within Maya grew.

Shaking, Maya stepped again. Again, Tessa and Sylvan followed. Again, the tingling amplified. Was it her imagination, or was Cassandra becoming smaller? Where before, she towered above them, Maya was now able to look her in the eye.

Trusting the proximity of the stones, Maya stepped again. Again, the other two moved in.

Close enough now to see proof of Cassandra's diminutive height, Maya's heart swelled with hope. Maya's eyes burned, and she struggled to concentrate as her body filled with the tingling sensation. The world in front of her indistinct, she closed her eyes, striving for control. When a throb began, she locked her hands around the stone. The blood in her body thumped.

102

ENTINEL SPED ACROSS THE TILE, his legs pumping. Try as he might, Teck couldn't catch him.

Hearing his name, Teck stopped to allow Wyliam and Patrick to reach him. Puffing, the priest pointed first to Sylvan and then to Tessa.

"Look. The pedagogues."

Teck swung back around. Like Sentinel, Striker and Nathaniel were rushing toward the women. They gained speed, moving faster than they should be able to. Right before they would be colliding with their apprentice, each made a move.

Striker tucked his wings and shot forward like an arrow.

Nathaniel leaped into the air, his body becoming translucent.

Sentinel pulled his swords, projecting himself off his feet toward his charge.

Teck sucked in a breath to yell, to shout a warning, to stop what he saw happening, but then the three pedagogues met the shining bodies of each of the women—and disappeared.

For a second, the women shone like the sun, pulsing balls of illumination.

And then the middle of the room exploded.

103

SITTING, MAYA GRASPED HER HEAD. What happened?
Sun shone through the dome, warm and inviting. Nothing moved. Everything—every bit of person, animal, and plant—was laid out in a circle as if blasted from the center of the dais.

Scoping the room again, Maya saw Tessa. The girl was on her back, her arms thrown wide. Pulling herself to her feet, Maya stumbled toward her daughter and flopped beside her, her stomach clenching when the girl moaned.

"Tessa." Maya grasped her shoulder and shook her.

Tessa moaned again, and her eyes squinted open. "Mama?"

"Yes. By the gods, Tessa. Are you hurt?"

Slowly sitting, Tessa looked herself over. "I don't think so." Then, looking around the room, she added, "What happened?"

Hearing others moving about, Maya glanced behind them. Striker lay prone on the ground.

"Striker," Maya said, and Tessa jerked. Crawling over to him, Tessa gently lifted him into her arms. When he blinked and shook his head, she sighed.

Maya was up and moving. When she approached Sentinel, he was sitting, holding his head.

Beyond him, Teck and Wyliam helped Patrick to his feet.

Soldiers, townsfolk, and children were rising. Soon everyone was talking in confusion.

Moving through the crowd, Maya saw Sylvan still lying among debris.

"Mother!" she cried and ran to her, dropping to her knees. Sylvan stirred. Her head flopped to the side, and a groan pushed past her lips.

"Mother," Maya said again. When Sylvan didn't respond, Maya grasped her shoulder. A sharp cry of pain came from the woman, and Maya released her. Looking around, she saw Teck moving toward her.

"Teck, she's injured."

He squatted beside them to look Sylvan over.

"Help her, please."

"I don't see anything wrong. There's no bleeding. Nothing seems broken."

"She's in pain," Maya cried.

"Maya." The soft whisper came from Sylvan and she flailed one hand. Grasping it, Maya leaned over her mother.

"Mother. Mother, I'm here."

Sylvan looked up. When she felt something bump into her arm, she winced, but the cat walked into her sight. "Nathaniel."

"My lady," the cat replied and curled his body half on hers. His purr seemed to soothe the woman.

"Let's move her, get her more comfortable."

When Maya and Teck supported her shoulders and tried to sit her up, Sylvan caught her breath.

"No," she cried, and they laid her back. "Maya."

Maya reached for her mother's hand, leaning over her, gaze intent on her face.

"I've always been proud of you," Sylvan said, staring into her daughter's eyes for a moment. "I'm glad I got to see you again. Got to see my girl all grown up." Laying a hand upon Nathaniel, Sylvan closed her eyes and took a final deep breath.

"Mother!" Maya cried, but Sylvan didn't respond.

Teck laid a palm along the side of her throat. His shoulders bowed and he glanced at Maya.

"I'm sorry, Maya."

A sob escaped, and Teck put an arm around her shoulders. Tessa did the same, Wyliam and Patrick behind her.

Maya gasped as Nathaniel first began to fade and then dissipated into the air. One moment he was there, and the next, just the imprint of him remained.

Breaking into tears, she threw herself into Teck's arms.

104

THE GROUP WAITED FOR BOARDING to begin. They had passage booked on a ship. One that would take them home.

Maya stood on the rise looking over the boarding area. Strapped on her back were crossed swords, and her red hair flashed in the sunlight.

When she heard footsteps, she turned to see Teck making his way to her. He wrapped an arm around her shoulders. She wrapped her arms around his waist.

"We'll be boarding soon."

"Yes," she agreed. "It will be good to leave this land. I'm ready to get home." It would be good to have so many at home. She felt relief and happiness that they were all together but sorrow for her lost mother. Knowing Sylvan had died in relative peace gave her comfort.

Sentinel looked at her and Teck for a moment and then turned to move toward the others, his hand resting on the hilt of his knife. Patrick stopped him to inquire about something. It would be good to have Patrick's sharp brain and quiet ways with them, Maya decided.

Wyliam and Tessa sat together in the dirt playing with a puppy, Sam still unsure of the bundle of energy. Teck had surprised her with him and they'd yet to think of a name. He yelped and ran around Tessa. Above her, on a branch of a newly leafing tree, Striker watched.

"It'll be good to have all of my family home," she said and held on like she'd never let him go.

Epilogue

C ALEB PEERED INTO THE SCRYING bowl at the small group of victors.

It was good.

He would watch out for them. Monitor their lives, and their children's lives. They were his now, and he would ensure they had all they needed for happiness and fulfillment.

Walking from the bowl, he reached within the folds of his cloak to pull out a stone.

Appearing on the day Cassandra ended, Caleb didn't know quite what to think of it. Red, etched with three lines joined at their tips, he felt the power pulsating from it.

Having the stone made him feel not quite so alone. Giving it one final look, Caleb slid the stone back within his clothing.

THE END

ACKNOWLEDGMENTS

Driven Digital Services

Kingsman Editing Services

Did you enjoy this book? Visit your favorite retailer
and leave a review to help other readers discover the magic
of *The Pedagogue Chronicles*.

* * * * *

VickiBWilliamson.com

Facebook.com/FindingPoppies

Made in the USA
Middletown, DE
14 November 2021